The Game-Players of Titan

Philip K. Dick was born in Chicago in 1928 and lived most of his life in California. He attended college for a year at Berkeley. Apart from writing, his main interest was music. He won the Hugo Award for his classic novel of alternative history, *The Man in the High Castle* (1962). He was married five times and had three children. He died in March 1982.

BY THE SAME AUTHOR

Novels

Solar Lottery
Eye in the Sky
Vulcan's Hammer
The Man Who Japed
The Cosmic Puppets
The World Jones Made
Time Out of Joint
Dr Futurity
The Man in the High Castle
The Game Players of Titan
Clans of the Alphane Moon
Flow My Tears, the
   Policeman Said
The Penultimate Truth
The Simulacra
Martian Time-Slip
Dr Bloodmoney, or How We
   Got Along After the Bomb
The Zap Gun
Now Wait for Last Year
Counter-Clock World
Ubik
Our Friends from Frolix 8
Glactic Pot-Healer
The Three Stigmata of
   Palmer Eldritch
A Scanner Darkly
Valis
The Divine Invasion
The Transmigration of
   Timothy Archer
Confessions of a Crap Artist
The Ganymede Takeover
   (with Ray Nelson)

Deus Irae
   (With Roger Zelazny)
A Maze of Death
Lies, Inc.
   (The Unteleported Man)
The Man Whose Teeth Were
   All Exactly Alike
In Milton Lumky Territory
Puttering About in a
   Small Land
Humpty Dumpty in Oakland
Radio Free Albemuth
We Can Build You
Mary and the Giant
The Broken Bubble

Short Stories

A Handful of Darkness
I Hope I Shall Arrive Soon
The Variable Man
The Book of Philip K. Dick
The Golden Man
The Preserving Machine
Collected Stories 1:
   Beyond Lies the Wub
Collected Stories 2:
   Second Variety
Collected Stories: 3
   The Father-Thing
Collected Stories 4:
   The Days of Perky Pat
Collected Stories 5:
   We Can Remember it for
   you Wholesale

Voyager

PHILIP K. DICK

The Game-Players of Titan

HarperCollins*Publishers*

Voyager
An Imprint of HarperCollins*Publishers*
77–85 Fulham Palace Road,
Hammersmith, London W6 8JB

The *Voyager* World Wide Web site address is
http://www.harpercollins.co.uk/voyager

This paperback edition 1996
3 5 7 9 8 6 4 2

Previously published in paperback by Grafton 1991

First published in Great Britain by
Sphere Books Ltd. 1963

ISBN 0 00 648249 X

Printed and bound in Great Britain by
Omnia Books Ltd, Glasgow

Chapter 1

It had been a bad night, and when he tried to drive home he had a terrible argument with his car.

'Mr Garden, you are in no condition to drive. Please use the auto-auto mech and recline in the rear seat.'

Pete Garden sat at the steering tiller and said as distinctly as he could manage, 'Look, I can drive. One drink, in fact several make you more alert. So stop fooling around.' He punched the starter button, but nothing happened. 'Start, darn it!'

The auto-auto said, 'You have not inserted the key.'

'Okay,' he said, feeling humiliated. Maybe the car was right. Resignedly, he inserted the key. The engine started up, but the controls were still dead. The Rushmore Effect was still taking place inside the hood, he knew; it was a losing argument. 'All right, I'll let you drive,' he said with as much dignity as possible. 'Since you're so eager. You'll probably louse it all up anyhow, like you always do when I'm – not feeling well.'

He crawled into the back seat, threw himself down, as the car lifted from the pavement and skimmed through the night sky, its signal lights blinking. God, he felt bad. His head was killing him.

His thoughts turned, as always, back to The Game.

Why had it gone so badly? Silvanus Angst was responsible. That clown, his brother-in-law or rather former brother-in-law. That's right, Pete said to himself; I have to remember. I'm not married to Freya anymore. Freya and I lost and so our marriage was dissolved and we're starting over again with Freya married to Clem Gaines and I'm not married to anybody yet because I haven't managed to roll a three, yet.

I'll roll a three tomorrow, he told himself. And when I do, they'll have to import a wife for me; I've used them all up in the group.

His car hummed on, finding its way above the deserted midsection of California, the desolate lands of abandoned towns.

'Did you know that?' he asked his car. 'That I've been married to every woman in the group now? And I haven't had any *luck*, yet, so it must be me. Right?'

The car said, 'It's you.'

'Even if it were me, it wouldn't be my fault; it's the Red Chinese. I hate them.' He lay supine, staring up at the stars through the transparent dome of the car. 'I love you, though; I've had you for years. You're never going to wear out.' He felt tears rise up in his eyes. 'Is that all right?'

'It depends on the preventative maintenance you faithfully follow.'

'I wonder what kind of woman they'll import for me.'

'I wonder,' the car echoed.

What other group was his group – Pretty Blue Fox – in closest contact with? Probably Straw Man Special, which met in Las Vegas and represented Bindmen from Nevada, Utah and Idaho. Shutting his eyes, he tried to remember what the women of Straw Man Special looked like.

When I get home to my apartment in Berkeley, Pete said to himself, I'll – and then he remembered something dreadful.

He could not go home to Berkeley. Because he had lost Berkeley in The Game, tonight. Walt Remington had won it from him by calling his bluff on square thirty-six. That was what had made it such a bad night.

'Change course,' he said hoarsely to the auto-auto circuit. He still held title deed to most of Marin County:

he could stay there. 'We'll go to San Rafael,' he said, sitting up and rubbing his forehead, groggily.

A male voice said, 'Mrs Gaines?'

Freya, combing her short blonde hair before the mirror, did not look around; absorbed, she thought, It sounds like that awful Bill Calumine.

'Do you want a ride home?' the voice asked, and then Freya realized that it was her new husband, Clem Gaines. 'You *are* going home, aren't you?' Clem Gaines, large and overstuffed, with blue eyes, she thought, like broken glass that had been glued there, and glued slightly awry, strolled across the Game room toward her. It pleased him, obviously, to be married to her.

It won't be for long, Freya thought. Unless, she thought suddenly, we have *luck*.

She continued brushing her hair, paying no attention to him. For a woman one hundred and forty years old, she decided critically, I look all right. But I can't take responsibility for it . . . none of us can.

They were preserved, all of them, by the absence of something, rather than the presence; in each of them the Hynes Gland had been removed at maturity and so for them the aging process was now imperceptible.

'I like you, Freya,' Clem said. 'You're a refreshing person; you make it obvious you don't like me.' He did not seem bothered; oafs like Clem Gaines never were. 'Let's go somewhere, Freya, and find out right away if *luck*wise you and I – ' He broke off, because a vug had come into the room.

Jean Blau, putting on her coat, groaned, 'Look, it wants to be friendly. They always do.' She backed away from it.

Her husband, Jack Blau, looked about for the group's vug-stick. 'I'll poke it a couple of times and it'll go away,' he said.

7

'No,' Freya protested. 'It's not doing any harm.'

'She's right,' Silvanus Angst said; he was at the sideboard, preparing himself a last drink. 'Just pour a little salt on it.' He giggled.

The vug seemed to have singled out Clem Gaines. It likes you, Freya thought. Maybe you can go somewhere with it, instead of me.

But that was not fair to Clem, because none of them consorted with their former adversaries; it was just not done, despite the efforts by the Titanians to heal the old rift of wartime dislike. They were a silicon-based life form, rather than carbon-based; their cycle was slow, and involved methane rather than oxygen as the metabolic catalyst. And they were bisexual . . . which was a rather non-B system indeed.

'Poke it,' Bill Calumine said to Jack Blau.

With the vug-stick, Jack prodded the jelly-like cytoplasm of the vug. 'Go home,' he told it sharply. He grinned at Bill Calumine. 'Maybe we can have some fun with it. Let's try to draw it into conversation. Hey, vuggy. You like make talk-talk?'

At once, eagerly, the Titanian's thoughts came to them, addressed to all the humans in the condominium apartment. 'Any pregnancies reported? If so, our medical facilities are available and we urge you to – '

'Listen, vuggy,' Bill Calumine said, 'if we have any *luck* we'll keep it to ourselves. It's bad luck to tell you; everybody knows that. How come *you* don't know that?'

'It knows it,' Silvanus Angst said. 'It just doesn't like to think about it.'

'Well, it's time the vugs faced reality,' Jack Blau said. 'We don't like them and that's it. Come on,' he said to his wife. 'Let's go home.' Impatiently, he waved Jean toward him.

The various members of the group filed out of the room

8

and down the front steps of the building to their parked cars. Freya found herself left with the vug.

'There have been no pregnancies in our group,' she told the vug, answering its question.

'Tragic,' the vug thought back in response.

'But there will be,' Freya said. 'I know we'll have *luck*, soon.'

'Why is your particular group so hostile to us?' the vug asked.

Freya said, 'Why, we hold you responsible for our sterility; you know that.' Especially our spinner Bill Calumine does, she thought.

'But it was your military weapon,' the vug protested.

'No, not ours. The Red Chinese.'

The vug did not grasp the distinction. 'In any case we are doing all we can to – '

'I don't want to discuss it,' Freya said. 'Please.'

'Let us help,' the vug begged.

She said to it, 'Go to hell.' And left the apartment, striding down the stairs to the street and her car.

The cold, dark night air of Carmel, California revived her; she took a deep breath, glanced up at the stars, smelled the freshness, the clean new scents. To her car she said, 'Open the door; I want to get in.'

'Yes, Mrs Garden.' The car door swung open.

'I'm not Mrs Garden anymore; I'm Mrs Gaines.' She entered, seated herself at the manual tiller. 'Try to keep it straight.'

'Yes, Mrs Gaines.' As soon as she put the key in, the motor started up.

'Has Pete Garden already left?' She scanned the gloomy street and did not see Pete's car. 'I guess he has.' She felt sad. It would have been nice to sit out here under the stars, so late at night, and chat a little. It would be as if they were still married . . . damn The Game, she

9

thought, and its spins. Damn *luck* itself, bad luck: that's all we seem to have, anymore. We're a marked race.

She held her wrist watch to her ear and it said in its tiny voice, 'Two-fifteen A.M., Mrs Garden.'

'Mrs Gaines,' she grated.

'Two-fifteen A.M., Mrs Gaines.'

How many people, she wondered, are alive on the face of Earth at this moment? One million? Two million? How many groups, playing The Game? Surely no more than a few hundred thousand. And every time there was a fatal accident, the population decreased irretrievably by one more.

Automatically, she reached into the glove compartment of the car and groped for a neatly-wrapped strip of rabbit-paper, as it was called. She found a strip – it was the old kind, not the new – and unwrapped it, put it between her teeth and bit.

In the glare of the dome light of the car she examined the strip of rabbit-paper. One dead rabbit, she thought, recalling the old days (they were before her time) when a rabbit had to die for this fact in question to be determined. The strip, in the dome light, was white, not green. She was not pregnant. Crumpling the strip, she dropped it into the disposal chute of the car and it incinerated instantly. Damn, she thought wretchedly. Well, what did I expect?

The car left the ground, started for her home in Los Angeles.

Too early though to tell about my *luck* with Clem, she realized. Obviously. That cheered her. Another week or two and perhaps something.

Poor Pete, she thought. Hasn't even rolled a three, isn't back in The Game, really. Should I drop by his bind in Marin County? See if he's there? But he was so stewed, so unmanageable. So bitterly unpleasant, tonight. There is no law or rule, though, that prevents us meeting outside

10

The Game. And yet – what purpose would it serve? We had no *luck*, she realized, Pete and I. In spite of our feeling for each other.

The radio of her car came on, suddenly; she heard the call-letters of a group in Ontario, Canada, broadcasting on all frequencies in great excitement. 'This is Pear Book Hovel,' the man declared exultantly. 'Tonight at ten P.M. our time we had *luck*! A woman in our group, Mrs Don Palmer, bit her rabbit-paper with no more idea of hoping than she ever did, and – '

Freya shut off the radio.

When he got home to his unlit, unused, former apartment in San Rafael, Pete Garden went at once to the medicine cabinet in the bathroom to see what medication he could find. I'll never get to sleep otherwise, he knew. It was an old story with him. Snoozex? It now took three 25-mg tablets of Snoozex to have any effect on him; he had taken too many for too long. I need something stronger, he thought. There's always phenobarbital, but it slugs you for the next day. Scopolamine hydrobromide; I could try that.

Or, he thought, I could try something much stronger. Emphytal.

Three of those, he thought, and I'd never wake up. Not in the strength capsules I've got. Here . . . he let the capsules lie on his palm as he stood considering. No one would bother me; no one would intervene –

The medicine cabinet said, 'Mr Garden, I am establishing contact with Dr Macy in Salt Lake City, because of your condition.'

'I have no condition,' Pete said. He quickly put the Emphytal capsules back in their bottle. 'See?' He waited. 'It was just momentary, a gesture.' Here he was, pleading with the Rushmore Effect of his medicine cabinet – macabre. 'Okay?' he asked it, hopefully.

11

A click. The cabinet had shut itself off.

Pete sighed in relief.

The doorbell sounded. What now? he wondered, walking through the faintly musty-smelling apartment, his mind still on what he could take as a soporific – without activating the alarm-circuit of the Rushmore Effect. He opened the door.

There stood his blonde-haired previous wife, Freya. 'Hi,' she said coolly. She walked into the apartment, gliding past him, self-possessed, as if it were perfectly natural for her to seek him out while she was married to Clem Gaines. 'What do you have in your fist?' she asked.

'Seven Snoozex tablets,' he admitted.

'I'll give you something better than that. It's going the rounds.' Freya dug into her leather mailbag-style purse. 'A new, new product manufactured in New Jersey by an autofac pharmaceutical house, there.' She held out a large blue spansule. 'Nerduwel,' she said, and then laughed.

'Ha-ha,' Pete said, not amused. It was a gag. Ne'er-do-well. 'Is that what you came for?' Having been his wife, his Bluff partner, for over three months, she of course knew of his chronic insomnia. 'I've got a hangover,' he informed her. 'And I lost Berkeley to Walt Remington, tonight. As you well know. So I'm just not capable of banter, right now.'

'Then fix me some coffee,' Freya said. She removed her fur-lined jacket and laid it over a chair. 'Or let me fix it for you.' With sympathy she said, 'You do look bad.'

'Berkeley – why did I put the title deed up, anyhow? I don't even remember. Of all my holdings – it must have been a self-destructive impulse.' He was silent, and then he said, 'On the way here tonight I picked up an all-points from Ontario.'

'I heard it,' she said nodding.

'Does their pregnancy elate or depress you?'

'I don't know,' Freya said somberly. 'I'm glad for them. But – ' She roamed about the apartment, her arms folded.

'It depresses me,' Pete said. He put a tea kettle of water on the range in the kitchen.

'Thank you,' the tea kettle – its Rushmore Effect – piped.

Freya said, 'We could have a relationship outside of The Game, you realize. It *has* been done.'

'It wouldn't be fair to Clem.' He felt a camaraderie with Clem Gaines; it overcame his feelings – temporarily, anyhow – for her.

And in any case he was curious about his future wife; sooner or later he would roll a three.

Chapter 2

Pete Garden was awakened the next morning by a sound so wonderfully impossible that he jumped from the bed and stood rigid, listening. He heard children. They were quarreling, somewhere outside the window of his San Rafael apartment.

It was a boy and a girl, and Pete thought, So there have been births in this county since I was last here. And of parents who are non-B, not Bindmen. Without property which would enable them to play The Game. He could hardly believe it, and he thought, I ought to deed the parents a small town . . . San Anselmo or Ross, even both. They deserve an opportunity to play. But maybe they don't want to.

'You're one,' the girl was declaring angrily.

'You're another.' The boy's voice, laden with accusation.

'Gimme that.' Sounds of a physical scuffle.

He lit a cigarette, then found his clothes and began to dress.

In the corner of the room, leaning against the wall, a MV-3 rifle . . . he caught sight of it and paused, remembering in a rush everything that the great old weapon had meant. Once, he had been prepared to stand off the Red Chinese with this rifle. But it had never seen use because the Red Chinese had never shown up . . . at least not in person. Their representatives, in the form of Hinkel Radiation, had arrived, however, but no amount of MV-3s doled out to California's citizen army could fight and conquer that. The radiation, from a Wasp-C satellite, had done the job expected and the United States had lost. But

14

People's China had not won. No one had. Hinkel Radiation waves, distributed on a world-wide basis, saw to that, god bless 'em.

Going over, Pete picked up the MV-3 and held it as he had long ago, in his youth. This gun, he realized, is one hundred and thirty years old, almost. An antique twice over. Would it still fire? Who cared . . . there was no one to kill with it, now. Only a psychotic could find grounds to kill in the nearly-empty cities of Earth. And even a psychotic might think it over and change his mind. After all, with fewer than ten thousand people in all California . . . he set the gun back down, carefully.

Anyhow the gun had not been primarily an anti-personnel weapon; its tiny A-cartridges had been intended to penetrate the armor plating of Soviet TL-90 tanks and cripple them. Remembering the training films they had been shown by Sixth Army brass, Pete thought, I'd like to catch sight of a 'human sea' these days. Chinese or not . . . we could use it.

I salute you, Bernhardt Hinkel, he thought caustically. The humane inventor of the ultimate in painless weapons . . . no, it hadn't hurt; you were correct. We felt nothing, didn't even know. And then –

Removal of the Hynes Gland in as many people as possible had been instigated, and it hadn't been a waste of effort; because of it there were people alive today. And certain combinations of male and female were not sterile; it was not an absolute condition, but rather a relative one. We can, in theory, have children; in fact, a few of us do.

The children outside his window, for instance . . .

Along the street a homeostatic maintenance vehicle swished, collecting trash and checking on the growth of lawns, first on one side of the street and then on the other. The steady whirring of the machine rose above the children's voices.

The empty city is kept tidy, Pete said to himself as the

15

machine halted to send out pseudopodia to grope peevishly at a camellia bush. Or rather, virtually empty city – a dozen or so non-B people lived here, at least according to the census he had last been shown.

Behind the maintenance vehicle came a second construct, this one even more elaborate; like a great twenty-legged bug it propelled itself down a driveway, hot on the scent of decay. The repair vehicle would rebuild whatever had fallen into ruin, Pete knew; it would bind up the wounds of the city, halt deterioration before it began. And for what? For whom? Good questions. Perhaps the vugs liked to look down from their observation satellites and see an intact civilization, rather than mere ruins.

Putting out his cigarette, Pete went into the kitchen, hoping to find food for breakfast. He had not inhabited this apartment for several years, but nonetheless he opened the vacuum-sealed refrigerator and found in it bacon and milk and eggs, bread and jam, all in good shape, everything he needed for breakfast. Antonio Nardi had been Bindman in Residence here before Pete; undoubtedly he had left these, not knowing that he was going to lose his title in The Game, would never be coming back.

But there was something more important than breakfast, something Pete had to do first.

Clicking on the vidphone he said, 'I'd like Walter Remington in Contra Costa County.'

'Yes, Mr Garden,' the vidphone said. And the screen, after a pause, lit up.

'Hi.' Walt Remington's dour, elongated features appeared and he gazed dully at Pete. Walt had not shaved yet this morning; stubble coated his jowls, and his eyes, small and red-rimmed, were puffy from lack of sleep. 'Why so early?' he mumbled. He was still in his pajamas.

Pete said, 'Do you remember what happened last night?'

16

'Oh yeah. Sure.' Walt nodded, smoothing his disordered hair in place.

'I lost Berkeley to you. I don't know why I put it up. It's been my bind, my residence, you know.'

'I know,' Walt said.

Taking a deep breath, Pete said, 'I'll trade you three cities in Marin County for it. Ross, San Rafael and San Anselmo. I want it back; I want to live there.'

Walt pointed out, 'You can live in Berkeley. As a non-B resident, of course; not as Bindman.'

'I can't live like that,' Pete said. 'I want to own it, not just be a squatter. Come on, Walt; you don't intend to live in Berkeley. I know you. It's too cold and foggy for you. You like the hot valley climate, like Sacramento. Where you are now, in Walnut Creek.'

'That's true,' Walt said. 'But – I can't trade Berkeley back to you, Pete.' The admission was dragged out of him, then. 'I don't have it. When I got home last night a broker was waiting for me; don't ask me how he knew I'd acquired it from you, but he did. A big wheeler and dealer from the East, Matt Pendleton Associates.' Walt looked glum.

'*And you sold Berkeley to them?*' Pete could hardly believe it. It meant that someone who was not part of their group had managed to buy into California. 'Why'd you do it?' he demanded.

'They traded me Salt Lake City for it,' Walt said, with morose pride. 'How could I turn that down? Now I can join Colonel Kitchener's group; they play in Provo, Utah. Sorry, Pete.' He looked guilty. 'I was still a little stewed, I guess. Anyhow it sounded too good to turn down at the time.'

Pete said, 'Who'd Pendleton Associates acquire it for?'

'They didn't say.'

'And you didn't ask.'

'No,' Walt admitted morosely. 'I didn't. I guess I should have.'

Pete said, 'I want Berkeley back. I'm going to track the deed down and get it back, even if I have to trade off all of Marin County. And in the meantime, I'll be looking forward to beating you at Game-time; look for me to take away everything you've got – no matter who your partner is.' Savagely, he clicked off the vidphone. The screen became dark.

How could Walt do it? he asked himself. Turn the title right over to someone outside the group – someone from the East.

I've got to know who Pendleton Associates would be representing in a deal like that, he said to himself.

He had a feeling, acute and ominous, that he knew.

Chapter 3

It was a very good morning for Mr Jerome Luckman of New York City. Because – and it flashed into his mind the moment he awoke – today was the first time in his life that he owned Berkeley, California. Operating through Matt Pendleton Associates he had at last been able to obtain a choice piece of California real estate, and this meant that now he could sit in on the Game-playing of Pretty Blue Fox which met at Carmel each night. And Carmel was almost as nice a town as Berkeley.

'Sid,' he called. 'Come into my office.' Luckman sat back in his chair, puffed on his after-breakfast delicado Mexican cigarette.

His secretary, non-Bindman Sid Mosk, opened the office door and put his head in. 'Yes, Mr Luckman.'

'Bring me that pre-cog,' Luckman said. 'I've finally got a use for him.' A use, he thought, which justifies the risk of disbarment from The Game. 'What's his name? Dave Mutreaux or something.' Luckman had a hazy memory of interviewing the pre-cog, but a man of his position saw so many people every day. And after all, New York City was well-populated; almost fifteen thousand souls. And many were children, hence new. 'Make sure he comes up a back way,' Luckman said. 'I don't want anybody to see him.' He had his reputation to maintain. And this was a touchy situation.

It was illegal, of course, to bring a person with Psionic talents to The Game, because Psi, in terms of Game-playing, represented a form of cheating pure and simple. For years, EEGs, electroencephalograms, had been given customarily by many groups, but this practice had died out. At least, Luckman hoped so. Certainly, it was done no longer in the East, because all the Psi-people were known, and the East set the style for the whole country, did it not?

One of Luckman's cats, a gray and white short-haired tom, hopped onto his desk; he absently scratched the cat's chin, thinking to himself, If I can't work that pre-cog into the Pretty Blue Fox group, I think I'll go myself. True, he hadn't played The Game in a year or more . . . but he had been the best player around. How else could he have become the Bindman for Greater New York City? And there had been strong competition in those days. Competition which Luckman had rendered non-B single-handedly.

There's no one that can beat me at Bluff, Luckman said to himself. *And everybody knows that.* Still, with a pre-cog . . . it was a sure thing. And he liked the idea of a sure thing because although he was an expert Bluff player he did not like to gamble. He had not played because he enjoyed it; he had played to win.

He had, for instance, run the great Game-player Joe Schilling right out of existence. Now Joe operated a little old phonograph record shop in New Mexico; his Game-playing days were over.

'Remember how I beat Joe Schilling?' he said to Sid. 'That last play, it's still in my mind, every detail. Joe rolled a five with the dice and drew a card from the fifth deck. He looked at it a long time, much too long. I knew then that he was going to bluff. Finally he moved his piece eight squares ahead; that put him on a top-win square; you know, that one about inheriting one hundred and fifty thousand dollars from a dead uncle. That piece of his sat on that square and I looked at it – ' He had, perhaps, a little Psionic talent of his own, because it had seemed to him that actually he could read Joe Schilling's mind. You drew a six, he had felt with absolute conviction. Your move eight squares ahead is a bluff.

Aloud, he said that, called Schilling's bluff. At that time, Joe had been New York City Bindman and could beat anyone at The Game; it was rare for any player to call one of Joe's moves.

Raising his great shaggy, bearded head, Joe Schilling had eyed him. There was silence. All the players waited.

'You really want to see the card I drew?' Joe Schilling asked.

'Yes.' He waited, unable to breathe; his lungs ached. If he were wrong, if the card really were an eight, then Joe Schilling had won again and his grip on New York City was even more secure.

Joe Schilling said quietly, 'It was a six.' He flipped over the card. Luckman had been right; it had been a bluff.

And the title deed to Greater New York City was his.

The cat on Luckman's desk yawped, now, hoping for breakfast; Luckman pushed it away and it hopped to the floor. 'Parasite,' Luckman said to it, but he felt fond of the cat; he believed devoutly that cats were lucky. He had had two toms with him in the condominium apartment that night when he had beaten Joe Schilling; perhaps they had done it, rather than a latent Psionic talent.

'I have Dave Mutreaux on the vid,' his secretary said. 'He's standing by. Do you want to speak to him personally?'

'If he's a genuine pre-cog,' Luckman said, 'he already knows what I want, so there's no need for me or anyone else to speak to the *zwepp*.' The paradoxes of precognition always amused and irked him. 'Cut the circuit, Sid, and if he never shows up here it proves he's no good.'

Sid, obediently, cut the circuit; the screen died. 'But let me point out,' Sid said, 'you never spoke to him, so there never was anything for him to preview. Isn't that right?'

'He can preview the actual interview with me,' Luckman answered. 'Here in my office. When I give him his instructions.'

'I guess that's right,' Sid admitted.

'Berkeley,' Luckman said musingly. 'I haven't been there in eighty or ninety years.' Like many Bindmen he did not like to enter an area which he did not own; it was a superstition, perhaps, but he considered it decidedly bad luck. 'I wonder if it's still foggy there. Well, I'll soon see.' From his desk drawer he brought forth the title deed which the broker had delivered to him. 'Let's see who was Bindman last,' he said, reading the deed. 'Walter Remington; he's the one who won it last night and then right away sold it. And before him, a fellow named Peter Garden. I wouldn't be surprised if this Peter Garden is angry as hell, right now, or will be when he finds out. He probably figured on winning it back.' And he'll never win it back now, Luckman said to himself. Not from me.

'Are you going to fly out there to the Coast?' Sid asked.

'Right,' Luckman said. 'As soon as I can get packed. I'm going to set up a vacation residence in Berkeley assuming I like it – assuming it isn't decayed. One thing I can't stand is a decayed town; I don't mind them empty, that you expect. But decay.' He shuddered. If there was one thing that was surely bad luck it was a town which had fallen into ruin, as many of the towns in the South had. In his early days he had been Bindman for several towns in North Carolina. He would never forget the *fshnuger* experience.

Sid asked, 'Can I be honorary Bindman while you're gone?'

'Sure,' Luckman said expansively. 'I'll write you out a parchment scroll in gold and seal it with red wax and ribbon.'

'Really?' Sid said, eying him uncertainly.

Luckman laughed. 'You'd like that, a lot of ceremony.

22

Like Pooh-bah in *The Mikado*. Lord High Honorary Bindman of New York City, and tax assessments fixed on the side. Right?'

Flushing, Sid murmured, 'I notice you worked hard for darn near sixty-five years to get to be Bindman for this area.'

'That's because of my social plans to improve the milieu,' Luckman said. 'When I took over the title deed there were only a few hundred people here. Now look at the population. It's due to me – not directly, but because I encouraged non-B people to play The Game, strictly for the pairing and re-pairing of mates, isn't that a fact?'

'Sure, Mr Luckman,' Sid said. 'That's a fact.'

'And because of that, a lot of fertile couples were uncovered that otherwise never would have paired off, right?'

'Yes,' Sid said, nodding. 'The way you've got this musical chairs you're practically single-handedly bringing back the human race.'

'And don't forget it,' Luckman said. Bending, he picked up another of his cats, this one a black Manx female. 'I'll take you along,' he told the cat as he petted her. 'I'll take maybe six or seven cats along with me,' he decided. 'For luck.' And also, although he did not say it, for company. Nobody on the West Coast liked him; he would not have his people, his non-Bs, to say hello to him every time he ventured forth. Thinking that, he felt sad. But, he thought, after I've lived there a while I'll have it built up like New York; it won't be an emptiness haunted by the past.

Ghosts, he thought, of our life the way it was, when our population was splitting the seams of this planet, spilling over onto Luna and even Mars. Populations on the verge of migration, and then those stupid jackasses, those Red Chinese, had to use that East German invention of that ex-Nazi, that – he could not even *think* the words that described Bernhardt Hinkel. Too bad Hinkel isn't still alive, Luckman said to himself. I'd like to have a few minutes alone with him. With no one else watching.

The only good thing you could say about the Hinkel Radiation was that it had finally reached East Germany.

There was one person who would know whom Matt Pendleton Associates would be fronting for, Pete Garden decided as he left the apartment in San Rafael and hurried to his parked car. It's worth a trip to New Mexico, to Colonel Kitchener's town, Albuquerque. Anyhow I have to go there to pick up a record.

Two days ago he had received a letter from Joe Schilling, the world's foremost rare phonograph record dealer; a Tito Schipa disc which Pete had asked for had finally been tracked down and was waiting for him.

'Good morning, Mr Garden,' his car said as he unlocked the door with his key.

'Hi,' Pete said, preoccupied.

Now, from the driveway of the apartment house across the street, the two children that he had heard earlier emerged to stare at him.

'Are you the Bindman?' the girl asked. They had made out his insignia, the brilliantly-colored armband. 'We never saw you before, Mr Bindman,' the girl said, awed. She was, Pete guessed, about eight years old.

He explained, 'That's because I haven't been here to Marin County in years.' Walking toward the two of them, he said, 'What are your names?'

'I'm Kelly,' the boy said. He appeared to be younger than the girl, Pete thought. Perhaps six at the most. Both of them were sweet-looking kids. He was glad to have them in his area. 'And my sister's name is Jessica. And we have an older sister named Mary Anne who isn't here; she's in San Francisco, in school.'

24

Three children in one family! Impressed, Pete said, 'What's your last name?'

'McClain,' the girl said. With pride, she said, 'My mother and father are the only people in all California with three children.'

He could believe that. 'I'd like to meet them,' he said.

The girl Jessica pointed. 'We live there in that house. It's funny you don't know my father, since you're the Bindman. It was my father who organized the street-sweeper and maintenance machines; he talked to the vugs about it and they agreed to send them in.'

'You're not afraid of the vugs, are you?' Pete said.

'No.' Both children shook their heads.

'We did fight a war with them,' he reminded the two children.

'But that was a long time ago,' the girl said.

'True,' Pete said. 'Well, I approve of your attitude.' He wished that he shared it.

From the house down the street a slender woman appeared, walking toward them. 'Mom!' the girl Jessica called excitedly. 'Look, here's the Bindman.'

The woman, dark-haired, attractive, wearing slacks and a brightly checkered cotton shirt, lithe and youthful-looking, approached. 'Welcome to Marin County,' she said to Pete. 'We don't see much of you, Mr Garden.' She held out her hand, and they shook.

'I congratulate you,' Pete said.

'For having three children?' Mrs McClain smiled. 'As they say, it's *luck*. Not skill. How about a cup of coffee before you leave Marin County? After all, you may never be back again.'

'I'll be back,' Pete said.

'Indeed.' The woman did not seem convinced; her handsome smile was tinged with irony. 'You know, you're almost a legend to us non-Bs in this area, Mr Garden.

Gosh, we'll be able to liven conversations for weeks to come, telling about our meeting you.'

For the life of him Pete could not tell if Mrs McClain was being sardonic; despite her words, her tone was neutral. She baffled him and he felt confused. 'I really will be back,' he said. 'I've lost Berkeley, where I – '

'Oh,' Mrs McClain said, nodding. Her effective, commanding smile increased. 'I see. Bad luck at The Game. That's why you're visiting us.'

'I'm on my way to New Mexico,' Pete said, and got into his car. 'Possibly I'll see you later on.' He closed the car door. 'Take off,' he instructed the auto-auto.

As the car rose the two children waved. Mrs McClain did not. Why such animosity? Pete wondered. Or had he only imagined it? Perhaps she resented the existence of the two separate groups, B and non-B; perhaps she felt it was unfair that so few people had a chance at the Gameboard.

I wouldn't blame her, Pete realized. But she doesn't understand that any moment any one of us can suddenly become non-B. We have only to recall Joe Schilling . . . once the greatest Bindman in the Western world and now non-B, probably for the rest of his life. The division is not as fixed as all that.

After all, he himself had been non-B once. He had obtained title to real estate the only way legally possible: he had posted his name and then waited for a Bindman somewhere to die. He had followed the rules set up by the vugs, had guessed a particular day, month and year. And sure enough, his guess had been lucky; on May 4, 2143, a Bindman named William Rust Lawrence had died, killed in an auto accident in Arizona. And Pete had become his heir, inherited his holdings and entered his Game-playing group.

The vugs, gamblers to the core, liked such chancy

systems for inheritance. And they abhorred cause and effect situations.

He wondered what Mrs McClain's first name was. Certainly she was pretty, he thought. He had liked her despite her peculiar bitter attitude, liked the way she looked, carried herself. He wished he knew more about the McClain family; perhaps they had once been Bindmen and had been wiped out. That would explain it.

I could ask around, he thought. After all, if they have three children they're certainly quite well known. Joe Schilling hears everything. I can ask him.

Chapter 4

'Sure,' Joseph Schilling said, leading the way through the dusty utter disorder of his record shop to the living quarters behind. 'I know Patricia McClain. How'd you happen to run into her?' He turned questioningly.

Pete said, 'The McClains are living in my bind.' He managed to thread a passage among the piles of records, packing cartons, letters, catalogues and posters from the past. 'How do you ever find anything in this place?' he asked Joe Schilling.

'I have a system,' Schilling said vaguely. 'I'll tell you why Pat McClain's so bitter. She used to be a B, but she was barred from The Game.'

'Why?'

'Pat's a telepath.' Joe Schilling cleared a place at the table in the kitchen and set out two handle-less teacups. 'Oolong tea?' he asked.

'Ah so,' Pete said, nodding.

'I've got your *Don Pasquale* record,' Schilling said as he poured tea from a black ceramic pot. 'The Schipa aria. Da-dum da-da da. A beautiful piece.' Humming, he produced lemon and sugar from the cupboard over the dish-filled sink. Then, in a low voice, he said, 'Look, I've got a customer out front.' He winked at Pete and pointed, peering past the dusty, stained curtain which separated the living quarters from the store. Pete saw a tall, skinny youth with horn-rimmed glasses and shaved head; the youth was examining a tattered, ancient record catalogue. 'A nut,' Schilling said softly. 'Eats yogurt and practices Yoga. And lots of vitamin E – for potency. I get all kinds.'

The youth called in a stammering voice, 'Say, do you h-have any Claudia Muzio records, Mr Sch-schilling?'

'Just the *Letter Scene* from *Traviata*,' Schilling said, making no move to rise from the table.

Pete said, 'I found Mrs McClain physically attractive.'

'Oh yes. Very vivacious. But not for you. She's what Jung described as an introverted feeling type; they run deep. They're inclined toward idealism and melancholy. You need a shallow, bright blonde type of woman, someone to cheer you up. Someone to get you out of your suicidal depressions that you're always either falling into or out of.' Schilling sipped his tea, a few drops spattering his reddish, thick beard. 'Well? Say something. Or are you in a depression right now?'

'No,' Pete said.

In the front of the store the tall, skinny youth called, 'M-mr Schilling, can I listen to this Gigli record of *Una Furtiva Lagrima*?'

'Sure,' Schilling said. He hummed that, absently, scratching his cheek. 'Pete,' he said, 'you know, rumors get to me. I hear you've lost Berkeley.'

'Yes,' Pete admitted. 'And Matt Pendleton Associates – '

'That would be Lucky Jerome Luckman,' Schilling said. '*Oy vey*, he's a hard man in The Game; I ought to know. Now he'll be sitting in with your group and pretty soon he'll own all of California.'

'Can't anybody play against Luckman and beat him?'

'Sure.' Joe Schilling nodded. 'I can.'

Pete stared at him. 'You're serious? But he wiped you out; you're a classic case!'

'Just bad luck,' Schilling said. 'If I had had more title deeds to put up, if I had been able to stay in a little longer – ' He smiled a bleak, crooked smile. 'Bluff's a fascinating game. Like poker, it combines chance and skill equally; you can win by either, or lose by either. I

29

lost by the former, on a single bad run – actually, on a single lucky guess by Luckman.'

'Not skill on his part.'

'Hell no! Luckman is to luck as I am to skill; we ought to be called Luckman and Skillman. If I ever get a stake and can start again . . .' Joe Schilling abruptly belched. 'Sorry.'

'I'll stake you,' Pete said, suddenly, on impulse.

'You can't afford to. I'm expensive, because I don't start winning right away. It takes time for my skill-factor to overcome any chance runs . . . such as the celebrated one by which Luckman wiped me out.'

From the front of the store came the sounds of the superb tenor Gigli singing; Schilling paused a moment to listen. Across from the table his huge dingy parrot Eeore shifted about in its cage, annoyed by the sharp, pure voice. Schilling gave the parrot a reproving glance.

'*Thy Tiny Hand is Frozen*,' Schilling said. 'The first of the two recordings Gigli made of that, and by far the better. Ever heard the latter of the two? From the complete opera and so bad as to be unbelievable. Wait.' He silenced himself, listening. 'A superb record,' he said to Pete. 'You should have it in your collection.'

'I don't care for Gigli,' Pete said. 'He sobs.'

'A convention,' Schilling said irritably. 'He was an Italian; it's traditional.'

'Schipa didn't.'

'Schipa was self-taught,' Schilling said.

The tall, skinny youth had approached, carrying the Gigli record. 'I'd l-like to buy this, Mr Schilling. H-how much?'

'One hundred and twenty-five dollars,' Schilling said.

'Wow,' the youth said, dismally. But nevertheless he got out his wallet.

'Very few of these survived the war with the vugs,'

Schilling explained, as he took the record and began wrapping it in heavy cardboard.

Two more customers entered the shop, then, a man and woman, both of them short, squat. Schilling greeted them. 'Good morning, Les. Es.' To Pete he said, 'This is Mr and Mrs Sibley; like yourself vocal addicts. From Portland, Oregon.' He indicated Pete. 'Bindman Peter Garden.'

Pete rose and shook hands with Les Sibley.

'Hi, Mr Garden,' Les Sibley said, in the deferential tone used by a non-B with a B. 'Where do you bind, sir?'

'Berkeley,' Pete said, and then remembered. 'Formerly Berkeley, now Marin County, California.'

'How do you doo,' Es Sibley said, in an ultra-fawning manner which Pete found – and always had found – objectionable. She held out her hand and when he shook it he found it soft and damp. 'I'll bet you have a really fine collection; I mean, ours isn't anything. Just a few Supervia records.'

'Supervia!' Pete said, interested. 'What do you have?'

Joe Schilling said, 'You can't eliminate, Pete. It's an unwritten agreement that my customers do not trade among themselves. If they do, I stop selling to them. Anyhow, you have all the Supervia records that Les and Es have, and a couple more besides.' He rang up the hundred and twenty-five dollars from the Gigli sale, and the tall, skinny youth departed.

'What do you consider the finest vocal recording ever made?' Es Sibley asked Pete.

'Aksel Schitz singing *Every Valley*,' Pete said.

'Amen to that,' Les said, nodding in agreement.

After the Sibleys had left, Pete paid for his Schipa record, had Joe Schilling wrap it extra-carefully, and then he took a deep breath and plunged into the issue at hand. 'Joe, can you win Berkeley back for me?' If Joe Schilling said yes it was good enough for him.

After a pause, Joe Schilling said, 'Possibly. If anybody can, I can. There is a ruling – little applied – that two persons of the same sex can play as Bluff partners. We could see if Luckman would accept that; we might have to put it to the vug Commissioner in your area for a ruling.'

'That would be a vug which calls itself US Cummings,' Pete said. He had had a number of squabbles with that particular vug; he had found the creature to be particularly trying, in a nit-picking manner.

'The alternative,' Joe Schilling said thoughtfully, 'would of course be to temporarily deed title to some of your remaining areas to me, but as I said before – '

'Aren't you out of practice?' Pete said. 'It's been years since you played The Game.'

'Possibly,' Schilling conceded. 'We'd soon find out, I hope, in time. I think – ' He glanced toward the front of the store; another auto-auto had parked outside and a customer was entering.

It was a lovely red-headed girl, and both Pete and Joe temporarily forgot their conversation. The girl, evidently at a loss in the chaotic, littered store, wandered about aimlessly from stack to stack.

'I better go help her,' Joe Schilling said.

'Do you know her?' Pete asked.

'Never saw her before.' Pausing, Joe Schilling straightened his wrinkled, old-fashioned necktie, smoothed his vest. 'Miss,' he said, walking toward the girl and smiling, 'can I assist you?'

'Perhaps,' the red-headed girl said in a soft, shy voice. She seemed self-conscious; glancing about her, not meeting Schilling's intent gaze, she murmured, 'Do you have any records by Nats Katz?'

'Good grief no,' Schilling said. He turned around and

said to Pete, 'My day's ruined. A pretty girl comes in and asks for a Nats Katz record.' In chagrin, he walked back to Pete.

'Who's Nats Katz?' Pete asked.

The girl, roused by amazement from her shyness, said, 'You've never heard of Nats Katz?' Clearly, she could not believe it. 'Why he's on TV every night; he's the greatest recording star of all time!'

Pete said, 'Mr Schilling here does not sell pops. Mr Schilling sells only ancient classics.' He smiled at the girl. It was hard, with the Hynes Gland operation, to assess a person's age, but it seemed to him that the red-headed girl was quite young, perhaps no more than nineteen. 'You should excuse Mr Schilling's reaction,' Pete said to her. 'He's an old man and set in his habits.'

Schilling grated, 'Come on, now. I just don't like popular ballad-belters.'

'*Everybody's* heard of Nats,' the girl said, still indignant. 'Even my mother and father, and they're distinctly fnool. Nats' last record, *Walkin' the Dog*, has sold over five thousand copies. You're both really strange people. You're real fnools, for real.' Now she became shy again. 'I guess I better go. So long.' She started toward the door of the shop.

'Wait,' Schilling said in an odd tone, starting after her. 'Don't I know you? Haven't I seen a news-wire picture of you?'

'Maybe,' the girl said.

Schilling said, 'You're Mary Anne McClain.' He turned to Pete. 'This is the third child of the woman you met today. It's synchronicity, her coming in here; you recall Jung's and Wolfgang Pauli's theory of the acausal connective principle.' To the girl, Schilling said, 'This man is Bindman for your area, Mary Anne. Meet Peter Garden.'

'Hi,' the girl said, unimpressed. 'Well, I have to go.' She disappeared out the door of the shop and got back into her car; Pete and Joe Schilling stood watching until the car took off and was gone.

'How old do you think she is?' Pete said.

'I know how old she is; I remember reading it. She's eighteen. One of twenty-nine students at San Francisco State College, majoring in history. Mary Anne was the first child born in San Francisco in the past hundred years.' His tone, now, was somber. 'God help the world,' he said, 'if anything happens to her, any kind of an accident or illness.'

Both of them were silent.

'She reminds me a little of her mother,' Pete said.

Joe Schilling said, 'She's stunningly attractive.' He eyed Pete. 'I suppose now you've changed your mind; you want to stake her instead of me.'

'She's probably never had an opportunity to play The Game.'

'Meaning?'

'She wouldn't make a good Bluff partner.'

'Right,' Joe said. 'Not nearly as good as me. And don't forget that. What's your marital status, right now?'

'When I lost Berkeley, Freya and I split up. She's now Mrs Gaines. I'm looking for a wife.'

'But you've got to have one who can play,' Joe Schilling said. 'A Bindman wife. Or you'll lose Marin County just like you lost Berkeley and then what'll you do? The world can't use two rare-record shops.'

Pete said, 'I've thought over and over again for years what I'd do if I were wiped out at the table. I'd become a farmer.'

Guffawing, Joe said, 'Indeed. Now you say, "I was never so serious in all my life."'

Pete said, 'I was never so serious in all my life.'

'Where?'

'In the Sacramento Valley. I'd raise grapes for wine. I've already looked into it.' He had, in fact, discussed it with the vug Commissioner, US Cummings; the vug authority would undoubtedly support him with farm equipment and cuttings. It was the type of project which they approved of in principle.

'By god,' Schilling said, 'I think you do mean it.'

'I'd charge you extra,' Pete said, 'because you're so rich from gouging record buyers all these years.'

'*Ich bin ein armer Mensch*,' Schilling protested. 'I'm poor.'

'Well, possibly we could trade. Wine for rare records.'

'Seriously,' Joe Schilling said, 'if Luckman enters your group and you have to play against him, I'll come into The Game as your partner.' He slapped Pete on the shoulder, encouragingly. 'So don't worry. Between the two of us we can take him. Of course, I'd expect you not to drink while you're playing.' He eyed Pete keenly. 'I heard about that; you were bagged when you put up Berkeley and lost it. You could hardly reel out of the con-apt to your car when it was over.'

With dignity, Pete stated, 'I drank *after* I lost. For consolation.'

'However it may have been, my ukase still stands. No drinking on your part, if we become partners; you have to swear off, and that includes any pills. I don't want your wits dulled by tranquilizers, especially the phenothiazine class . . . I particularly distrust them, and I know you take them regularly.'

Pete said nothing; it was so. He shrugged, wandered about the store, poking at a stack of records here and there. He felt discouraged.

'And I'll practice,' Joe Schilling said. 'I'll train, sincerely put myself in top shape.' He poured himself a fresh cup of oolong tea.

'Maybe I'm going to wind up a lush,' Pete said. And, with a possible life-span of two hundred and some years . . . it could be pretty dreadful.

'I don't think so,' Joe Schilling said. 'You're too morose to become an alcoholic. I'm more afraid of – ' He hesitated.

'Go ahead and say it,' Pete said.

'Suicide.'

Pete slid an ancient HMV record from a stack and examined the label. He did not look directly at Schilling; he avoided meeting the man's wise, blunt gaze.

'Would you be better off back with Freya?' Schilling inquired.

'Naw.' Pete gestured. 'I can't explain it, because on a rational basis we made a good pair. But something intangible didn't work. In my opinion, that's why she and I lost at the table; somehow we never could really pull together as a couple.' He recalled his wife before Freya, Janice Marks, now Janice Remington. They had cooperated successfully; at least it had seemed so to him. But of course they had not had any *luck*.

As a matter of fact, Pete Garden had never had any *luck*; in all the world he had no progeny. The goddam Red Chinese, he said to himself . . . he wrote it off with the customary envenomed phrase. And yet –

'Schilling,' he said, 'do you have any issue?'

'Yes,' Schilling said. 'I thought everyone knew. A boy, eleven years old, in Florida. His mother was my – ' He counted for a time. 'My sixteenth wife. I only had two more wives before Luckman wiped me out.'

'How much issue has Luckman exactly? I've heard it placed at nine or ten.'

'About eleven, by now.'

'Christ!' Pete said.

'We should face the fact,' Joe Schilling said, 'that Luckman, in many ways, *is the finest, most valuable human being alive today*. The most direct issue, the greatest success in Bluff; his amelioration of the status of the non-Bs in his area.'

36

'All right,' Pete said irritably. 'Let's drop it.'

'And,' Schilling continued, unperturbed, 'the vugs like him.' He added, 'As a matter of fact virtually everyone likes him. You've never met him, have you?'

'No.'

'You'll see what I mean,' Joe Schilling said, 'when he gets out to the West Coast and joins Pretty Blue Fox.'

To the pre-cog Dave Mutreaux, Luckman said expansively, 'I'm glad to see you got here.' It pleased him because it demonstrated the reality of the man's talent. It was, so to speak, a *de facto* case for using Mutreaux.

The lanky, well-dressed, middle-aged Psi-man – he was in fact a minor Bindman in his own right, possessing the title to a meager county in Western Kansas – seated himself sprawlingly in the deep chair facing Luckman's desk and drawled, 'We've got to be careful, Mr Luckman. Extremely careful. I've been severely limiting myself, trying to keep my talent out of sight. I can preview what you want me to do; fact is, I previewed it coming over here by auto-auto. Frankly I'm surprised that a man of your *luck* and stature would want to employ me.' A slow, insulting grin crossed the pre-cog's features.

Luckman said, 'I'm afraid when the players out on the Coast see me sitting in they won't want to play. They'll band together against me and conspire to keep their really valuable deeds in their safety deposit boxes instead of putting them out on the table. You see, David, they may not know it's me who obtained the Berkeley deed, because I – '

'They know,' Mutreaux said, still grinning lazily.

'Oh.'

'The rumor's already going around . . . I heard it on that crooner's TV show, that Nats Katz. It's big news, Luckman, that you've managed to buy into the West

37

Coast. Real big news. "Watch Lucky Luckman's smoke," Nats said; I recall his words.'

'Hmm,' Luckman said, disconcerted.

'I'll tell you something else,' the pre-cog said. He crossed his long legs, slouched down in the chair, his arms folded. 'I can preview a spread of possible *this-evenings*, some of them with me out there in Carmel, California, sitting in at The Game with the Pretty Blue Fox folks, and some with you.' He chuckled. 'And in a couple of the possible *this-evenings*, those folks are sending out for an EEG machine. Don't ask me why. They don't normally keep one handy, so it must be a hunch.'

'Bad luck,' Luckman said, grumblingly.

'If I go there and they give me an EEG,' Mutreaux said, 'and find out I'm Psionic, you know what that means? I lose all the deeds I hold. See what I'm getting at, Luckman? Are you prepared to reimburse me, if that occurs?'

'Sure,' Luckman said. But he was thinking of something else; if an EEG was run on Mutreaux, the Berkeley deed would be forfeited, and who would make *that* up? Maybe I better go myself and not use Mutreaux, he said to himself. But some primal instinct, some near-Psionic hunch inside his mind, told him not to go. Stay away from the West Coast, it said. Stay here!

Why should he feel such a powerful, acute aversion to venturing forth from New York City? Was it merely the old superstition that a Bindman stayed in his own bind . . . *or was it something more?*

'I'm going to send you anyhow, Dave,' Luckman said. 'And risk the EEG.'

Mutreaux drawled, 'However, Mr Luckman, I decline to go; I don't care to take the risk myself.' Unwinding his limbs he rose awkwardly to his feet. 'I guess you'll just have to go yourself,' he said with a smile bordering on an outright smirk.

Damn it, Luckman said to himself. These little two-bit Bindmen are haughty; you can't get to them.

'What have you got to lose by going?' Mutreaux asked. 'As far as I can preview, Pretty Blue Fox plays with you, and it appears, from here, that your luck holds out; I see you winning a second California deed the first night you play.' He added, 'This forecast I give you free. No obligation.' He touched his forehead in a mock salute.

'Thanks,' Luckman snapped. Thanks for nothing, he thought. Because the biting, weak fright was still there in him, the pre-rational aversion to the trip. Gawd, he thought, I'm hooked; I paid plenty for Berkeley. I've *got* to go! Anyhow, it's unreasonable, this fear.

One of his cats, an orange tom, had ceased washing and was now staring at Luckman with its tongue absurdly protruding. I'll take you, Luckman decided. You can provide me with your magic protection. You and your – what was the old belief? – your nine or ten lives.

'Put your *geschlumer* tongue back in,' he ordered the cat peevishly. The cat irritated him; it was so ignorant of fate, of reality.

Extending his hand, Dave Mutreaux said, 'It's good to see you again, fellow Bindman Luckman, and maybe I can be of use to you some other time. I'm heading back to Kansas now.' He glanced at his watch. 'It's getting late; almost time to begin this evening's play.'

Luckman said, as he shook hands with the pre-cog, 'Should I start this soon with Pretty Blue Fox? Tonight?'

'Why not?'

'Seeing the future must give you a hell of a lot of confidence,' Luckman said, complainingly.

'It is useful,' Mutreaux agreed.

'I wish I had it on my trip,' Luckman said, and then he thought, I'm tired of catering to my superstitions. I don't need any Psionic power to protect me; I've got a lot more than that.

Sid Mosk, entering the office, glanced from Luckman to Mutreaux and then back at his employer again. 'You're going?' he said.

'That's right.' Luckman nodded. 'Pack my things for me and load them into an auto-auto; I intend to set up a temporary residence in Berkeley before The Game begins this evening. So I'll feel comfortable; you know, as if I belong.'

'Will do,' Sid Mosk agreed, making a note of the request.

Before I go to bed tonight, Luckman realized, I'll have sat in with Pretty Blue Fox, will have begun almost a new life . . . I wonder what it'll bring?

Once more, fervently, he wished for Dave Mutreaux' talent.

Chapter 5

In the condominium apartment in Carmel which the Bluff-playing group of Bindmen, Pretty Blue Fox, owned jointly, Mrs Freya Gaines, making herself comfortable, not sitting too close to her husband Clem, watched the others arrive one by one.

Bill Calumine, sauntering aggressively through the open door in his loud sports shirt and tie, nodded to her and Clem. 'Greetings.' His wife and Bluff partner Arlene followed after him, a preoccupied frown of worry on her rather wrinkled face. Arlene had taken advantage of the Hynes operation somewhat later in life than had the others.

'Hi ya,' Walt Remington said gloomily, glancing furtively around as he entered with his alert, bright-eyed wife Janice. 'I understand we've got a new member,' he said in a self-conscious, uncomfortable voice; guilt was written all over him as he shakily removed his coat and laid it over a chair.

'Yes,' Freya said to him. And you know why, she thought.

Now the sandy-haired baby of the group, Stuart Marks, put in his appearance, and with him his tall, masculine, no-nonsense wife Yule, wearing a black suede leather jacket and jeans. 'I was listening to Nats Katz,' Stuart said, 'and he said – '

'He was correct,' Clem Gaines answered. 'Lucky Luckman is already on the West Coast, setting up residence in Berkeley.'

Carrying a bottle of whiskey wrapped up in a paper

bag, Silvanus Angst strolled in, smiling broadly at everyone, in a good mood as always. And immediately after him came swarthy Jack Blau, his dark eyes flickering as he looked at everyone in the room; he jerked his head in greeting but did not speak.

Jean, his wife, greeted Freya. 'You might be interested . . . we looked into the business of getting Pete a new wife; we were with Straw Man Special for two whole hours, today.'

'Any luck?' Freya asked, trying to make her voice sound casual.

'Yes,' Jean Blau said. 'There's a woman named Carol Holt coming over from Straw Man Special, this evening; she should be here any time.'

'What's she like?' Freya said, preparing herself.

Jean said, 'Intelligent.'

'I mean,' Freya said, 'what does she look like?'

'Brown hair. Small. I really can't describe her; why don't you just wait?' Jean glanced toward the door, and there stood Pete Garden; he had come in and was standing listening.

'Hi,' Freya said to him. 'They found you a wife.'

Pete said to Jean, 'Thanks.' His voice was gruff.

'Well, you must have a partner to play,' Jean pointed out.

'I'm not sore,' Pete said. Like Silvanus Angst, he carried a bottle wrapped up in a paper bag; he now set it down on the sideboard next to Silvanus' and took off his coat. 'In fact I'm glad,' he said.

Silvanus giggled and said, 'What Pete's worried about is the man who got hold of the Berkeley deed, isn't it, Pete? Lucky Luckman, they say.' Short and plump, Silvanus waddled over to Freya and stroked her hair. 'You worried, too?'

Carefully disengaging Angst's fingers from her hair, Freya said, 'I certainly am. It's a terrible thing.'

'It is,' Jean Blau agreed. 'We'd better discuss it before Luckman gets here; there must be something we can do.'

'Refuse to seat him?' Angst said. 'Refuse to play against him?'

Freya said, 'No vital deeds should be offered during the play. His getting a toe-hold here in California is bad enough; if he gains more – '

'We mustn't permit it,' Jack Blau agreed. He glared at Walt Remington. 'How could you do it? We ought to expel you. And you're such a jackass you probably haven't got any idea what you've done.'

'He understands,' Bill Calumine said. 'He didn't intend to; he sold to brokers and they right away – '

'That's no excuse,' Jack Blau said.

Clem Gaines said, 'One thing we can do, we can insist that he submit to an EEG. I took the liberty of bringing a machine along. That might bar him. We ought to be able to bar him *somehow*.'

'Should we check with US Cummings and see if it has any idea?' Jean Blau asked. 'I know it's contrary to their intentions to have one man dominate both coasts; they were upset when Luckman pushed Joe Schilling out of New York City, in fact – I remember that distinctly.'

'I'd prefer not to turn to the vugs,' Bill Calumine said. He looked around at the group. 'Anybody else have any ideas? Speak up.'

There was an uneasy silence.

'Aw come on,' Stuart Marks said. 'Can't we just – ' He gestured. 'You know. Scare him physically. There're six men, here. Against one.'

After a pause Bill Calumine said, 'I'm for that. A little force. At least we can agree to combine against him during The Game itself. And if – '

He broke off. Someone had come in.

Rising to her feet, Jean Blau said, 'Folks, this is the new player who's come to us from Straw Man Special,

43

Carol Holt.' Jean advanced to take the girl by the arm and lead her into the room. 'Carol, this is Freya and Clem Gaines, Jean and Jack Blau, Silvanus Angst, Walter and Janice Remington, Stuart Marks, Yule Marks, and over here is your Bluff partner, Pete Garden. Pete, this is Carol Holt; we spent two hours picking her out for you.'

'And I'm Mrs Angst,' Mrs Angst said, entering the room after Carol. 'My, but this is an exciting night. Two new people, I understand.'

Freya studied Carol Holt and wondered what Pete's reaction was; he showed nothing on the surface, only polite formality as he greeted the girl. He seemed abstracted tonight. Perhaps he hadn't entirely recovered from the shock of the night before. She herself had not, certainly.

The girl from Straw Man Special, Freya decided, was not too terribly bright-looking. And yet she appeared to have personality; her hair was nicely bound up in the currently-modish ratnest knot and her eye make-up was well-applied. Carol wore low-heeled slippers, no stockings, and a madras wrap-around skirt which made her seem, Freya thought, a trifle hefty at the midsection. But she had nice fair skin, and her voice, when she spoke, was pleasant enough.

Even so, Freya concluded, Pete won't go for her; she's just not his kind. And what is Pete's kind? she asked herself. Me? No, not herself either. Their marriage had been one-sided; she had felt all the deep emotions and Pete had simply been gloomy, anticipating in some vague way the calamity which would end their relationship: the loss of Berkeley.

'Pete,' Freya reminded him, 'you still have to roll a three.'

Turning to Bill Calumine, their spinner, Pete said, 'Give me the device and I'll begin now. How many turns am I allowed?' A complex rule governed the situation, and Jack Blau went off to get the rules book to look it up.

Together, Bill Calumine and Jack Blau decided that tonight Pete was entitled to six throws.

Carol said, 'I didn't realize he hadn't rolled his three, yet. I hope I haven't made a trip all the way here for nothing.' She seated herself on the arm of a couch, smoothed her skirt over her knees – fair, smooth knees, Freya noted – and lit a cigarette, looking bored.

Seated with the spinning device, Pete rolled. His first roll was a nine. To Carol he said, 'I'm doing the best I can.' In his voice there was an overtone of resentment. His new relationship, Freya saw, was getting into motion in the customary way. She smiled to herself. It was impossible not to take a measure of enjoyment in the situation.

Scowling, Pete rolled again. This time it was ten.

'We can't start playing anyhow,' Janice Remington said brightly. 'We have to wait for Mr Luckman to get here.'

Carol Holt snorted smoke from her nostrils and said, 'Good god, is Lucky Luckman a part of Pretty Blue Fox? Nobody told me that!' She shot a brief, tense glare in Jean Blau's direction.

Seated with the spinner, Pete said, 'I got it.' He rose stiffly to his feet.

Bending, Bill Calumine said, 'He sure did. A real, authentic three.' He picked up the spinner; it was over. 'Now the ceremony and except for waiting on Mr Luckman we can go ahead.'

Patience Angst said, 'I'm vows-giver this week, Bill. I'll administer the ceremony.' She brought out the group ring which she passed to Pete Garden; Pete stood beside Carol Holt, who had not yet recovered from the news about Lucky Luckman. 'Carol and Peter, we are gathered here to witness your entering into holy matrimony. Terran and Titanian law cojoin to empower me to ask you if you

45

voluntarily acquiesce in this sacred and legal binding. Do you, Peter, take Carol to be your lawful wedded wife?'

'Yes,' Pete said, glumly. Or so it seemed to Freya.

'Do you, Carol – ' Patience Angst paused, because a new figure had appeared in the doorway of the condominium apartment. It stood silently watching.

Lucky Luckman, the big winner from New York, the greatest Bindman in the Western world, had arrived. Everyone in the room turned at once to look.

'Don't let me interrupt,' Luckman said, and did not budge.

Patience, then, murmuringly continued the ceremony to its conclusion.

So this is what the one and only Lucky Luckman looks like, Freya said to herself. A brawny man, stockily-built, with a round, apple-shaped face, all his coloration pale and straw-like, a peculiar vegetable quality as if Luckman had been nourished indoors. His hair had a soft, thin texture and did not hide the pinkish scalp. At least Luckman had a clean, well-washed look, Freya observed. His clothes, neutral in cut and quality, showed taste. But his hands . . . she found herself staring at his hands. Luckman's wrists were thick and furred with the same pale whisker-like hair; the hands themselves were small, the fingers short, and the skin near his knuckles was spotted with what appeared perhaps to be freckles. His voice was oddly high-pitched, mild. She did not like him. There was something wrong with him; he had a capon-like quality, like a defrocked, barred priest. He looked soft where he should be hard.

And we really have worked out no strategy against him, Freya said to herself. We don't know how to work together and now it's too late.

I wonder how many of us in this room will be playing a week from now, she thought.

46

We must find a way to stop this man, she said to herself.

'And this is my wife Dotty,' Jerome Luckman was saying, introducing to the group an ample, crow-haired, Italian-looking woman who smiled nicely around at them all. Pete Garden scarcely paid any attention. Let's get the EEG machine in here, he thought. He went over to Bill Calumine and squatted down beside him.

'It's EEG time,' he said softly to Calumine. 'As a starter.'

'Yes.' Calumine nodded, rose and disappeared into the other room, along with Clem Gaines. Presently he returned, the Crofts-Harrison machine tagging along behind him, a wheeled egg with coiled receptors, rows of meters sparkling. It had not been used for a long time; the group was quite stable. Until now.

But now, Pete thought, it's all changed; we have two new members, one of whom is unknown, the other a patent enemy who must be fought with all we've got. And he felt the struggle personally because the deed had been his. Luckman, entranced at the Claremont Hotel in Berkeley, now dwelt in Pete's own bind. What could constitute a more intimate invasion than that? He stared at Luckman and now the short, light-haired big Bindman from the East stared back. Neither man said anything; there was nothing to say.

'An EEG,' Luckman said, as he made out the Crofts-Harrison machine. An unusual, twisting grimace touched his features. 'Why not?' He glanced at his wife. 'We don't mind, do we?' He held out his arm, and Calumine strapped the anode belt tightly in place. 'You won't find any Psi-power in me,' Luckman said as the cathode terminal was fixed to his temple. He continued to smile.

Presently the Crofts-Harrison machine excreted its short spool of printed tape. Bill Calumine, as official group spinner, examined it, then passed it to Pete. Together, they read the tape, silently conferring.

No Psionic cephalic activity, Pete decided, at least not at the moment. It might come and go; that's common, certainly. So anyhow, dammit, we can't legitimately bar Luckman on this count. Too bad, he thought, and returned the tape to Calumine, who then passed it to Stu Marks and Silvanus Angst.

'Am I clean?' Luckman asked, genially. He seemed utterly confident, and why not? It was they who should worry, not he. Obviously, Luckman knew it.

Walt Remington said hoarsely, 'Mr Luckman, I'm personally responsible for your having this opportunity to invade Pretty Blue Fox.'

'Oh, Remington,' Luckman said.. He extended his hand, but Walt ignored it. 'Say, don't blame yourself; I would have gotten in eventually anyhow.'

Dotty Luckman spoke up. 'That's so, Mr Remington. Don't feel bad; my husband can get into any group he likes.' Her eyes shone proudly.

'What am I,' Luckman growled, 'some sort of monster? I play fair; nobody ever accused me of cheating. I play the same as you do, to win.' He looked from one of them to the next, waiting for an answer. He did not seem much perturbed, however; it was evidently a merely formal question. Luckman did not expect to change their feelings, and perhaps he did not even want to.

Pete said, 'We feel, Mr Luckman, that you already have more than your share. The Game wasn't contrived as an excuse to achieve economic monopoly and you know it.' He was silent, then, because that fairly well expressed it. The others in the group were nodding in agreement.

'I tell you what,' Luckman said. 'I like to see everyone happy about things; I don't see any reason for this suspicion and gloom. Maybe you're not very confident in your own abilities; maybe that's it. Anyhow, how about this? For every California title deed I win – ' He paused, enjoying their tension. 'I'll contribute to the group a title deed for a town in some other state. So no matter what happens, you'll all still wind up Bindmen . . . maybe not here on the Coast, but somewhere.' He grinned, showing teeth so regular that – to Pete Garden, anyhow – they seemed palpably false.

'Thanks,' Freya said frigidly.

No one else spoke.

Is it meant to be an insult? Pete wondered. Maybe Luckman sincerely intends it; maybe he's that primitive, that naïve about human feelings.

The door opened and a vug came in.

It was, Pete saw, the District Commissioner, U. S. Cummings. What did it want? he wondered. Had the Titanians heard about Luckman's move to the West Coast? Now the vug, after its fashion, greeted the members of the group.

'What do you want?' Bill Calumine asked it sourly. 'We're just about to sit down to play.'

The vug's thoughts came to them. 'Sorry for this intrusion. Mr Luckman, what is the meaning of your presence here? Produce your document of validation that entitles you to enter this group.'

'Oh, come on,' Luckman said. 'You know I've got the deed.' He reached into his coat, brought out a large envelope. 'What is this, a gag?'

Extending pseudopodia, the vug inspected the deed, then returned it to Luckman. 'You neglected to notify us of your entry into this group.'

'I don't have to,' Luckman said. 'It's not mandatory.'

'Nevertheless,' U. S. Cummings declared, 'it's protocol. What is your intention here at Pretty Blue Fox?'

Luckman said, 'I intend to win.'

The vug seemed to contemplate him; it was silent for a time.

49

'That's my legal right,' Luckman added. He seemed a little nervous. 'You don't have any power to intercede in this. You're not our masters; let me refer you to the Concordat of 2095 signed between your military and the UN. All you can do is make recommendations and give assistance to us when it's requested. I didn't hear anybody request your presence here in this room tonight.' He looked around at the group for agreement.

Bill Calumine said to the vug, 'We can handle this.'

'That's right,' Stuart Marks said. 'So beat it, vuggy. Go on.' He went to get the vug-stick; it was propped up in the corner of the room.

U. S. Cummings, with no further thoughts in their direction, departed.

As soon as it had gone, Jack Blau said, 'Let's begin playing.'

'Right,' Bill Calumine agreed. Producing his key, he went to the locked closet; a moment later he was laying out the large Game-board on the table in the center of the room. The others began drawing up their chairs, making themselves comfortable, deciding whom they wanted to sit beside.

Coming up to Pete, Carol Holt said, 'We probably won't do too well at first, Mr Garden. Since we're not used to each other's styles.'

It was time, Pete judged, to tell her about Joe Schilling. 'Listen,' he said. 'I hate to say this but you and I may not be partners very long.'

'Oh?' Carol said. 'Why not?' She eyed him.

Pete said, 'I'm frankly more interested in winning Berkeley back than I am in anything else – than in *luck*, as the popular phrase has it. In the biological sense.' Despite the fact, he thought, that both the Terran and Titanian authorities who set up The Game considered it primarily a means to that end, rather than to the economic end.

'You've never seen me play,' Carol said. She walked swiftly over to the corner of the room and stood with her hands behind her back, regarding him. 'I'm quite good.'

'Perhaps good,' Pete agreed, 'but hardly good enough to beat Luckman. And that's the issue. I'll play with you tonight, but tomorrow I want to bring in someone else. No offense meant.'

'But I am offended,' Carol said.

He shrugged. 'Then you'll have to be offended.'

'Who is this person you want to bring in?'

'Joe Schilling.'

'The rare-record man?' The girl's honey-colored eyes widened with amazement. 'But – '

'I know Luckman beat him,' Pete said. 'But I don't think he can do it again. Schilling is a good friend of mine; I have confidence in him.'

'Which is more,' Carol Holt said, 'than you can say about me, right? You're not even interested in seeing how I play. You've already decided. I wonder why you bothered to go through with the marriage ceremony.'

Pete said, 'For tonight – '

'I suggest,' Carol said, 'that we not even bother about tonight.' Her cheeks had flushed dark red now; she was quite angry.

'Now listen,' Pete said, uneasy now, wanting to mollify her. 'I didn't intend to – '

'You don't want to hurt me,' Carol Holt said, 'but you have, very much. At Straw Man Special my friends had all the respect in the world for me. I'm not used to this.' She blinked rapidly.

'For god's sake,' Pete said, horrified. He took her by the hand, propelled her from the room and outside, into the night darkness. 'Listen. I just wanted to prepare you in case I brought Joe Schilling in; Berkeley was my place of bind and I'm just not going to give up on it, don't you understand? It has nothing to do with you. You may be

51

the best Bluff-player on Earth, for all I know.' He took hold of her by the shoulders, gripping her. 'Now let's stop this bickering and go back in; they're starting to play.'

Carol sniffed. 'Just a minute.' She found a handkerchief in her skirt pocket and blew her nose.

'Come on, you fellows,' Bill Calumine called, from within the apartment.

Silvanus Angst appeared in the doorway. 'We're starting.' He giggled, seeing them. 'The economic part right now, Mr Garden, if you please.'

Together, Pete and Carol returned to the lighted living room and The Game. 'We were discussing our strategy,' Pete said to Calumine.

'But as regards to what?' Janice Remington said, and winked.

Freya glanced first at Pete and then at Carol; she said nothing however. The others were already involved in carefully watching Luckman; they did not care about anything else. Title deeds were starting to appear. Reluctantly, one by one they were put into the pot basket.

'Mr Luckman,' Yule Marks said bluntly, 'you have to put up the Berkeley deed; it's the only California real estate you own.' She and the rest of the group watched intently as Luckman deposited the large envelope in the basket. 'I hope,' Yule said, 'that you lose it and never show up here again.'

'You're an outspoken woman,' Luckman said, with a wry smile. His expression, then, seemed to harden; it became rigid, fixed in place.

Pete thought, He intends to beat us. He's made up his mind; he has no more liking for us than we have for him.

It's going to be a dirty, hard business.

'I withdraw my offer,' Luckman said. 'Of giving you title deeds to towns outside California.' He picked up the stack of numbered cards and began to shuffle them

52

magnificently. 'In view of your hostility. It's clear that we can't have even the semblance of cordiality.'

'That's right,' Walt Remington said in answer.

No one else spoke, but it was as evident to Luckman as it was to Pete Garden that each person in the room felt the same way.

'Draw for first play,' Bill Calumine said, and took a card from the shuffled deck.

To himself Jerome Luckman thought, These people are going to pay for their attitude. I came here legally and decently; I did my part and they wouldn't have that.

His turn to draw a card came; he drew, and it was a seventeen. My luck's showing up already, he said to himself. He lit a delicado cigarette, leaned back in his chair and watched as the others drew.

It's a good thing Dave Mutreaux refused to come here, Luckman realized. The pre-cog was right; they did have the EEG machine to try out as a ploy; they would have had him dead to rights.

'Evidently you go first Luckman,' Calumine said. 'With your seventeen you're high man.' He seemed resigned, as did the others.

'The Luckman luck,' Luckman said to them as he reached for the round metal spinner.

Watching Pete out of the corner of her eye, Freya Gaines thought, He and she had a fight outside there; Carol, when she came back in, looked as if she had been crying. Too bad, Freya said to herself with relish.

They won't be able to play as partners, she knew. Carol won't be able to put up with Pete's melancholy, his hypochondria. And in her he's simply not going to find a woman who'll put up with him. I know he'll turn back to me in a relationship outside The Game. He'll have to, or crack up emotionally.

It was her turn to play. This initial round was played without the element of bluff; the visible spinner was used, not the cards. Freya spun, obtained a four. Damn, she thought as she moved her piece four spaces ahead on the board. That brought her to a sadly-familiar square: *Excise tax Pay $500.*

She paid, silently; Janice Remington, the banker, accepted the bills. How tense I am, Freya thought. Everyone here is, including Luckman himself.

Which of us, she wondered, will be the first to call Luckman on a bluff? Who'll have the courage? And if they challenge him, will they succeed? Will they be right? She herself shrank from it. Not me, she said to herself.

Pete would, she decided. He'll be the first; he really hates the man.

It was Pete's turn, now; he spun a seven and began moving his piece. His face was expressionless.

Chapter 6

Being somewhat poor, Joe Schilling owned an ancient, cantankerous, moody auto-auto which he called Max. Unfortunately he could not afford a newer one.

As usual, today Max balked at the instructions given it. 'No,' it said. 'I'm not going to fly out to the Coast. You can walk.'

'I'm not asking you, I'm telling you,' Joe Schilling told it.

'What business do you have out on the Coast anyhow?' Max demanded in its surly fashion. Its motor had started, however. 'I need repair-work done,' it complained, 'before I undertake such a long trip. Why can't you maintain me properly? Everybody else keeps up their cars.'

'You're not worth keeping up,' Joe Schilling said, and got into the auto-auto, seated himself at the tiller, then remembered that he had forgotten his parrot, Eeore. 'Damn it,' he said, 'don't leave without me; I have to go back for something.' He got out of the car and strode back to the record shop, key in hand.

The car made no comment as he returned with the parrot; it seemed resigned, now, or perhaps the articulation circuit had collapsed.

'Are you still there?' Schilling asked the car.

'Of course I am. Can't you see me?'

'Take me to San Rafael, California,' Schilling said. The time was early morning; he would probably be able to catch Pete Garden at his pro-tem apartment.

Pete had called late last night to report on the first encounter with Lucky Luckman. The moment he heard

Pete's gloomy tone of voice Joe Schilling had known the result of The Game; Luckman had won.

'The problem now,' Pete said, 'is that he's got two California title deeds, so he doesn't have to risk Berkeley anymore. He can put up the other one.'

'You should have had me right from the start,' Schilling said.

After a pause Pete said, 'Well, I've got a little problem. Carol Holt Garden, my new wife, she rates herself a fine Bluff-player.'

'Is she?'

'She's good,' Pete said. 'But – '

'But you still lost. I'll start out for the Coast tomorrow morning.' And now here he was, as promised, starting out with two suitcases of personal articles and his parrot Eeore, ready to play against Luckman.

Wives, Schilling thought. More of a problem than an asset. The economic aspects of our lives should never have been melded hopelessly with the sexual; it makes things too complex. Blame that on the Titanians and their desire to solve our difficulties with one neat solution covering all. What they've actually done is gotten us entangled even more thoroughly.

Pete hadn't said any more about Carol.

But marriage had always been primarily an economic entity, Schilling reflected as he steered his auto-auto up into the early-morning New Mexico sky. The vugs hadn't invented that; they had merely intensified an already existing condition. Marriage had to do with the transmission of property, of lines of inheritance. And of cooperation in career-lines as well. All this emerged explicitly in The Game and dominated conditions; The Game merely dealt openly with what had been there implicitly before.

The car radio came on then, and a male voice addressed

56

Schilling. 'This is Kitchener; I'm told you're leaving my bind. Why?'

'Business on the West Coast.' It irritated him that the Bindman of the area should burst into the situation and meddle. But that was Colonel Kitchener, a fussy, elderly spinster-type retired officer who nosed into everybody's business.

'I didn't give you permission,' Kitchener complained.

'You and Max,' Schilling said.

'Pardon?' Kitchener berated him, 'Maybe I just won't want to let you back into my bind, Schilling. I happen to know you're going to Carmel to play The Game, and if you're as good as all that – '

'As good as all what?' Schilling broke in. 'That's to be demonstrated, as yet.'

'If you're good enough to play at all,' Kitchener said, 'you ought to be playing for me.' It was obvious that most of the story had leaked out. Schilling sighed. That was one difficulty with such a diminished world-population; the planet had become like one extensive small town, with everyone knowing everyone else's business. 'Maybe you could practice in my group,' Kitchener offered. 'And then play against Luckman when you're back in shape. After all, you won't do your friends any good coming in cold as you are. Don't you agree?'

'I may be cold,' Schilling said, 'but I'm not that cold.'

'First you denied being good and now you deny being bad,' Kitchener said. 'You're confusing me, Schilling. I'll permit you to go, but I hope if you do show your old talent you'll bring some of it to our table, out of a sense of loyalty to your own Bindman. Good day.'

'Good day, Kitch,' Schilling said, and broke the circuit. Well, his trip to the Coast had already earned him two enemies, his auto-auto and Colonel Kitchener. A bad harbinger, Schilling decided. Most unlucky. The car, he could afford to have antagonistic to his enterprise, but not a man as powerful as Kitchener. After all, the Colonel was right; if he did have any talents at The Game they should be used to support his own Bindman, not someone else.

All at once Max spoke up. 'You see what you got yourself into?' it said accusingly.

'I realize I should have checked with my Bindman and gotten his approval,' Schilling agreed.

'You hoped to sneak out of New Mexico unnoticed,' Max said.

It was true; Schilling nodded. Yes, it was decidedly a bad beginning.

Waking in the still-unfamiliar apartment in San Rafael, Peter Garden jumped in surprise at the sight of the tousled head of brown hair beside him, the bare, smooth shoulders, so eternally inviting – and then remembered who she was and what had happened the evening before. He got out of bed without waking her, went into the kitchen in his pajamas to search for a package of cigarettes.

A second California deed had been lost and Joe Schilling was on his way from New Mexico; that's how things stood, he recalled. And he now had a wife who – How exactly did he evaluate Carol Holt Garden? It would be good to know precisely where he stood in relation to her before Joe Schilling put in his appearance . . . and that could be any time, now.

He lit a cigarette, put the tea kettle on the burner. As the tea kettle started to thank him he said, 'Be quiet. My wife's asleep.'

The tea kettle obediently warmed in silence.

He liked Carol; she was pretty and, to say the least, great guns in bed. It was as simple as that. She was not terribly pretty and many of his wives had been as good in bed and better and he did not like her inordinately;

58

everything about his feelings was commensurate with reality. Her feelings, however, were excessive. To Carol this new marriage challenged her sense of identity by way of her prestige. As a woman, a wife, as a Game-player. That was a lot.

Outside the apartment, on the street below, the two McClain children played quietly; he heard their tense, muted voices. Going to the kitchen window he looked out and saw them, the boy Kelly, the girl Jessica, involved in some sort of knife game. Absorbed, they were oblivious to anything else, to him, to the vacant, auto-maintained city around them.

I wonder how their mother is, Pete said to himself. Patricia McClain, whose story I know . . .

Returning to the bedroom he got his clothes, carried them to the kitchen and silently dressed, not waking up Carol.

'I'm ready,' the tea kettle said, all at once.

He took it from the burner, started to make instant coffee, and then changed his mind. Let's see if Mrs McClain will fix breakfast for the Bindman, he said to himself.

Before the full-length mirror in the apartment's bathroom he stared at himself, concluded that he looked, while not stunning, at least adequate. And then, noiselessly, he set off, out of the apartment and down the stairs to the ground floor.

'Hi, kids,' he said to Kelly and Jessica.

'Hi, Mr Bindman,' they murmured, absorbed.

'Where can I find your mother?' he asked them.

They both pointed.

Pete, taking a deep breath of sweet early-morning air, walked that way with fast strides, feeling hungry in several ways – deep and intricate ways.

His auto-auto, Max, landed at the curb before the apartment building in San Rafael, and Joe Schilling stiffly slid across the seat, opened the door manually and stepped out.

He rang the proper buzzer and an answering buzz unlocked the massive front door. Carefully locked to bar intruders who no longer exist, he said to himself as he climbed the carpeted stairs to the fourth floor.

The apartment door stood open but it was not Pete Garden waiting for him; it was a young woman with disorderly brown hair and a sleepy expression. 'Who are you?' she said.

'A friend of Pete's,' Joe Schilling said. 'Are you Carol?'

She nodded, drew her robe around her self-consciously. 'Pete's not here. I just got up and he's gone; I don't know where.'

'Can I come in?' Schilling asked. 'And wait?'

'If you like. I'm going to have breakfast.' She padded away from the door and Schilling followed; he found her once more, in the kitchen of the apartment, cooking bacon on the range.

The tea kettle announced, 'Mr Garden was here but he left.'

'Did he say where he was going?' Schilling asked it.

'He looked out the window and then left.' The Rushmore Effect built into the tea kettle did not amount to much; the tea kettle was little help.

Schilling seated himself at the kitchen table. 'How are you and Pete getting along?'

'Oh, we had a dreadful first evening,' Carol said. 'We lost. Pete was so morose about it . . . he didn't say one word all the way home here from Carmel, and even after we got here he hardly said anything to me, as if he thought it was my fault.' She turned sadly toward Joe Schilling. 'I just don't know how we're going to go on; Pete seems almost – suicidal.'

'He's always been that way,' Schilling said. 'Don't blame yourself.'

'Oh,' Carol said, nodding. 'Well, thanks for letting me know.'

'Could I have a cup of coffee?'

'Certainly,' she said, putting the tea kettle back on. 'Are you by any chance the friend he vidphoned last night after The Game?'

'Yes,' Schilling said. He felt embarrassed; he had come here to replace this woman at the Game table. How much did she know of Pete's intentions? In many ways, Schilling thought, Pete's a heel when it comes to women.

Carol said, 'I know what you're here for, Mr Schilling.'

'Umm,' Schilling said, cautiously.

'I'm not going to step aside,' she said, as she spooned ground coffee into the mid-part of the aluminum pot. 'Your history of playing isn't a good one. I believe I can do better than you.'

'Hmm,' Schilling said, nodding.

After that he drank his coffee and she ate breakfast in awkward, strained silence, both of them waiting for Pete Garden to return.

Patricia McClain was dust-mopping the living room of her apartment; she glanced up, saw Pete, and then she smiled a slow, secretive smile. 'The Bindman cometh,' she said, and continued dust-mopping.

'Hello,' Pete said, self-consciously.

'I can read your mind, Mr Garden. You know quite a bit about me, from having discussed me with Joseph Schilling. So you met Mary Anne, my oldest daughter. And you find her "stunningly attractive," as Schilling put it . . . as well as much like me.' Pat McClain glanced up at him; her dark eyes sparkled. 'Don't you think Mary Anne is a little young for you? You're one hundred and forty or thereabouts and she's eighteen.'

Pete said, 'Since the Hynes Gland operations – '

'Never mind,' Patricia said. 'I agree. And you're also

thinking that the real difference between me and my daughter is that I'm embittered and she's still fresh and feminine. This, coming from a man who steadily contemplates, ruminates about, suicide.'

'I can't help it,' Pete said. 'Clinically, it's obsessive thinking; it's involuntary. I wish I could get rid of it. Doctor Macy told me that decades ago. I've taken every pill there is . . . it goes away for a time and then returns.' He entered the McClain apartment. 'Had breakfast?'

'Yes,' Patricia said. 'And you can't eat here; it isn't proper and I don't care to fix it for you. I'll tell you truthfully, Mr Garden; I don't wish to get involved with you emotionally. In fact the idea of it repels me.'

'Why?' he said, as evenly as possible.

'Because I don't like you.'

'And why's that?' he said, not retreating either physically or psychologically.

'Because you're able to play The Game and I'm not,' Patricia said. 'And because you have a wife, a new one, and yet you're here, not there. I don't like your treatment of her.'

'Being a telepath is quite a help,' Pete said, 'when it comes to making evaluations of other people's vices and weaknesses.'

'It is.'

'Can I help it,' Pete said, 'if I'm attracted to you and not to Carol?'

'You can't help what you feel, but you could avoid doing what you're doing; I'm perfectly aware of your reason for being here, Mr Garden. But don't forget *I'm married, too*. And I take my marriage seriously, which you do not. But of course you don't; you have a new wife every few weeks or so. Every time there's a severe setback at The Game.' Her disgust was manifest; her lips were tightly compressed and her black eyes flashed.

62

He wondered what she had been like before discovery of her Psionic talent had barred her from The Game.

'Much like I am now,' Patricia said.

'I doubt that,' he said. He thought about her daughter. I wonder if she'll be this way in time, he speculated. I suppose it depends on whether she has her mother's telepathic talent or not, and if so –

'Mary Anne doesn't have it,' Patricia said. 'None of the children do; we've looked into it already.'

Then she won't wind up like you have, he thought.

'Perhaps not,' Patricia said, soberly. All at once she said, 'I won't let you stay here, Mr Garden, but you can drive me into San Francisco if you wish. I have shopping to do there. And we can stop at a restaurant and have breakfast, if you care to.'

He started to agree and then he remembered Joe Schilling. 'I can't. Because of business.'

'Strategy talks about The Game.'

'Yes.' Obviously, he couldn't deny it.

'You put that first, before anything else. Even with your so-called "deep feelings" toward me.'

'I asked Joe Schilling to come here. I have to be around to greet him.' That seemed self-evident to him. Apparently it did not seem so to her, however, but there was nothing he could do about that. Her cynicism was too deeply embedded for him to affect it in any way.

'Don't judge me,' Patricia McClain said. 'You may be right, but – ' She moved away from him, holding her hand up to her forehead, as if physically suffering. 'I still can't stand it, Mr Garden.'

'Sorry,' he said. 'I'll leave, Pat.'

'I tell you what,' she said. 'I'll meet you this afternoon at one-thirty, in downtown San Francisco. At Market and Third. We can have lunch together. Do you think you can slip away from your wife and your Game-playing friend for that?'

'Yes,' he said.

'Then it's agreed,' Patricia said. And she went on dust-mopping.

Pete said, 'Tell me why you changed your mind about seeing me. *What did you pick up in my mind?* It must have been fairly important.'

'I'd rather not say,' Patricia answered.

'Please.'

'The telepathic faculty has one basic drawback. You may not know this. It tends to pick up too much; it's too sensitive to marginal or merely latent thoughts in people, what the old psychologists called the "unconscious mind." There's a relationship between the telepathic faculty and paranoia; the latter is the involuntary reception of other people's suppressed hostile and aggressive thoughts.'

'What did you read in my unconscious, Pat?'

'I – read a syndrome of potential action. If I were a pre-cog I could tell you more. You *may* do it; you may not. But – ' She glanced up at him. 'It's a violent act, and it has to do with death.'

'Death,' he echoed.

'Perhaps,' Patricia said, 'you'll attempt suicide. I don't know; it's inchoate, still. It has to do with death – and with Jerome Luckman.'

'And it's so bad that it would make you reverse yourself in your decision not to have anything to do with me.'

Patricia said, 'It would be wrong of me, after picking up such a syndrome, to simply abandon you.'

'Thanks,' he said, tartly.

'I don't want it on my conscience. I'd hate to hear on Nats Katz' program tomorrow or the day after that you'd taken that overdose of Emphytal that you're obsessively preoccupied with.' She smiled at him, but it was a colorless smile, devoid of joy.

'I'll see you at one-thirty,' Pete said. 'At Third and Market.' Unless, he thought, the inchoate syndrome

64

having to do with violence and death and Jerome Luckman becomes actual before then.

'It may,' Patricia said somberly. 'That's another quality of the unconscious, it stands outside of time. You can't tell, in reading it, whether you're picking up something minutes away from actualization or days away or even years. It's all blurred together.'

Wordlessly, Pete turned and strode out of the apartment, away from her.

The next he knew he was riding in his car, high over the desert.

He knew, instantly, that it was much later.

Snapping on the radio transmitter he said, 'Give me a time signal.'

The mechanical voice from the speaker said, 'Six P.M. Mountain Standard Time, Mr Garden.'

Where am I? he asked himself. 'Where is this?' he said to the car. 'Nevada?' It looked like Nevada, barren and empty.

The car said, 'Eastern Utah.'

'When did I leave the Coast?'

'Two hours ago, Mr Garden.'

'What have I done during the last five hours?'

The car said, 'At nine-thirty you drove from Marin County, California to Carmel, to the Game Room in the Carmel condominium apartment building.'

'Whom did I see?'

'I don't know.'

'Continue,' he said, breathing shallowly.

'You stayed there one hour. Then you came out and took off for Berkeley.'

'Berkeley!' he said.

'You landed at the Claremont Hotel. You stayed there only a short time, only a few minutes. Then you took off for San Francisco. You landed at San Francisco State College and went into the administration building.'

'You don't know what I did there, do you?'

'No, Mr Garden. You were there an hour. Then you came out and took off once more. This time you landed at a parking lot in downtown San Francisco, at Fourth and Market; you parked me there and set out on foot.'

'Going which way?'

'I didn't notice.'

'Go ahead.'

'You returned at two-fifteen, got back in, and directed me to fly in an East course. I have done so ever since.'

'And we didn't land anywhere since San Francisco?'

'No, Mr Garden. And by the way, I'm very short of fuel. We should come down at Salt Lake City, if possible.'

'All right,' he said. 'Head that way.'

'Thank you, Mr Garden,' the car said, and altered its course.

Pete sat for a time and then he switched on the transmitter and vidphoned his apartment in San Rafael.

On the small screen Carol Holt Garden's face appeared. 'Oh hello,' she said. 'Where are you? Bill Calumine called; he's getting the group together early this evening to discuss strategy. He wants to be sure both you and I are there.'

'Did Joe Schilling show up?'

'Yes. What do you mean? You came back to the apartment early this morning and sat out in your car talking to him; you talked out there so I wouldn't hear.'

Pete said hoarsely, 'What happened after that?'

'I don't understand your question.'

'What did I do?' he demanded. 'Did I go anywhere with Joe Schilling? Where is he now?'

'I don't know where he is now,' Carol said. 'What on earth is the matter with you? Don't you know what you did today? Do you always have periods of amnesia?'

Pete grated, 'Just tell me what happened.'

'You sat in the car talking to Joe Schilling and then he

went off, I guess. Anyhow you came back upstairs alone and said to me – Just a second, I have something on the stove.' She disappeared from the screen; he waited, counting the seconds, until at last she returned. 'Sorry. Let's see. You came back upstairs – ' Carol paused, meditating. 'We talked. Then you went downstairs again, and that's the last I've seen of you, until you called just now.'

'What did you and I talk about?'

'You told me that you wanted to play with Mr Schilling as your partner tonight.' Carol's voice was cold, withdrawn emotionally. 'We shall I say, *discussed* it. Argued about it, actually. In the end – ' She glared at him. 'If you don't know – '

'I don't,' he said.

Carol said, 'There's no reason why I should tell you. Ask Joe, if you want to know; I'm sure you informed him.'

'Where is he?'

'I have no idea,' Carol said, and broke the connection. The tiny image of her on the vidscreen died.

I'm sure, he said to himself, that I arranged with Joe for him to play as my partner, tonight. But that's not the problem.

The problem – it was not what did I do? but why don't I remember? I may have done nothing at all; that is, nothing that was unusual or important. Although going to Berkeley . . . perhaps I wanted to pick up some of my things which I'd left, he decided.

But according to the Rushmore Effect of the car, he had not gone to his old apartment; he had gone to the Claremont, and that was where Lucky Luckman was staying.

Evidently he had seen – or had tried to see – Luckman.

He thought, I'd better get hold of Joe Schilling. Find him and talk to him. Tell him that for reasons unknown to me I'm missing almost an entire day. The shock of what Pat McClain said – could that explain it?

And evidently he had met Patricia in downtown San Francisco as they had agreed.

If so, what had they done?

What was his relationship with her, now? Perhaps he had been successful; perhaps, on the other hand, he had only antagonized her further. No way to tell. And the visit to San Francisco State College . . .

Evidently he had sought out Pat's daughter, Mary Anne.

Good lord. What a day to lose!

Using the car's transmitter he phoned Joe Schilling's record shop in New Mexico and got a Rushmore variety of answering device. 'Mr Schilling is not currently here. He and his parrot are on the Pacific Coast; you can contact him through Marin County Bindman Peter Garden at San Rafael.'

Oh no you can't, Pete said to himself. And cut the connection with a wild swipe of his hand.

After a time he vidphoned Freya Garden Gaines.

'Oh, hello there, Peter,' Freya said, looking pleased to hear from him. 'Where are you? We're all supposed to get together at – '

'I'm hunting for Joe Schilling,' he said. 'You know where he is?'

'No. I haven't seen him. Did you bring him out to the Coast to play against Luckman?'

'If you hear from him,' Pete said, 'tell him to go to my apartment in San Rafael and stay there.'

'Okay,' Freya said. 'Is something wrong?'

'Maybe so,' he said, and rang off.

I wish to hell I knew, he said to himself.

To the car he said, 'Do you have enough fuel to head directly back to San Rafael without stopping at Salt Lake City?'

'No, Mr Garden,' the car said.

'Get your damn fuel, then,' he told it, 'and then let's get back to California as fast as possible.'

'All right, but there's no point in being angry at me; it was your instructions that brought us to this place.'

He cursed at the car. And sat impatiently waiting as it nosed down toward deserted, vast Salt Lake City below.

Chapter 7

When finally he got back to San Rafael it was evening; he switched on the landing lights of the car and came to rest at the curb before his apartment building.

As he stepped out, a shape emerged from the darkness, hurrying toward him. 'Pete!'

It was, he made out, Patricia McClain; she wore a long heavy coat and her hair was tied back in a knot. 'What is it?' he said, catching her air of alarm and urgency.

'Just a second.' She came close to him, breathless, gasping, her eyes dilated with fear. 'I want to scan your mind.'

'What's happened?'

'My god,' she said. 'You don't remember. The whole day's lost to you; Pete, *be careful.* I better go – my husband's waiting. Goodbye. I'll see you as soon as I can; don't try to get in touch with me, I'll call you.' She stared at him for an instant and then she disappeared down the street, rushing away into the evening darkness.

He went on, then, up the stairs to his apartment.

In the living room, large, red-bearded Joseph Schilling sat waiting; seeing him, Schilling at once rose to his feet. 'Where have you been?'

Pete said, 'Is Carol here or are you alone?' He glanced around him. There was no sign of her.

'I haven't seen her since this morning. Since the three of us were together here in the apartment. I was talking to your former wife, Freya, and she told me that you – '

'How did you get in,' Pete said, 'if Carol isn't here?'

'The apartment was unlocked.'

Pete said, 'Listen, Joe. Something's happened, today.'

70

'You mean Luckman's disappearance?'

Staring at him, chilled, Pete said, 'I didn't know Luckman had disappeared.'

'Of course you do; you're the one who told me.' Now Schilling stared back at him.

They were both silent.

Schilling said, 'You called me from your car; you caught me at the con-apt in Carmel; I was studying recordings of your group's past Gameplays. And then later on I heard it over Nats Katz' afternoon program. Luckman disappeared this morning.'

'And he hasn't been found?'

'No.' Schilling grabbed Pete by the shoulder. '*Why don't you remember?*'

'I had an encounter. With a telepath.'

'Pat McClain? You told me; you were remarkably upset. I could tell, I know you. You alluded to something she had picked up in your unconscious, something having to do with your obsessive suicidal impulses, you said. And then you suddenly signed off and broke the circuit.'

'I saw her again just now,' Pete said. Her warning; probably it had to do with Luckman's disappearance. Did Patricia think he had something to do with it?

Schilling said, 'I'll fix you a drink.' He went over to the cabinet by the large living-room windows. 'While I was waiting for you I managed to find where you keep it. This scotch isn't bad, but as far as I'm concerned there's nothing quite like – '

'I haven't eaten dinner,' Pete said. 'I don't want a drink.' He went into the kitchen, to the refrigerator, with the vague idea of preparing some sort of meal.

'There's some very fine kosher-style corn beef; I picked it up at a delicatessen in San Francisco, it and dark bread and slaw.'

'Okay.' Pete got the food out.

71

'We don't have much time to get to Carmel. We're supposed to be there early. But if Luckman doesn't show up – '

'Are the police looking for him? Have they been called in?'

'I don't know. You didn't say and neither did Katz.'

Pete said, 'Did I tell you how I happened to know about it?'

'No.'

'This is terrible,' Pete said. He cut two thick slices of the dark bread; his hands were shaking.

'Why?'

'I don't know why. Doesn't it strike you that way?'

Schilling shrugged. 'Maybe it would be a good thing if someone did him in. We should have such bad luck every day. Wouldn't this solve our collective problems? His widow would have to play his hand and we can beat Dotty Luckman; I know her system and it's mediocre.' He, too, cut himself some of the dark bread and helped himself to the kosher-style corn beef.

The vidphone rang.

'You get it,' Pete said. He felt dread.

'Sure.' Schilling strode into the living room. 'Hello,' his voice came to Pete.

Bill Calumine's voice: 'Something's come up. I want everyone at Carmel immediately.'

'Okay, we'll leave now.' Schilling returned to the kitchen.

'I heard,' Pete said.

'Leave a note for your wife Carol.'

'Telling her what?'

'Don't you know that either? Telling her to get down to Carmel; the agreement we arrived at – remember? – is for me to play the hands but for her to sit in and watch from behind me, seeing what I draw and how I play each turn. You don't remember that either, do you?'

Pete said, 'No.'

'She wasn't very pleased.' Schilling got his hat and coat from the closet. 'But you figured you'd come up with something just dandy, there. Come on; it's time to leave. Bring your corn-beef sandwich along.'

As they left the apartment and came out into the hall they met Carol Holt Garden; she was stepping from the elevator. Her face looked tired. Seeing them, she halted.

'Well?' she said listlessly. 'I suppose you heard.'

Schilling said, 'We heard from Bill Calumine, if that's what you mean.'

'I mean,' Carol said, 'about Luckman. Since I've already called the police. If you want to see, come downstairs.'

By the elevator, the three of them descended to the ground floor, and Carol led them to her car, parked behind Schilling's and Pete's at the curb.

'I discovered it in mid-flight,' she said woodenly, leaning against the hood of the car, hands in her coat pockets. 'I was flying along and I happened to wonder if I'd left my purse at my old apartment, where I and my previous husband lived. I was there today, getting some things I had forgotten.'

Pete and Joe Schilling opened the door to her car.

'I switched on the dome light,' Carol said. 'And saw it. It must have been put in while I was parked at my old apartment, but it's barely possible that it was done even earlier, when I was here this morning.' She added, 'You can see that he – it – is way down on the floor, out of sight. I – touched it, trying to find my purse.' She was silent, then.

By the glare of the dome light, Pete saw the body jammed behind the front seats of the car. It was Luckman; no doubt of it. Even in death, the round, plump-cheeked

73

face was recognizable. It was not ruddy, now. It was, in the artificial light, a pulpy gray.

'I called the police at once,' Carol said, 'and arranged to meet them here.' Sirens were now audible in the black sky above them, a long way off.

Chapter 8

Facing the members of the group Pretty Blue Fox, Bill Calumine said, 'Ladies and gentlemen, Jerome Luckman has been murdered and every one of us is a suspect. That's the situation. There isn't much more I can tell you at this time. Naturally, there will be no Game-playing tonight.'

Silvanus Angst giggled and said, 'I don't know who did it, but whoever it is – congratulations.' He laughed, waiting for the others to join in.

'Be quiet,' Freya said to him sharply.

Coloring, Angst said, 'But I'm right; it's the best news – '

'It's not good news that we're under suspicion,' Bill Calumine said shortly. 'I don't know who did it, or even if any of us did it. And I'm not even sure that it's to our advantage; we may find enormous legal complications in getting back the two California title deeds which we lost to him. I just don't know; it's too soon. What we need is legal advice.'

'Right,' Stuart Marks said, and around the room the other members of the group nodded. 'We should jointly hire an attorney, a good one.'

'To help protect us,' Jack Blau said, 'and to advise us how best to get those two deeds back.'

'A vote,' Walt Remington said.

Irritably, Bill Calumine said, 'We don't need to vote; it's obvious we need an attorney. The police will be here any time, now. Let me ask this,' he glanced around the room, 'if one of you did it – and I stress the word *if* – does that person want to declare himself now?'

There was silence. No one moved.

With a brief smile, Calumine said, 'That takes care of that, anyhow. If one of us killed Luckman he's not going to say.'

'Would you want him to?' Jack Blau asked.

'Not particularly,' Calumine said. He turned to the vidphone. 'If no one objects I'll call Bert Barth, my attorney in Los Angeles, and see if he can get right up here. All right?' Again he glanced around.

No one objected.

'All right, then,' Calumine said, and dialed.

Schilling said, 'Whoever did it, for whatever motives,' his voice was harsh, 'putting it in Carol Holt Garden's car was a vicious and brutal act. Wholly inexcusable.'

Freya smiled. 'We can condone the murder but not putting the body in Mrs Garden's car. An odd era we're living in.'

'You know I'm right,' Schilling said to her.

Freya shrugged.

Into the vidphone, Bill Calumine was saying, 'Give me Mr Barth; it's an emergency.' He turned toward Carol, who sat by Pete and Joe Schilling on the large center sofa. 'I'm particularly thinking of your protection, Mrs Garden, in our hiring of legal counsel. Since it was found in your car.'

'Carol's no more a suspect than anyone else,' Pete said. At least, he thought, I hope not. Why should she be? After all, she notified the police as soon as she found it.

Lighting a cigarette, Schilling said to him, 'So I arrived too late. I'll never have my opportunity to get back at Lucky Luckman.'

Stuart Marks murmured, 'Unless you already have.'

'Meaning what?' Schilling said, turning toward him and surveying him.

'Hell, what do you think I mean?' Marks said.

On the vidscreen the firm, elongated features of the

Los Angeles attorney Bert Barth had formed and Barth was already in the process of advising the group. 'They'll come as a team,' he was explaining to Bill Calumine. 'One vug, one Terran; that's customary in capital crimes. I'll get up there as soon as I can but it'll take me at least half an hour. Be prepared for them both to be excellent telepaths; that's customary, too. But remember: evidence obtained through telepathic scanning is not legal in a Terran court of law; that's been solidly established.'

Calumine said, 'It sounds to me like a violation of the provision in the US Constitution against a citizen being forced to testify against himself.'

'That, too,' Barth said, nodding. Now the whole group was silent, listening to the conversation between Calumine and their attorney. 'The police telepaths can scan you and determine if you're guilty or innocent, but other evidence has to be produced for it to stand up in court. They will use their telepathic faculties to the hilt however; you can be sure of that.'

The Rushmore Effect of the apartment now chimed and then announced, 'Two persons are outside wishing to enter.'

'Police?' Stuart Marks asked.

'One Titanian,' the Rushmore Effect said, 'and one Terran. Are you police?' It was addressing the visitors. 'They are police,' it informed the group. 'Shall I admit them?'

'Have them come on up,' Bill Calumine said, after an exchange of glances with his attorney.

Barth continued, 'What your people must be prepared for is this. By law, the authorities can disband your group until this crime is solved. In principle, it's supposed to act as a determent to future crimes committed by Game-playing groups. Actually, it works out more as a simple punitive gesture, punishing everyone involved.'

Dismally, Freya said, 'Disband the group – oh no!'

77

'Sure,' Jack Blau said grimly. 'Didn't you know that? It's the first thing I thought of when I heard about Luckman's death; I knew they'd disband us.' He glared around the room, as if seeking for the person responsible for the crime.

'Well, maybe they won't,' Walt Remington said.

There was a knock at the apartment door itself. The police.

'I'll stay on the vidphone,' Bert Barth offered, 'instead of trying to make it up there. I can probably advise you better this way.' From the vidscreen he looked toward the door.

Freya opened the door. There stood a lean, tall young Terran and, beside him, a vug. The Terran said, 'I'm Wade Hawthorne.' He produced a black-backed leather wallet, which contained their identification; the vug merely rested in its customary fashion, overtaxed by the ascent to this floor. Stitched to it was the name-thread E. B. Black.

'Come in,' Bill Calumine said, striding toward the door. 'I'm the group's spinner, Bill Calumine's my name.' He held the door wide, and the two officers entered the apartment, the vug E. B. Black coming first.

'We wish first to talk to Mrs Carol Holt Garden,' the vug thought-propagated to the group. 'Since the corpse was found in her car.'

'I'm Carol Garden.' She rose to her feet, stood steady and calm as the team of police turned to face her.

'Do we have your permission to scan you telepathically?' Wade Hawthorne asked her.

She glanced at the vidscreen.

'Tell them yes,' Bert Barth said. To the two police he said, 'I'm Barth, their legal counselor, in Los Angeles. I've advised my clients, this group, Pretty Blue Fox, to cooperate with you fully. They will all be open for telepathic scanning, but they understand – and I know

78

you do, too – that any evidence you obtain in this fashion can't be entered in a court of law.'

'That's correct,' Hawthorne said, and walked over to Carol.

The vug slid slowly after him, and there was silence.

'It appears to be as Mrs Garden related on the phone,' the vug E. B. Black said, presently. 'She discovered the corpse in mid-flight and at once notified us.' To its companion the vug continued, 'I find no indication that Mrs Garden had any prior knowledge of the corpse's presence in her car. She does not appear to have had anything to do with Luckman prior to that discovery. Do you agree?'

'I agree,' Hawthorne said slowly. 'But – ' He glanced around the room. 'There is something in connection with her husband, Mr Peter Garden. I'd like to examine you next, Mr Garden.'

Pete, his throat dry, rose to his feet. 'Can I talk with our attorney a moment in private?' he said to the policeman Hawthorne.

'No,' Hawthorne said in a pleasant, even voice. 'He's already advised you on this matter; I see no reason to permit you to – '

'I'm aware of what his advice is,' Pete said. 'I'm interested in learning the consequences if I were to refuse.' He walked across the room to the vidphone. 'Well?' he said to Barth.

'You'll become a prime suspect,' Barth said. 'But it's your right; you can refuse. I'd advise you not to, because if you do they'll never stop hounding you. They'll scan you sooner or later anyhow.'

Pete said, 'I have an aversion to having my mind read.' Once they discovered his amnesia, he realized, they would be certain he had killed Luckman. And perhaps he had. The obvious was confronting him brutally.

'What's your decision?' Hawthorne asked him.

'You've probably begun to scan me already,' Pete said. Barth of course was right; if he refused they would scan him anyhow, if not now, then some other time. 'Go ahead,' he said, and felt sick and weary. He walked over to the two of them and stood with his hands in his pockets.

Time passed. No one spoke.

'I've picked up the matter which Mrs Garden was thinking about,' the vug thought-radiated to its companion. 'Have you?'

'Yes,' Hawthorne said, nodding. To Pete he said, 'You have no actual memory of today, do you? You've reconstructed it from remarks made by your auto-auto or at least by *alleged* remarks.'

'You can question the Rushmore of my car,' Pete said.

'It informed you,' Hawthorne said slowly, 'that you paid a visit to Berkeley, today. But you don't actually know if it was to see Luckman, and if so, whether you did see him or not. I can't imagine why this block in your mind exists; was it self-imposed? And if so, how?'

'I can't tell you the answer to that,' Pete said. 'As you can certainly read for yourself.'

Hawthorne said drily, 'Anyone intending to commit a capital crime would of course know that telepaths would be brought in; he would have to deal with that, and nothing could possibly benefit him more than a segment of amnesia entering to block out that period of his activities.' To E. B. Black he said, 'I would presume we should take Mr Garden into custody.'

The vug answered, 'Perhaps. But we must examine the others, as a matter of course.' To the group it declared, 'You are ordered to disband as a Game-playing organization; from this moment on it is illegal for any of you to come together for the purpose of playing Bluff. This ruling will hold until the murderer of Jerome Luckman has been found.'

They turned, instinctively, to the vidscreen.

Barth said, 'It's legal. As I warned you.' He seemed resigned.

'Speaking for the group,' Bill Calumine said to the two police, 'I protest this.'

Hawthorne shrugged. He did not seem particularly worried by Calumine's protest.

'I have picked up something unusual,' the vug said to its companion. 'Please scan the rest of the group as a whole and see if you agree.'

Glancing at him, Hawthorne nodded; he walked slowly about the room, from person to person, and then back to the vug. 'Yes,' he said. 'Mr Garden is not the only person here unable to recall what he did today. In all, six persons in this group show similar lapses of memory. Mrs Remington, Mr Gaines, Mr Angst, Mrs Angst, Mrs Calumine, and Mr Garden. None of them have intact memories.'

Astonished, Pete Garden looked around the room, and saw by the expressions on the faces of the other five that it was true. They were in the same situation that he was. And probably, like himself, each of them had believed his situation unique. So none of them had discussed it.

'I can see,' Hawthorne said, 'that we're going to have difficulty establishing the identity of the murderer of Mr Luckman, in view of this. However, I'm sure it can be done; it merely will take longer.' He glared at the group with displeasure.

In the kitchen of the con-apt, Janice Remington and Freya Gaines fixed coffee. The others remained in the living room with the team of detectives.

'How was Luckman killed?' Pete asked Hawthorne.

'By a heat-needle, evidently. We're having an autopsy performed, of course; we'll have certain knowledge then.'

'What the hell is a "heat-needle"?' Jack Blau asked.

Hawthorne said, 'A side-arm left over from the war; they were all called in, but a large number of servicemen

81

kept theirs and we find them being used every now and then. It employs a laser beam and is accurate from quite a distance, assuming there is no intervening structure.'

Coffee was brought; Hawthorne accepted a cup and seated himself. His companion, the vug E. B. Black, declined.

On the vidscreen, the miniature image of their attorney Bert Barth said, 'Mr Hawthorne, whom do you intend to hold? All six persons with defective memories? I'd like to know now because I'm going to have to ring off this line, soon; I have other commitments.'

'It seems probable we'll hold the six and release the others. Do you find that objectionable, Mr Barth?' Hawthorne seemed amused.

Mrs Angst broke in, 'They're not going to hold me, not without a charge.'

'They can hold you – anybody – seventy-two hours at least,' Barth said. 'For observation. There are several blanket charges they can bring in. So don't fight that, Mrs Angst; after all, a man has been killed. This is a serious matter.'

'Thanks for the help,' Bill Calumine said to Barth, a little bit ironically, it seemed to Pete. 'I'd like to ask you one more thing; can you begin work getting the stricture on our meeting for Game-playing removed?'

'I'll see what I can do,' Barth said. 'Give me some time. There was a case last year in Chicago. A group there was dissolved under the same statute for several weeks and naturally they took it to court. As I recall the group won its case; anyhow I'll look into it.' Barth rang off.

'We're lucky,' Jean Blau said, 'that we've got legal representation.' She looked frightened; going over to her husband she stood close by him.

Silvanus Angst said, 'I still say we're better off; Luckman would have wiped us out.' He grinned at the two police. 'Maybe I did it. Like you say, I don't remember.

Frankly, if I did it I'm glad.' He did not appear to have any fear of the police. Pete envied him.

'Mr Garden,' Hawthorne said, 'I catch a very interesting thought from you. Early this morning you were warned by someone – I can't catch by whom – that you were about to commit an act of violence having to do with Luckman. Am I correct?' Rising, he walked over to Pete. 'Would you mind thinking as clearly as possible about this?' His tone was informal.

Pete said, 'This is a violation of my rights.' He wished that the attorney were still on the vidphone; as soon as Barth had rung off the attitude of the police had stiffened. The group was now at their mercy.

'Not precisely,' Hawthorne said. 'We're governed by many regulations; our pairing off bi-racially is to protect the rights of those we investigate. Actually we're hampered by such an arrangement.'

Bill Calumine said, 'Did both of you agree on shutting down our group? Or was that its idea?' He jerked his head in the direction of E. B. Black.

'I fully concur in the action of banning Pretty Blue Fox,' Hawthorne said. 'Despite what your inborn prejudices may tell you.'

Pete said, 'You're wasting your time baiting him for his association with the vugs.' It was obvious that Hawthorne was used to it by now. He probably encountered it everywhere the two detectives went.

Coming over beside Pete, Joe Schilling said softly, 'I'm just not satisfied with the attitude of that Bert Barth. He's giving in too easily; a good aggressive lawyer would stand up for us more.'

'Perhaps so,' Pete said. It had seemed that way to him, too.

'I have my own attorney back in New Mexico; his name is Laird Sharp. I've known him professionally and socially a long time; I'm familiar with his way of operating and it's in great contrast to Barth's. And since they're evidently going to book you I'd like to see you get him instead of this attorney of Calumine's. I know he could get you right out.'

'The problem,' Pete said, 'is that military law still prevails in many situations.' The Concordat between Terrans and Titanians had been a military one. He felt pessimistic. 'If the police want to take us in they probably can,' he said to Schilling. Something was terribly wrong. Something with enormous power was in operation; it had acted against six members of the group already, and who knew what its limits were? If it could deplete them of their recent memories –

The vug E. B. Black said, 'I agree with you, Mr Garden. It is unique and disconcerting. Up to now we have not run into anything exactly like it. Individuals, to avoid being scanned, have procured electroshock and managed to obliterate memory-cells. But that does not seem to be the case here.'

'How can you be sure of that?' Stuart Marks said. 'Maybe these six people acted together to get electroshock equipment; they could have done it through almost any psychiatrist and psychiatric hospital. The machinery is readily available.' He glowered at Pete hostilely. 'Look what you've done. Because of you our group has been banned!'

'Because of me?' Pete said.

'Because of the six of you.' Marks looked suddenly around at all of them. 'Obviously, one or more of you killed Luckman. You should have looked into the legal situation before you did it.'

Mrs Angst said, 'We did not kill Luckman.'

'You don't know that,' Stuart Marks said. 'You don't remember. Right? So don't try to have it both ways, remembering that you didn't do it and not remembering that you did.'

Bill Calumine spoke up; his voice was icy. 'Marks, damn it, you have no moral right for acting this way. What do you mean by accusing your fellow group-members? I'm going to insist that we continue to act together and not let ourselves be split apart this way. If we start to fight among ourselves and begin accusing each other, the police will be able to – ' He broke off.

'Be able to what?' Hawthorne said mildly. 'Be able to locate the slayer? That's all we intend to do and you know it.'

Calumine said to the group, 'I still insist we should stick together, those with intact memories and those without; we're still a group, and it's up to the police to voice the accusations, not us.' To Stuart Marks he said, 'If you do that again I'll ask for a vote to have you dropped from the group.'

'That's not legal,' Marks said. 'And you know it. I still say what I said; one or more of these six people killed Luckman and I don't see why we should protect them. It means the obliteration of our group. It's to our best interests to have the slayer discovered. Then we can resume playing.'

Walt Remington said, 'Whoever killed Luckman didn't do it for himself; he did it for all of us. It may have been the act of an individual, an individual decision, but we all benefited; that person saved our hides, and as far as I'm concerned it's ethically loathsome for a member of the group to assist the police in apprehending him.' Shaking with anger, he faced Stuart Marks.

'We didn't like Luckman,' Jean Blau said, 'and we were terribly afraid of him but that didn't create a mandate for someone to go out and kill him, supposedly in the name of the group. I agree with Stuart. We should cooperate with the police in determining who did it.'

'A vote,' Silvanus Angst said.

'Yes,' Carol agreed. 'We should decide on policy. Are

85

we to hang together or are we, as individuals, to betray one another? I'll tell you my vote right now; it's thoroughly wrong for any of us to – '

The policeman Wade Hawthorne interrupted her. 'You have no choice, Mrs Garden; you *must* cooperate with us. It's the law. You can be compelled to.'

'I doubt that,' Bill Calumine said.

Joe Schilling said, 'I'm going to contact my own attorney in New Mexico.' He crossed the room to the vidphone, clicked it on and began to dial.

'Is there any way,' Freya was saying to Hawthorne, 'that the lapsed memories can be restored?'

'Not if the braincells in question have been destroyed,' Hawthorne answered. 'And I assume that's the case. It's hardly likely that these six members of Pretty Blue Fox have simultaneously suffered hysterical loss of memory.' He smiled briefly.

Pete said to him, 'My day was fairly well reconstructed by the Rushmore Effect of my car, and it didn't put me at any time near a psychiatric hospital where I could have obtained electroshock.'

'You stopped at San Francisco State College,' Hawthorne said. 'And their psych department possesses ETS equipment; you could have gotten it there.'

'What about the other five?' Pete said.

'Their days have not been reconstructed by Rushmore circuitry as has yours,' Hawthorne said. 'And there are major omissions in yours; a good deal of your activity today is far from clear.'

Joe Schilling said, 'I have Sharp on the vid. You want to talk to him, Pete? I've sketched the situation briefly.'

The vug E. B. Black said suddenly, 'Just a moment, Mr Garden.' It conferred telepathically for a time with its colleague, and then it said to Pete, 'Mr Hawthorne and I have decided not to book any of you; there's no *direct* evidence involving any one of you in the crime. But if we let you go, you must agree to carry tattletales with you at all times. Inquire of your attorney Mr Sharp if that will be acceptable.'

'What the hell is a "tattletale"?' Joe Schilling asked.

'A tracing device,' Hawthorne said. 'It will inform us where each of you are at all times.'

'Does it have a telepathic content?' Pete asked.

'No,' Hawthorne said. 'Although I wish it had.'

On the vidscreen, Laird Sharp, youthful and active-looking, said, 'I heard the proposal and without going into it any further I'd be inclined to label it as a clear violation of these people's rights.'

'Suit yourself,' Hawthorne said. 'Then we'll have to book them.'

'I'll have them out at once,' Sharp said. To Pete he said, 'Don't allow them to hook any sort of monitoring devices to you, and if you discover they have, rip them off. I'll fly right out there. It's obvious to me that your rights are being resoundingly violated.'

Joe Schilling said to Pete, 'Do you want him?'

'Yes,' Pete said.

Bill Calumine said, 'I – have to agree. He seems to have more on the ball than Barth.' Turning to the group Calumine said, 'I offer the motion that we retain this man Sharp collectively.'

Hands went up. The motion carried.

'I'll see you shortly, then,' Sharp said, and broke the connection.

'A good man,' Schilling said, and reseated himself.

Pete felt a little better now; it was a good feeling, he thought, to have someone battling hard on your side.

The group as a whole seemed less stunned, now. They were coming out of their stupor.

'I'm going to make a motion,' Freya said to the group. 'I move that we order Bill Calumine to step down and

87

that we elect someone else, someone more vigorous, as group spinner.'

Astonished, Bill Calumine said, 'W-why?'

'Because you sicked that do-nothing attorney on us,' Freya said. 'That Bert Barth who just let the police walk all over us.'

Jean Blau said, 'True, but it's still better to let him remain as spinner than to stir up trouble.'

'But trouble,' Pete said, 'is something we can't avoid. We're in it already.' After an interval he said, 'I second Freya's motion.'

Taken by surprise, the group began to murmur.

'Vote,' Silvanus Angst said. Snickering, he added, 'I agree with Pete; I vote for Calumine's removal.'

Bill Calumine stared at Pete and said hoarsely, 'How could you second a motion like that? *Do you want someone more vigorous?* I would think you wouldn't.'

'Why not?' Pete said.

'Because,' Calumine said, his face red with anger, his voice trembling, 'you personally have so much to lose.'

'What causes you to say that?' the detective Hawthorne asked him.

Calumine said, 'Pete killed Jerome Luckman.'

'How do you know that?' Hawthorne said, frowning.

'He called me and told me he was going to do it,' Calumine said. 'Early this morning. If you had scanned me more thoroughly you would have found that; it wasn't very far down in my mind.'

For a moment Hawthorne was silent, evidently scanning Calumine. Then he turned to the group. Thoughtfully, he said, 'What he says is true. The memory is there in his mind. But – *it wasn't there earlier when I scanned him a little while ago.*' He glanced at his partner, E. B. Black.

'It was not there,' the vug replied in agreement. 'I scanned him, too. Yet it's clearly there now.'

They both turned toward Pete.

Chapter 9

Joe Schilling said, 'I don't think you killed Luckman, Pete. I also don't think you called Bill Calumine and told him you were going to. I think someone or something is manipulating our minds. That thought was not in Calumine's head originally; both cops scanned him.' He was silent then.

The two of them were at the Hall of Justice in San Francisco, awaiting the arraignment. It was an hour later.

'When do you think Sharp will be here?' Pete said.

'Any time.' Schilling paced about. 'Calumine obviously is sincere; he actually believes you said that to him.'

There was a commotion down the corridor and Laird Sharp appeared, wearing a heavy blue overcoat and carrying a briefcase; he strode toward them. 'I've already talked to the district attorney. I got them to lower the charge from homicide to simply knowledge of a homicide and deliberate concealment of the knowledge from the police. I pointed out that you're a Bindman, you own property in California. You can be trusted out on bail. We'll have a bond broker in here and get you right out.'

Pete said, 'Thanks.'

'It's my job,' Sharp said. 'After all, you're paying me. I understand you've had a change of authority in your group; who's your spinner, now that Calumine is out?'

'My quondam wife, Freya Garden Gaines,' Pete said.

'Your quondam or your goddam wife?' Sharp asked, cupping his ear. 'Anyhow, the real question is can you swing the group so that they'll help pay my fee? Or are you alone in this?'

Joe Schilling said, 'It doesn't matter; in any case I'll guarantee your fee.'

'I ask,' Sharp said, 'because my fee would differ according to whether it's an individual or a group.' He examined his watch. 'Well, let's get the arraignment over and the bond broker in here, and then let's go somewhere and have a cup of coffee and talk the situation over.'

'Fine,' Schilling said, nodding. 'We've got a good man, here,' he said to Pete. 'Without Laird you'd be in here on an unbailable offense.'

'I know,' Pete said, tensely.

'Let me ask you point blank,' Laird Sharp said, across the table to Pete. 'Did you kill Jerome Lucky Luckman?'

Pete said, 'I don't know.' He explained why.

Scowling, Laird Sharp said, 'Six persons, you say. Name of god; what's going on, here? So you could have killed him. You or anyone of you or several or even all.' He fingered a sugar cube. 'I'll tell you a piece of bad news. The Widow Luckman, Dotty, is putting great pressure on the police to break this case. That means they're going to try for a conviction as soon as possible, and it'll be before a military court . . . it's that damn Concordat; we've never gotten out from under it.'

'I realize that,' Pete said. He felt tired.

'The police have given me a written transcript of the investigating officers' report,' Sharp said, reaching into his briefcase. 'I had to pull a few strings, but here it is.' He brought a voluminous document from his briefcase and pushed his coffee cup aside to lay it out on the table. 'I've already glanced at it. This E. B. Black found in your memory an encounter with a woman named Patricia McClain who told you that you were about to perform an act of violence having to do with Luckman's death.'

'No,' Pete said. 'Having to do with Luckman *and* death. It's not quite the same thing.'

The lawyer eyed him keenly. 'Very true, Garden.' He returned to the document.

'Counselor,' Schilling said, 'they have no real case against Pete. Outside of that phony memory that Calumine has – '

'They've got nothing.' Sharp nodded. 'Except the amnesia, and you share that with five other group-members. But the problem is that they'll be digging around trying to get more dope on you, beginning from the assumption that you are guilty. And by starting with that as a premise, god knows what they may be able to find. You say your auto-auto said you dropped by Berkeley sometime today . . . where Luckman was staying. You don't know why or even if you managed to reach him. God, you may have done it all right, Garden. But we'll presume you didn't, for the purposes of our case. Is there anyone that you personally suspect, and if so, why?'

'No one,' Pete said.

'Incidentally,' Sharp said, 'I happen to know something about Mr Calumine's attorney, Bert Barth. He's an excellent man. If you deposed Calumine on Barth's account you were in error; Barth is inclined to be cautious, but once he gets started you can't pull him loose.'

Pete and Joe Schilling glanced at each other.

'Anyhow,' Sharp said, 'the die is cast. I think your best bet, Garden, is to look up your Psionic woman friend Pat McClain and find out what you and she did today and what she read in your mind while you were with her.'

'Okay,' Pete said. He agreed.

'Shall we go there now?' Sharp said, putting his document away in his briefcase and rising to his feet. 'It's only ten o'clock; we may be able to catch her before she goes to bed.'

Also standing up, Pete said, 'There's a problem. She has a husband. Whom I've never met. If you understand me.'

Sharp nodded. 'I see.' He meditated. 'Maybe she'd be willing to fly here to San Francisco; I'll give her a call. If not, is there any other place you can think of?'

'Not your apartment,' Joe Schilling said. 'Carol's there.' He regarded Pete somberly. 'I have a place now. You don't remember, but you found it for me, in your present bind, San Anselmo. It's about two miles from your own apartment. If you want, I'll call Pat McClain; she no doubt remembers me. Both she and Al, her husband, have bought Jussi Bjoerling records from me. I'll tell her to meet us at my apartment.'

'Fine,' Pete said.

Joe Schilling went to the vidphone in the back of the restaurant to call.

'He's a nice guy,' Sharp said to Pete as they waited.

'Yes,' Pete agreed.

'Do you think he killed Luckman?'

Startled, Pete jerked his head, stared at his lawyer.

'Don't become unglued,' Sharp said smoothly. 'I was just curious. *You* are my client, Garden; as far as I'm professionally concerned, everyone else is a suspect over and above you, even Joe Schilling whom I've known for eighty-five years.'

'You're a jerry?' Pete said, surprised. With such energy, Pete had assumed Sharp to be no more than forty or fifty.

'Yes,' Sharp said. 'I'm a geriatric, like yourself. One hundred and fifteen years old.' He sat broodingly twisting a match folder up into a ball. 'Schilling could have done it; he's hated Luckman for years. You know the story of how Luckman reduced him to penury.'

'Then why did he wait until now?'

Glancing at him, Sharp said, 'Schilling came out here to play Luckman again. Right? He was positive he could beat Luckman if they ever tangled again; he's been telling himself that all this time, ever since Lucky beat him.

Maybe Joe got out here, all prepared to play for your group against Luckman, then lost his nerve . . . discovered at the last moment that when it came right down to it he *couldn't* beat Luckman after all – or at least feared he couldn't.'

'I see,' Pete said.

'So he was in an untenable position, committed to playing and beating Luckman, not merely for himself but for his friends . . . and he knew he simply could not do it. What other way out than to – ' Sharp broke off; Joe Schilling was crossing the near-empty restaurant, returning to the table. 'It's a compelling theory, anyhow,' Sharp said, and turned to greet Joe Schilling.

'What's an interesting theory?' Joe said, seating himself.

Sharp said, 'The theory that a single enormously powerful agency is at work manipulating the minds of the members of Pretty Blue Fox, turning them into a corporate instrument of its will.'

'You put it a little grandiosely,' Joe said, 'but in the main I feel that must be the case. As I said to Pete.'

'What did Pat McClain say?' Pete asked.

'She'll meet us here,' Joe said. 'So let's have a second cup of coffee; it'll take her another fifteen minutes. She had gone to bed.'

A half hour later Pat McClain, wearing a light trench coat, low-heeled slippers and slacks, entered the restaurant and walked toward their table. 'Hello, Pete,' she said to him; she looked pale, and her eyes were unnaturally dilated. 'Mr Schilling.' She nodded to Joe. 'And – ' She studied Laird Sharp as she seated herself. 'I'm a telepath, you know, Mr Sharp. Yes, I read that you know; you're Pete's lawyer.'

Pete thought, I wonder how – if at all – Pat's telepathic talent could assist me, at this point. I had no doubts about

Sharp, and I don't in any way, shape, or form accept his theory about Joe Schilling.

Glancing at him, Pat said, 'I'll do all I can to help you, Pete.' Her voice was low but steady; she had herself under control; the panic of a few hours ago was gone. 'You don't remember anything that happened between us, this afternoon.'

'No,' he admitted.

'Well,' Pat said, 'you and I got on astonishingly well, for two people who are married to someone else entirely.'

Sharp asked her, 'Was there anything in Pete's mind, when he met you this afternoon, about Lucky Luckman?'

'Yes,' she said. 'A tremendous desire for Luckman's death.'

'Then he didn't know Luckman was dead,' Joe said.

'Is that correct?' Sharp asked her.

Pat nodded. 'He was terribly afraid. He felt that – ' She hesitated. 'He felt that Luckman would beat Joe again, as he did years ago; Pete was going into a psychological fugue, a retreat from the whole situation regarding Luckman.'

'No plans to kill Luckman, I assume,' Sharp said.

'No,' Pat said.

'If it can be established that Luckman was dead by one-thirty,' Joe Schilling said, 'wouldn't that clear Pete?'

'Probably,' Sharp said. To Pat he said, 'You'd testify to this in court?'

'Yes.' She nodded.

'Despite your husband.'

After a pause she again nodded.

Sharp said, 'And would you let the telepaths of the police scan you?'

'Oh Christ,' she said, drawing back.

'Why not?' Sharp said. 'You're telling the truth, aren't you?'

'Y-yes,' Pat said. 'But – ' She gestured. 'There's so much more, so many personal matters.'

Schilling said wryly, 'Ironic. As a telepath she's been scanning people's private ruminations all her life. Now, when it's a question of a telepath scanning her – '

'But you don't understand!' Pat said.

'I understand,' Schilling said. 'You and Pete had an assignation today; you're having an affair. Correct? And your husband isn't to know and Pete's wife isn't to know. But that's the stuff life is made of; you know that perfectly well. If you allow the telepathic police to scan you, possibly you will save Pete's life; isn't that worth being scanned for? Or perhaps you're not telling the truth, and they'd find out.'

'I'm telling the truth,' Pat said angrily, her eyes blazing. 'But – I can't allow the police telepaths to scan me and that's that.' She turned to Pete. 'I'm sorry. Maybe some-day you'll know why. It has nothing to do with you, or with my husband finding out. There really isn't anything to find out anyhow; we met, walked, had lunch, then you left.'

Sharp said astutely, 'Joe, this girl's obviously mixed up in something extra-legal. If the police scan her she's lost.'

Pat said nothing. But the expression on her face showed that it was so; the attorney was right.

What could she be involved with? Pete wondered. Strange . . . he would never have imagined it about her; Pat McClain seemed too withdrawn, too encapsulated.

'Maybe it's a pose,' she said, picking up his thought.

Sharp said, 'So we can't get you to testify for Pete, even though it's direct evidence that he did not know of Luckman's death.' He eyed her intently.

'I heard on TV,' she said, 'that Luckman is believed to have been killed sometime late today, near dinner time. So,' she gestured, 'my testimony wouldn't help anyhow.'

'Did you hear that?' Sharp said. 'Odd. I listened, too,

on the way here from New Mexico. And according to Nats Katz, the time of Luckman's death had still to be established.'

There was silence.

'It's too bad,' Sharp said acidly, 'that we can't read your mind, Mrs McClain, as you can read ours. It might prove somewhat interesting.'

'That clown Nats Katz,' Pat said. 'He's not a newscaster anyhow; he's a pop singer and disc jockey. He sometimes is six hours behind in his so-called news briefs.' With steady fingers she got out a cigarette and lit up. 'Go out and track down a news vendor; get a late edition of the *Chronicle*. It's probably in that.'

Sharp said, 'It doesn't matter. Because in any case you won't testify for my client.'

To Pete, she said, 'Forgive me.'

'Hell,' Pete said, 'if you won't testify you won't.' And anyhow he tended to believe her about the time of death having been established as late in the day.

'What sort of extra-legal activity would a pretty woman like you be mixed up in?' Sharp asked her.

Pat said nothing.

'It could be noised about,' Sharp pointed out to her. 'And then the authorities would want to scan you whether you testify in this or not.'

'Let it drop,' Pete said to him.

Sharp glanced his way, shrugged. 'Whatever you say.'

'Thank you, Pete,' Pat said. She sat smoking silently.

'I have a request,' Sharp said, after a time, 'to make of you, Mrs McClain. As you have probably already gleaned from Mr Garden's mind, five other members of Pretty Blue Fox have shown up with amnesia regarding the day's activities.'

'Yes.' Pat nodded.

'Undoubtedly they will all be attempting to determine what they did and did not do today in the manner that

Pete employed, checking with various Rushmore units and so on. Would you be willing to assist us by scanning these five people in the next day or so to determine what they've learned?'

'Why?' Joe said.

'I don't know why,' Sharp answered. 'And I won't know until she gives us the information. But,' he hesitated, chewing his lower lip and scowling, 'I'd like to find out if the paths of these six people intersected at any moment during the day. During the now-forgotten interval.'

'Give us your operational theory,' Joe said.

Sharp said, 'It's possible that all six acted in concert, as part of a complicated, far-reaching plan. They may have elaborated it some time in the past and had *that* removed by electroshock also.'

With a grimace Joe Schilling said, 'But they didn't know until just the other day that Lucky Luckman was coming out here.'

'The death of Luckman may be nothing more than a symptom of a greater strategy,' Sharp said. 'His presence here may have spoiled the effective operation of this larger plan.' He eyed Pete. 'What do you say to this?'

'I say you've got a theory much more ornate than the situation itself,' Pete said.

'Possibly,' Sharp said. 'But evidently it was necessary to mentally blind six people today, when one would expect two or three to be sufficient. Two in addition to the murderer himself would have made prosecution difficult enough, I think. But I could be wrong; whoever is behind this may simply be playing it as cautious as he can.'

'The Master Game-player,' Pete said.

'Pardon?' Sharp said. 'Oh yes. Bluff, the game Mrs McClain can never play because she's too talented. The Game that cost Joe Schilling his status and Luckman his life. Doesn't this homicide make you a trifle less bitter, Mrs McClain? Maybe you're not so badly off, after all.'

'How did you know that?' Pat asked him. 'About what you term my "bitterness." I've never seen you before tonight, have I? Or is my "bitterness" that well-known?'

'It's all in the briefcase,' Sharp said, patting the leather side of it. 'The police got it from Pete's mind.' He smiled at her. 'Now let me ask you something, Mrs McClain. As a Psi-person, *do you have contact with very many other Psi-individuals*?'

'Sometimes,' Pat said.

'Do you know first hand the range of Psionic ability? For instance, we all know about the telepath, the pre-cog, the psycho-kinetic, but what about the rarer talents? For example, is there a sub-variety of Psi which deals with the alteration of the contents of other people's psyches? A sort of mental psycho-kinesis?'

Pat said, 'Not – to my knowledge, no.'

'You understand my question.'

'Yes.' She nodded. 'But to my knowledge, which is limited, no Psi talents exist which could explain the amnesia of the six members of Pretty Blue Fox nor the alteration in Bill Calumine's mind regarding what Pete did or did not say to him.'

'You say your knowledge is limited.' Sharp scrutinized her as he spoke. 'Then it's not impossible that such a talent – and such a Psi-person – could exist.'

'Why would a Psionic individual want to kill Luckman?' Pat asked.

'Why would anyone want to?' Sharp said. 'Obviously, someone did.'

'But someone in Pretty Blue Fox. They had reasons to.'

Sharp said quietly, 'There is nothing in the make-up of the members of Pretty Blue Fox which would account for the capacity to cripple the memories of six people and alter the memory of a seventh.'

'Does such a capacity exist anywhere that you know of?' Pat asked him.

'Yes,' Sharp said. 'During the war both sides used techniques of that sort. It goes all the way back to mid-twentieth-century Soviet brainwashing procedures.'

'Horrible,' Pat said with a shudder. 'One of the worst periods in our history.'

At the door of the restaurant an automated news vending machine appeared, with a late edition of the *Chronicle*. Its Rushmore Effect bleated out, 'Special coverage of the Luckman murder case.' The restaurant, except for their party, was empty; the news vending machine, being homotropic, headed toward them, still bleating. 'The *Chronicle*'s own circuit investigates and discloses startling new details not found in the *Examiner* or the *News Call-Bulletin*.' It waved the newspaper in their faces.

Getting out a coin, Sharp inserted it in the slot of the machine; it at once presented him with a copy of the paper and rolled back out of the restaurant, to hunt for more people.

'What does it say?' Pat asked, as Sharp read the lead article.

'You're correct,' Sharp said, nodding. 'Time of death believed to be late in the afternoon. Not too long before Mrs Garden found the body in her car. So I owe you an apology.'

Joe Schilling said, 'Maybe Pat's also a pre-cog. The news wasn't out yet when she told you that. She previewed this edition in advance of its release. How useful she'd be in the newspaper business.'

'Not very funny,' Pat said. 'That's one of the reasons why Psis become so cynical; we're so mistrusted, no matter what we do.'

'Let's go somewhere that we can get a drink,' Joe Schilling said. To Pete he said, 'What's a good bar in the

Bay Area? You must know the situation around here; you're a sophisticate, urbane and cosmopolitan.'

Pete said, 'We can go to the Blind Lemon in Berkeley. It's almost two centuries old. Or should I stay out of Berkeley?' he asked Sharp.

'No reason to avoid it,' Sharp said. 'You're not going to run into Dotty Luckman at a bar; that's certain. You don't have a bad conscience about Berkeley, do you?'

'No,' Pete said.

'I have to go home,' Pat McClain said. 'Goodbye.' She rose to her feet.

Accompanying her to her car, Pete said, 'Thanks for coming.'

On the dark San Francisco sidewalk she stood by her car, stubbing her cigarette out with the toe of her slipper. 'Pete,' she said, 'even if you did kill Luckman or helped kill him, I – still want to know you better. We were just beginning to become acquainted, this afternoon. I like you a lot.' She smiled at him. 'What a mess this all is. You crazy Game-players; taking it so seriously. Willing, at least some of you, to kill a human being because of it. Maybe I am glad I had to leave it; maybe I'm better off.' She stood on tiptoe, kissed him. 'I'll see you. I'll vidphone you when I can.'

He watched her car shoot rapidly into the night sky, its signal lights winking red, on and off.

What's she mixed up in? he asked himself as he walked back into the restaurant. She'll never tell me. Perhaps I can find out through her children. For some reason it seemed important for him to know.

'You don't trust her,' Joe Schilling said to him, as he sat down once more at the table. 'That's too bad. I think she's fundamentally an honest person, but god knows what she's got herself involved in. You're probably right to be suspicious.'

'I'm not suspicious,' Pete said. 'I'm just concerned.'

Sharp said, 'Psi-people are different from us. You can't put your finger on exactly what it is – I mean, in addition to their talent. That girl . . .' He shook his head. 'I was sure she was lying. How long has she been your mistress, Garden, did you say?'

'She's not,' Pete said. At least he didn't think so. A shame to forget something like that, not to be certain in that aspect of one's life.

'I don't know whether to wish you luck or not,' Laird Sharp said, thoughtfully.

'Wish me luck,' Pete said. 'I can always use it in that area.'

'So to speak,' Schilling said, and smiled.

When he got home to his apartment in San Rafael, Pete Garden found Carol standing at the window, gazing sightlessly out. She barely greeted him; her voice was distant and muted.

'Sharp got me out on bail,' Pete said. 'They've got me charged with – '

'I know.' Her arms folded, Carol nodded. 'They were here. The two detectives, Hawthorne and Black. Mutt and Jeff, only I can't figure out which is the easy-going one and which is supposed to be tough. They both seem tough.'

'What were they doing here?' he demanded.

'Searching the apartment. They had a warrant. Hawthorne told me about Pat.'

After a pause, Pete said, 'That's a shame.'

'No, I think it's very good. Now we know exactly where we stand, you and I, in relationship to each other. You don't need me in The Game; Joe Schilling does that. And you don't need me here, either. I'm going back to my own group. I've decided.' She pointed toward the bedroom of the apartment and he saw, on the bed, two suitcases. 'Maybe you can help carry them downstairs to the car,' Carol said.

'I wish you'd stay,' he said.

'To be jeered at?'

'Nobody's jeering at you.'

'Of course they are. Everybody in Pretty Blue Fox is, or will be. And it'll be in the papers.'

'Maybe so,' he said. He hadn't thought of that.

'If I hadn't found Luckman's body,' Carol said, 'I wouldn't know about Pat. And if I didn't know about Pat I would have tried – and possibly succeeded – in being a good wife of yours. So you can blame whoever killed Luckman for destroying our marriage.'

'Maybe that's why they did it,' he said. 'Killed Luckman.'

'I doubt it. Our marriage is hardly that important. How many wives have you had, in all?'

'Eighteen.'

Carol nodded. 'I've had fifteen husbands. That's thirty-three combinations of male and female. And no *luck*, as they say, from any of them.'

'When did you last bite into a piece of rabbit-paper?'

Carol smiled thinly. 'Oh, I do all the time. It wouldn't show up from us, yet. It's too early.'

'Not with the new West German kind,' Pete said. 'I read about it. It records even an impregnation only an hour old.'

'Good grief,' Carol said. 'Well, I don't have any of the new kind; I didn't even know it existed.'

'I know an all-night drugstore,' Pete said, 'in Berkeley. Let's fly over there and pick up a packet of the new rabbit-paper.'

'Why?'

'There's always the chance, the possibility. And if we had *luck*, you wouldn't want to dissolve our relationship.'

'All right,' Carol said. 'You take my two suitcases down to the car and we'll fly over to the all-night drugstore.

102

And if I am pregnant, I'll come back here with you. And if I'm not, then goodbye.'

'Okay,' he said. There wasn't much else he could say; he couldn't force her to remain.

'Do you want me to stay?' Carol asked, as he carried the two heavy suitcases downstairs to her car.

'Yes,' he said.

'Why?'

He didn't know why. 'Well – ' he began.

'Forget it,' Carol said, and got into her car. 'You follow me in yours. I don't feel like riding with you, Pete.'

Presently he was in the air over San Rafael, riding on the beam created by her tail lights. He felt melancholy. Damn those cops, he thought. Anything to split the members of the group apart, so they can be picked off one at a time. But it wasn't the two police that he blamed; it was himself. If she hadn't found out this way she would have run onto it by another.

I let my life become overly complex, he decided. Too much for me to keep straight and handle. Carol has certainly received a bad handful of cards since she came to Pretty Blue Fox. First Luckman arrives; then I bring Schilling in to take her place at the Game table; then Luckman's body turns up in her car; now this. No wonder she wants to leave.

Why should she stay? he asked himself. Give me one good reason.

He couldn't.

They flew over the Bay and soon they were gliding down to land at the deserted parking lot of the drugstore. Carol, slightly ahead of him, stood waiting as he got out of his car and walked over to her.

'It's a nice night,' she said. 'So you used to live here. What a shame you lost it. Just think, Pete; if you hadn't lost it I'd never have met you.'

'Yeah,' he said, as they ascended the ramp and entered

the drugstore. That and so much else would never have come about.

The Rushmore Effect of the drugstore greeted them; they were its only customers. 'Good evening, sir and madame. How may I assist you, please?' The obedient mechanical voice issued from a hundred speakers hidden throughout the great lit-up place. The entire structure had focused its attention on the two of them.

Carol said, 'Do you know anything about a new instant rabbit-paper?'

'Yes madame,' the drugstore answered eagerly. 'A recent scientific breakthrough, from A. G. Chemie at Bonn. I'll get it for you.' From an orifice at the end of the glass counter a package tumbled; it slithered to a halt directly before them and Pete picked it up. 'The same price as the old.'

He paid the drugstore and then he and Carol walked back out onto the dark, deserted parking lot.

'All for us,' Carol said. 'This enormous place with a thousand lights on and that Rushmore circuit clamoring away. It's like a drugstore for the dead. A spectral drugstore.'

'Hell,' Pete said, 'it's very much for the living. The only problem is, there just aren't enough of the living.'

'Maybe there's one more than there was,' Carol said; she removed a strip of rabbit-paper from the pack, unwrapped it, placed it between her even, white teeth and bit. 'What color does it turn?' she asked, as she examined it. 'Same as the old?'

'White for non,' Pete said, 'green for positive.'

In the dim light of the parking lot it was hard to tell.

Carol opened her car door; the dome light switched on and she inspected the strip of rabbit-paper by it.

The paper was green.

Carol looked up at him and said, 'I'm pregnant. We've had *luck*.' Her voice was bleak; her eyes filled with tears and she looked away. 'I'll be goddamned,' she said brokenly. 'The first time I've ever been in all my whole life. And with a man who's already – ' She was silent, breathing with difficulty and staring fixedly past him into the night darkness.

'This calls for a celebration!' he said.

'It does?' She turned to face him.

'We got to go on the radio and broadcast it to the whole world!'

'Oh,' Carol said, nodding. 'Yes, that's right; that's the custom. Won't everyone be jealous of us? My!'

Crawling into her car, Pete snapped on the transmitter of the radio to the emergency all-wave broadcast position. 'Hey!' he exclaimed. 'You know what? This is Pete Garden of Pretty Blue Fox at Carmel, California. Carol Holt Garden and I have only been married a day or so, and tonight we made use of the new type of West German rabbit-paper – '

'I wish I were dead,' Carol said.

'You what?' He stared at her in disbelief. 'You're nuts! This is the most important event of our lives! We've added to the population. This makes up for Luckman's death, it balances it out. Right?' He caught hold of her hand and compressed it until she moaned. 'Say something into the mike, Mrs Garden.'

Carol said, 'I wish all of you the same *luck* I've had tonight.'

'You're goddam right!' Pete shouted into the microphone. 'Every single one of you listening to me!'

'So now we stay together,' Carol said softly.

'Yes,' Pete agreed. 'That's right; that's what we decided.'

'And what about Patricia McClain?'

'The hell with everybody else in the world except you,' Pete said. 'Except you and me and the baby.'

Carol smiled a little. 'Okay. Let's drive back.'

'Do you think you're able to drive? We'll leave your car here and both go back in mine and I'll drive.' Quickly, he carried her suitcases to his own car, then took her by the arm and led her. 'Just sit down and take it easy,' he said, seating her in his car and fastening the safety belt in place.

'Pete,' she said, 'do you realize what this means in terms of The Game?' She had turned pale. 'Every deed in the pot belongs to us, automatically. But – there is no Game right now! There aren't any deeds in the pot, because of the police ban. But we must get something. We'll have to look it up in the manual.'

'Okay,' he said, only half-listening to her; he was busy carefully guiding his car up into the sky.

'Pete,' she said, '*maybe you win back Berkeley*.'

'Not a chance. There was at least one Game subsequent to that, the one we played last night.'

'True.' She nodded. 'We'll have to apply to the Rules Committee in the Jay Satellite for an interpretation, I guess.'

He frankly did not care about The Game at this moment. The idea of a child, a son or daughter . . . it obliterated everything else in his mind, all that had happened of late, everything connected with Luckman's arrival and death and the banning of the group.

Luck, he thought, this late in my life. One hundred and fifty years. After so many tries; after the failure of so many, many combinations.

With Carol beside him he drove his car back across the dark Bay to San Rafael and their apartment.

When they got there, and had gone upstairs, Pete headed at once for the medicine cabinet in the bathroom.

'What are you doing?' Carol asked, following after him.

Pete said, 'I'm going out on a whing-ding; I'm going to get drunker than I've ever before been in my life.' From the medicine cabinet he got down five Snoozex tablets and, after hesitating, a handful of methamphetamine tablets. 'These will help,' he explained to Carol. 'Goodbye.' He swallowed the pills, gulping them down all together, and then headed for the hall door. 'It's a custom.' He paused briefly at the door. 'When you learn you're going to have a child. I've read about it.' He saluted her gravely and then shut the door after him.

A moment later he was downstairs, back in his car, starting out alone in the dark night, searching for the nearest bar.

As the car shot upward into the sky, Pete thought, God knows where I'm going or when I'll get back. I certainly don't know – and don't care.

'Wheeoo!' he shouted exultantly, as the car climbed.

The sound of his voice echoed back to him and he shouted again.

Chapter 10

Roused from her sleep, Freya Gaines groped for the switch of the vidphone; groggily she found it and snapped it on.

'Lo,' she mumbled, wondering what time it was. She made out the luminous dial of the clock beside the bed. Three A.M. Good grief.

Carol Holt Garden's features formed on the vidscreen. 'Freya, have you seen Pete?' Carol's voice was jerky, anxiety-stricken. 'He went out and he still hasn't come back; I can't go to sleep.'

'No,' Freya said. 'Of course I don't know where he is. Did the police let him go?'

'He's out on bail,' Carol said. 'Do – you have any idea what places he might stop at? The bars are all closed, now; I was waiting for two o'clock thinking he'd show up no later than two-thirty. But – '

'Try the Blind Lemon in Berkeley,' Freya said, and started to cut the connection. Maybe he's dead, she thought. Threw himself off one of the bridges or crashed his car – finally.

Carol said, 'He's celebrating.'

'Good god why?' Freya said.

'I'm pregnant.'

Fully awake, Freya said, 'I see. Astonishing. Right away. You must be using that new rabbit-paper they're selling.'

'Yes,' Carol said. 'I bit a piece tonight and it turned green; that's why Pete's out. I wish he'd come back. He's so emotional, first he's depressed and suicidal and then – '

'You worry about your problems. I'll worry about mine,' Freya cut in. 'Congratulations, Carol. I hope it's a baby.' And then she did break the connection; the image faded into darkness.

The bastard, Freya said to herself with fury and bitterness. She lay back, supine, staring up at the ceiling, clenching her fists and fighting back the tears. I could kill him, she said to herself. I hope he's dead; I hope he never comes back to her.

Would he come here? She sat up, stricken. What if he does? she asked herself. Beside her, in the bed, Clem Gaines snored on. If he shows up here I won't let him in, she decided; I don't want to see him.

But, for some reason, she knew Pete would not come here anyhow. He's not looking for me, she realized. I'm the last person he's looking for.

She lit a cigarette and sat in bed, smoking and staring straight ahead of her, silently.

The vug said, 'Mr Garden, when did you first begin to notice these disembodied feelings, as if the world about you is not quite real?'

'As long ago as I can remember,' Pete said.

'And your reaction?'

'Depression. I've taken thousands of amitriptyline tablets and they only have a temporary effect.'

'Do you know who I am?' the vug asked.

'Let's see,' Pete said, cogitating. The name *Doctor Phelps* floated through his mind. 'Doctor Eugen Phelps,' he said hopefully.

'Almost right, Mr Garden. It's Doctor E. R. Philipson. And how did you happen to look me up? Do you perhaps recall that?'

Pete said, 'How could I help looking you up?' The answer was obvious. 'Because you're there. Or rather, here.'

'Stick out your tongue.'

'Why?'

'As a mark of disrespect.'

Pete stuck out his tongue. 'Ahhh,' he said.

'Additional comment is unnecessary; the point's made. How many times have you attempted suicide?'

'Four,' Pete said. 'The first when I was twenty. The second when I was forty. The third – '

'No need to go on. How close did you come to success?'

'Very close. Yes sir. Especially the last time.'

'What stopped you?'

'A force greater than myself,' Pete said.

'How droll.' The vug chuckled.

'I mean my wife. Betty, that was her name. Betty Jo. She and I met at Joe Schilling's rare record shop. Betty Jo had breasts as firm and ripe as melons. Or was her name Mary Anne?'

'Her name was not Mary Anne,' Doctor E. R. Philipson said, 'because now you're speaking of the eighteen-year-old daughter of Pat and Allen McClain and she has never been your wife. I am not qualified to describe her breasts. Or her mother's. In any case you scarcely know her; all you know about her in fact is that she devoutly listens to Nats Katz whom you can't stand. You and she have nothing in common.'

'You lying son of a bitch,' Pete said.

'Oh no. I'm not lying. I'm facing reality and that's exactly what you've failed to do; that's why you're here. You're involved in an intricate, sustained illusion-system of massive proportion. You and half of your Game-playing friends. Do you want to escape from it?'

'No,' Pete said. 'I mean yes. Yes or no; what does it matter?' He felt sick at his stomach. 'Can I leave now?' he said. 'I think I've spent all my money.'

The vug Doctor E.R. Philipson said, 'You have twenty-five dollars in time left.'

'Well, I'd rather have the twenty-five dollars.'

'That raises a nice point of professional ethics in that you have already paid me.'

'Then pay me back,' Pete said.

The vug sighed. 'This is a stalemate. I think I will make the decision for both of us. Do I have twenty-five dollars' worth of help left that I can give you? It depends on what you want. You are in a situation of insidiously-growing difficulty. It will probably kill you shortly, just as it killed Mr Luckman. Be especially careful for your pregnant wife; she is excruciatingly fragile at this point.'

'I will. I will.'

Doctor E. R. Philipson said, 'Your best bet, Garden, is to bend with the forces of the times. There's little hope that you can achieve much, really; you're one person and you do, in some respects, properly see the situation. But physically you're powerless. Who can you go to? E. B. Black? Mr Hawthorne? You could try. They might help you; they might not. Now, as to the time-segment missing from your memory.'

'Yes,' Pete said. 'The time-segment missing from my memory. How about that?'

'You have fairly well reconstructed it by means of the Rushmore Effect mechanisms. So don't fret unduly.'

'But did I kill Luckman?'

'Ha, ha,' the vug said. 'Do you think I'm going to tell you? Are you out of your mind?'

'Maybe so,' Pete said. 'Maybe I'm being naïve.' He felt even sicker, now, too sick to go on any further. 'Where's the men's room?' he asked the vug. 'Or shall I say the humans' room?' He looked around, squinting to see. The colors were all wrong and when he tried to walk he felt weightless or at least much lighter. *Too* light. He was not on Earth. This was not one-G pulling at him; it was only a fraction.

He thought, *I'm on Titan.*

'Second door to the left,' the vug Doctor E. R. Philipson said.

'Thank you,' Pete said, walking with care so that he would not float up and rebound from one of the white-painted walls. 'Listen,' he said, pausing. 'What about Carol? I'm giving up Patricia; nothing means anything to me except the mother of my child.'

'Nothing means anything, you mean,' Doctor E. R. Philipson said. 'A joke, and a poor one. I'm merely commenting on your state of mind. "Things are seldom what they seem; Skim-milk masquerades as cream." A wonderful statement by the Terran humorist, W. S. Gilbert. I wish you luck and I suggest you consult E. B. Black; he's reliable. You can trust him. I'm not so sure about Hawthorne.' The vug called loudly after Pete. 'And close the bathroom door after you so I won't have to listen. It's disgusting when a Terran is sick.'

Pete shut the door. How do I get out of here? he asked himself. I've got to escape. How'd I get here to Titan in the first place?

How much time has passed? Days – weeks, perhaps.

I have to get home to Carol. God, he thought. They may have killed her by now, the way they killed Luckman. They? Who?

He did not know. It had been explained to him . . . or had it? Had he really gotten one hundred and fifty dollars' worth? Perhaps. It was his responsibility, not theirs, to retain the knowledge.

A window, high up in the bathroom. He moved the great metal paper towel drum over, stood on it and managed to reach the window. Stuck shut, painted shut. He smashed upward against its wooden frame with the heels of his hands.

Creaking, the window rose.

Room enough. He hoisted himself up, squeezed through. Darkness, the Titanian night . . . he dropped,

112

fell, listening to himself whistle down and down like a feather, or rather like a bug with large surface-area in proportion to mass. Whooee, he shouted, but he heard no sound except the whistle of his falling.

He struck, pitched forward, lay suffering the pain in his feet and legs. I broke my goddam ankle, he said to himself. He hobbled up to his feet. An alley, trashcans and cobblestones; he hobbled toward a street light. To his right, a red neon sign. Dave's Place. A bar. He had come out the back, out of the men's washroom, minus his coat. He leaned against the wall of a building, waiting for the numbing pain in his ankles to subside.

A Rushmore circuit cruising past, automatic policeman. 'Are you all right, sir?'

'Yes,' Pete said. 'Thank you. Just stopped to – you know what. Nature called.' He laughed. 'Thanks.' The Rushmore cop wheeled on.

What city am I in? he asked himself. The air, damp, smelled of ashes. Chicago? St Louis? Warm, foul air, not the clean air of San Francisco. He walked unsteadily down the street, away from Dave's Place. The vug inside, cadging drinks, clipping Terran customers, rolling them in an educated way. He felt for his wallet in his pants' pocket. Gone. Jesus Christ! He felt at his coat; there it was. He sighed in relief.

Those pills I took, he thought, didn't mix with the drinks, or rather did mix; that's the problem. But I'm okay, not hurt, just a little shaken up and scared. And I'm lost. I've lost myself and my car. And separately.

'Car,' he called, trying to summon its auto-auto mech system. Its Rushmore Effect. Sometimes it responded; sometimes not. Chance factor.

Lights, twin beams. His car rolled along the curb, bumped to a halt by him. 'Mr Garden. Here I am.'

'Listen,' Pete said, fumbling, finding the door handle. 'Where are we, for chrissakes?'

113

'Pocatello, Idaho.'

'For chrissakes!'

'It's god's truth, Mr Garden; I swear it.'

Pete said. 'You're awfully articulate for a Rushmore circuit, aren't you?' Opening the car door he peered in, blinking in the glare of the dome light. Peered suspiciously, and in fright.

Someone sat behind the tiller.

After a pause the figure said, 'Get in, Mr Garden.'

'Why?' he said.

'So I can drive you where you want to go.'

'I don't want to go anywhere,' he said. 'I want to stay here.'

'Why are you looking at me so funny? Don't you remember coming and getting me? It was your idea to do the town – do several towns, as a matter of fact.' She smiled. It was a woman; he saw that now.

'Who the hell are you?' he said. 'I don't know you.'

'Why, you certainly do. You met me at Joseph Schilling's rare record shop in New Mexico.'

'Mary Anne McClain,' he said, then. He got slowly into the car beside her. 'What's been going on?'

Mary Anne said calmly, 'You've been celebrating your wife Carol's pregnancy.'

'But how'd I get mixed up with you?'

'First you dropped by the apartment in Marin County. I wasn't there because I was at the San Francisco public library doing research. My mother told you and you flew to San Francisco, to the library, and picked me up. And we drove to Pocatello because you had the idea that an eighteen-year-old girl would be served in a bar in Idaho, and she isn't in San Francisco as we found out.'

'Was I right?'

'No. So you went in alone, to Dave's Place, and I've

114

been sitting out here in the car waiting for you. And you just now came out of that alley and began yelling.'

'I see,' he said. He lay back against the seat. 'I feel sick. I wish I was home.'

Mary Anne McClain said, 'I'll drive you home, Mr Garden.' The car now had lifted into the sky; Pete shut his eyes.

'How'd I get mixed up with that vug?' he said, after a time.

'What vug?'

'In the bar. I guess. Doctor something Philipson.'

'How would I know? They wouldn't let me in.'

'Well, was there a vug in there? Didn't you see in?'

'I saw in; I went in at first. But there was no vug while I was there. But of course I came right back out; they made me leave.'

'I'm quite a heel,' Pete said, 'staying inside drinking while you sat out here in the car.'

'I didn't mind,' Mary Anne said. 'I had a nice conversation with the Rushmore unit. I learned a lot about you. Didn't I, car?'

'Yes, Miss McClain,' the car said.

'It likes me,' Mary Anne said. 'All Rushmore Effects like me.' She laughed. 'I charm them.'

'Evidently,' Pete said. 'What time is it?'

'About four.'

'A.M.?' He couldn't believe it. How come the bar was still open? 'They don't allow bars open that late, in any state.'

'Maybe I looked at the clock wrong,' Mary Anne said.

'No,' Pete said. 'You looked at it right. But something's wrong; something's terribly wrong.'

'Ha, ha,' Mary Anne said.

He glanced at her. At the tiller of the car sat the shapeless slime of a vug. 'Car,' Pete said instantly. 'What's at the tiller? Tell me.'

'Mary Anne McClain, Mr Garden,' the car said.

But the vug still sat there. He saw it.

'Are you sure?' Pete said.

'Positive,' the car said.

The vug said, 'As I said, I can charm Rushmore circuits.'

'Where are we going?' Pete said.

'Home. To take you back to your wife Carol.'

'And then what?'

'And then I'm going home to bed.'

'*What are you?*' he said to it.

'What do you think? You can see. Tell someone about it; tell Mr Hawthorne the detective or better yet tell E. B. Black the detective. E. B. Black would get a kick out of it.'

Pete shut his eyes.

When he opened them again it was Mary Anne McClain sitting there beside him, at the tiller of the car.

'You were right,' he said to the car. Or were you? he wondered. God, he thought; I wish I was home, I wish I hadn't come out tonight. I'm scared. Joe Schilling, he could help me. Aloud he said, 'Take me to Joe Schilling's apartment, Mary Anne or whatever your name is.'

'At *this* time of night? You're crazy.'

'He's my best friend. In all the world.'

'It'll be five A.M. when we get there.'

'He'll be glad to see me,' Pete said. 'With what I have to tell him.'

'And what's that?' Mary Anne said.

Cautiously, he said, 'You know. About Carol. The baby.'

'Oh yes,' Mary Anne said. She nodded. 'As Freya said, "I hope it's a baby."'

'Freya said that? Who to?'

'To Carol.'

'How do you know?'

116

Mary Anne said, 'You telephoned Carol from the car before we went to Dave's Place; you wanted to be sure she was all right. She was very upset and you asked why and she said that she had called Freya, looking for you, and Freya had said that.'

'Damn that Freya,' Pete said.

'I don't blame you for feeling like that. She's a hard, schizoid type, it sounds like. We studied about that in psych.'

'Do you like school?'

'Love it,' Mary Anne said.

'Do you think you could be interested in an old man of one hundred and fifty years?'

'You're not so old, Mr Garden. Just confused. You'll feel better after I get you home.' She smiled at him, briefly.

'I'm still potent,' he said. 'As witness Carol's impregnation. Whooee!' he cried.

'Three cheers,' Mary Anne said. 'Just think: one more Terran in the world. Isn't that delightful?'

'We don't generally refer to ourselves as Terrans,' Pete said. 'We generally say "people." You made a mistake.'

'Oh,' Mary Anne said, nodding. 'Mistake noted.'

Pete said, 'Is your mother part of this? Is that why she didn't want the police to scan her?'

'Yep,' Mary Anne said.

'How many are in it?'

'Oh, thousands,' Mary Anne – or rather the vug – said. Despite what he saw he knew it to be a vug. 'Just thousands and thousands. All over the planet.'

'But not everyone's in on it,' Pete said. 'Because you still have to hide from the authorities. I think I will tell Hawthorne.'

Mary Anne laughed.

Reaching into the glove compartment, Pete fumbled about.

'Mary Anne removed the gun,' the car informed him. 'She was afraid if the police stopped you and they found it they'd put you back in jail.'

'That's right,' Mary Anne said.

'You people killed Luckman. Why?'

She shrugged. 'I forget. Sorry.'

'Who's next?'

'The thing.'

'What thing?'

Mary Anne, her eyes sparkling, said, 'The thing growing inside Carol. Bad luck, Mr Garden; it's not a baby.'

He shut his eyes.

The next he knew, they were over the Bay Area.

'Almost home,' Mary Anne said.

'And you're just going to let me off?' he said.

'Why not?'

'I don't know.' He was sick, then, in the corner of the car, like an animal would be. Mary Anne said nothing after that and he said nothing either. What a terrible night this had been, he thought to himself. It should have been wonderful; my first *luck*. And instead –

And now he could not reasonably dwell on the theme of suicide, because the situation had become worse, was too bad for that to be a solution. My own problems are problems of perception, he realized. Of understanding and then accepting. What I have to remember is *that they're not all in it*. The detective E. B. Black isn't in it and Doctor Philipson; he or it isn't in it either. I can get help from something, somewhere, sometime.

'Right you are,' Mary Anne said.

'Are you a telepath?' he said to her.

'I very much certainly darn right am.'

'But,' he said, 'your mother said you weren't.'

'My mother lied to you.'

Pete said, 'Is Nats Katz the center of all this?'

'Yes,' she said.

118

'I thought so,' he said, and lay back against the seat, trying not to be sick again.

Mary Anne said, 'Here we are.' The car dipped down, skimmed above the deserted pavement of a San Rafael street. 'Give me a kiss,' she said, 'before you get out.' She brought the car to a halt at the curb and looking up he saw his apartment building. The light was on in his window; Carol was still up, waiting for him, or else she had fallen asleep with the lights on.

'A kiss,' he echoed. 'Really?'

'Yes really,' Mary Anne said, and leaned expectantly toward him.

'I can't,' he said.

'Why not?'

'Because,' he said, 'of what you are, the thing that you are.'

'Oh how absurd,' Mary Anne said. 'What's the matter with you, Pete? You're lost in dreams!'

'I am?'

'Yes,' she said, glaring at him in exasperation. 'You took dope tonight and got drunk and you were terribly excited about Carol and also you were afraid because of the police. You've been hallucinating like mad for the last two hours. You thought that psychiatrist, Doctor Philipson, was a vug, and then you thought *I* was a vug.' To the car, Mary Anne said, 'Am I a vug?'

'No, Mary Anne,' the Rushmore circuit of the car answered, for the second time.

'See?' she said.

'I still can't do it,' he said. 'Just let me out of the car.' He found the door handle, opened the door, stepped out on the curb, his legs shaking under him.

'Good night,' Mary Anne said, eying him.

'Good night.' He started toward the door of the apartment building.

The car said, after him, 'You got me all dirty.'

119

'Too bad,' Pete said. He opened the apartment building door with his key and passed on inside; the door shut after him.

When he got upstairs he found Carol standing in the hall in a short, sheer yellow nightgown. 'I heard the car drive up,' she said. 'Thank god you're back! I was so worried about you.' She folded her arms, self-consciously blushing. 'I should be in my robe, I know.'

'Thanks for waiting up.' He passed on by her, went into the bathroom and washed his face and hands with cold water.

'Can I fix you something to eat or drink? It's so late now.'

'Coffee,' he said, 'would be fine.'

In the kitchen she fixed a pot of coffee for both of them.

'Do me a favor,' Pete said. 'Call Pocatello information, the vidphone autocorp, and find out if there's a Doctor E. R. Philipson listed.'

'All right.' Carol clicked on the vidphone. She talked for a time with a sequence of homeostatic circuits and then she rang off. 'Yes.'

'I was seeing him,' Pete said. 'It cost me one hundred and fifty dollars. Their rates are high. Could you tell from what the vidphone said if Philipson is a Terran?'

'They didn't say. I got his number.' She pushed the pad toward him.

'I'll call him and ask.' He clicked the vidphone back on.

'At *five-thirty* in the morning?'

'Yes,' he said, dialing. A long time passed; the phone, at the other end, rang and rang. '"Walkin' the dog, see-bawh, see-bawh,"' Pete sang. '"He have-um red whisker, he have-um green paw." Doctors expect this,' he said to Carol. There was a sharp click, then, and on the vidscreen a face, a wrinkled human face, formed. 'Doctor Philipson?' Pete asked.

120

'Yes.' The doctor shook his head blearily, then scrutinized Pete. 'Oh, it's you.'

'You remember me?' Pete said.

'Of course I do. You're the man Joe Schilling sent to me; I saw you for an hour earlier tonight.'

Joe Schilling, Pete said to himself. I didn't know that. 'You're not a vug, are you?' Pete said to Doctor Philipson.

'Is that what you called me up to ask?'

'Yes,' Pete said. 'It's very important.'

'I am not a vug,' Doctor Philipson said, and hung up.

Pete shut off the vidphone. 'I think I'll go to bed,' he said to Carol. 'I'm worn out. Are you okay?'

'Yes,' she said. 'A little tired.'

'Let's go to bed together,' he said to her.

Carol smiled. 'All right. I'm certainly glad to have you back; do you always do things like this, go out on binges until five-thirty A.M.?'

'No,' he said. And I'll never do it again, he thought.

As he sat on the edge of the bed removing his clothes he found something, a match folder stuffed into his left shoe, beneath his instep. He set the shoe down, held the match folder under the lamp by the bed and examined it. Carol, beside him, had already gotten into bed and apparently had gone directly to sleep.

On the match folder, in his own hand, penciled words:

WE ARE ENTIRELY SURROUNDED
BY BUGS RUGS VUGS

That was my discovery tonight, he remembered. My bright, crowning achievement, and I was afraid I'd somehow forget it. I wonder when I wrote that? In the bar? On the way home? Probably when I first figured it out, when I was talking to Doctor Philipson.

'Carol,' he said, 'I know who killed Luckman.'

121

'Who?' she said, still awake.

'We all did,' Pete said. 'All six of us who've lost our memories. Janice Remington, Silvanus Angst and his wife, Clem Gaines, Bill Calumine's wife and myself; we did it acting under the influence of the vugs.' He held out the match folder to her. 'Read what I wrote, here. In case I didn't remember; in case they tampered with my mind again.'

Sitting up, she took the match folder and studied it. '"We are entirely surrounded by vugs." Excuse me – but I have to laugh.'

He glared at her grimly.

'That's why you placed that call to the dóctor in Idaho and asked him what you did; now I understand. But he isn't a vug; you saw him yourself on the screen and heard him.'

'Yeah, that's so,' he admitted.

'Who else is a vug? Or, as you started to write it – '

'Mary Anne McClain. She's the worst of them all.'

'Oh,' Carol said, nodding. 'I see, Pete. That's who you were with, tonight. I wondered. I knew it was someone. Some woman.'

Pete clicked on the vidphone by the bed. 'I'm going to call Hawthorne and Black, those two cops. They're not in on it.' As he dialed he said to Carol, 'No wonder Pat McClain didn't want to be scanned by the police.'

'Pete, don't do it tonight.' She reached out and cut the circuit off.

'But they may get me tonight. Any time.'

'Tomorrow.' Carol smiled at him coaxingly. 'Please.'

'Can I call Joe Schilling, then?'

'If you want. I just don't think you should talk to the police right now, the way you're feeling. You're in so much trouble with them already.'

He dialed information, got Joe Schilling's new number in Marin County.

122

Presently Schilling's hairy, ruddy face formed on the screen, fully alert. 'Yes? What is it? Pete – listen, Carol called and told me the good news, about your *luck*. My god, that's terrific!'

Pete said, 'Did you send me to a Doctor Philipson in Pocatello?'

'*Who?*'

Pete repeated the name. Joe Schilling's face screwed up in bafflement. 'Okay,' Pete said. 'Sorry I woke you. I didn't think you did.'

'Wait a minute,' Schilling said. 'Listen, about two years ago when you were at my shop in New Mexico we had a conversation – what was it about? It was something about the side effects of a methamphetamine hydrochloride. You were taking them then, and I warned you against them; there was an article in *Scientific American* by a psychiatrist in Idaho; I think it was this Philipson you mentioned, and he said that the methamphetamines can precipitate a psychotic episode.'

'I have a dim memory,' Pete said.

'Your theory, your answer to the article, was that you were *also* taking a trifluoperazine, a dihydrochloride of some sort which you swore compensated for the side effects of the methamphetamines.'

Pete said, 'I took a whole bunch of methamphetamine tablets, tonight. 7.5-milligram ones, too.'

'And you also drank?'

'Yes.'

'*Oy gewalt.* You remember what Philipson said in his article about a mixture of the methamphetamines and alcohol.'

'Vaguely.'

'They potentiate each other. Did you have a psychotic episode, tonight?'

'Not by a long shot. I had a moment of absolute truth. Here, I'll read it to you.' To Carol, Pete said, 'Hand me

123

back that match folder.' She passed it to him and he read from it. 'That was my revelation, Joe. My experience. 'There are vugs all around us.'

Schilling was silent a moment and then he said, 'About this Doctor Philipson in Idaho. Did you go to him? Is that why you ask?'

'I paid one hundred and fifty dollars to him tonight,' Pete said. 'And in my opinion I got my money's worth.'

After a pause, Schilling said, 'I'm going to suggest something to you that'll surprise you. Call that detective, Hawthorne.'

'That's what I wanted to do,' Pete said. 'But Carol won't let me.'

'I want to talk to Carol,' Joe Schilling said.

Rising to a sitting position in the bed, Carol faced the vidscreen. 'I'm right here, Joe. If you think Pete should call Hawthorne – '

'Carol, I've known your husband for years. He has suicidal depressions. Regularly. To be blunt, dear, he's a manic-depressive; he has an affective psychosis, periodically. Tonight, because of the news about the baby, he's gone into a manic phase and I for one don't blame him. I know how it feels; it's like being reborn. I want him to call Hawthorne for a very good reason. Hawthorne has had more to do with vugs than anyone else we know. There's no use my talking to Pete; I don't know a darn thing about vugs; maybe they're all around us, for all I know. I'm not going to try to argue Pete out of it, especially at five-thirty in the morning. I suggest you follow the same course.'

'All right,' Carol said.

'Pete,' Joe Schilling said. 'Remember this, when you talk to Hawthorne. Anything you say may turn up later on in the prosecutor's case against you; Hawthorne is not a friend, pure and simple. So go cautiously. Right?'

'Yes,' Pete agreed. 'But tell me what you think; was it the mixture of methamphetamines and alcohol?'

Joe Schilling said, sidestepping the question, 'Tell me something. What did Doctor Philipson say?'

'He said a lot of things. He said, for one, that he thought this situation was going to kill me as it had Luckman. And for me to take special care of Carol. And he said – ' He paused. 'There's little I can do to change matters.'

'Did he seem friendly?'

'Yes,' Pete said. 'Even though he's a vug.' He broke the connection, then, waited a moment and then dialed the police emergency number. One of the friendly ones, he said to himself. One who's on our side, maybe.

It took the police switchboard twenty minutes to locate Hawthorne. During that time Pete drank coffee and felt more and more sober.

'Hawthorne?' he said at last, when the image formed. 'Sorry to bother you so late at night. I can tell you who killed Luckman.'

Hawthorne said, 'Mr Garden, we know who killed Luckman. We've got a confession. That's where I've been, at Carmel headquarters.' He looked drawn and weary.

'Who?' Pete demanded. 'Which one of the group?'

'It was nobody in Pretty Blue Fox. We moved our investigations back to the East Coast, where Luckman started out. The confession is by a top employee of Luckman's, a man named Sid Mosk. As yet we haven't been able to establish the motive. We're working on that.'

Pete clicked off the vidphone and sat in silence.

What now? he asked himself. What do I do?

'Come to bed,' Carol said, lying back down and covering herself up with the blankets.

Shutting off the lamp, Pete Garden went to bed.

It was a mistake.

Chapter 11

He awoke – and saw, standing by the bed, two figures, a man and a woman. 'Be quiet,' Pat McClain said softly, indicating Carol. The man beside her held the heat-needle pointed steadily at Pete. He was a man Pete had never seen before in his life.

The man said, 'If you make trouble we'll kill her.' The heat-needle, now, was aimed at Carol. 'Do you understand?'

The clock on the bedside table read nine-thirty; bright, pale, morning sunlight spilled into the bedroom from the windows.

'Okay,' Pete said. 'I understand.'

Patricia McClain said, 'Get up and get dressed.'

'Where?' Pete said, sliding from the bed. 'Here in front of the two of you?'

Glancing at the man, Patricia said, 'In the kitchen.' The two of them followed after him, from the bedroom to the kitchen; Patricia shut the door. 'You stay with him while he dresses,' she said to the man. 'I'll watch his wife.' Bringing out a second heat-needle, she returned stealthily to the bedroom. 'He won't make any trouble if Carol's in danger; I can pick that up from his mind. It's acutely pronounced.'

As the unfamiliar man held the heat-needle on him, Pete dressed.

'So your wife's had *luck*,' the man said, 'Congratulations.'

Glancing at him, Pete said, 'Are you Pat's husband?'

'That's right,' the man said. 'Allen McClain. I'm glad

126

to meet you at last, Mr Garden.' He smiled a thin, brief smile. 'Pat's told me so much about you.'

Presently the three of them were walking down the corridor of the apartment building, toward the elevator.

'Did your daughter get home all right last night?' Pete said.

'Yes,' Patricia said. 'Very late, however. What I scanned in her mind was interesting, to say the least. Fortunately she didn't go to sleep right away; she lay thinking. And so I got it all.'

Allen McClain said, 'Carol won't wake up for another hour. So there's no immediate problem of her reporting him missing. Not until almost eleven.'

'How do you know she won't wake up?' Pete said.

Allen said nothing.

'You're a pre-cog?' Pete asked.

There was no answer. But it was obviously so.

'And,' Allen McClain said to his wife, 'he' – he jerked his head at Pete – 'Mr Garden, here, won't try to escape. At least, most of the parallel possibilities indicate that. Five out of six futures. A good statistic, I think.' At the elevator he pressed the button.

Pete said to Patricia, 'Yesterday you were concerned about my safety. Now this.' He gestured at the two heat-needles. 'Why the change?'

'Because in the meantime you were out with my daughter,' Patricia said. 'I wish you hadn't been. I told you that she was too young for you; I warned you away from her.'

'However,' Pete pointed out, 'as you read in my mind at the time, I found Mary Anne to be stunningly attractive.'

The elevator came; the doors slid open.

In the elevator stood the detective Wade Hawthorne. He gaped at them, then fumbled inside his coat.

Allen McClain said, 'Being a pre-cog helps. You can

never be surprised.' With his heat-needle he shot Hawthorne in the head. Hawthorne crashed back against the far wall of the elevator, then fell sloppily and lay sprawled face-first on the floor of the elevator.

'Get in,' Patricia McClain said to Pete. He got in and so did the McClains; with the body of Wade Hawthorne they descended to the ground floor.

Pete said to the Rushmore unit of the elevator, 'They're kidnapping me and they've killed a detective. Get help.'

'Cancel that last request,' Patricia McClain said to the elevator. 'We don't need any help, thank you.'

'All right, miss,' the Rushmore Effect said, obediently.

The elevator doors opened; the McClains followed behind Pete, through the lobby and out onto the sidewalk.

To Pete, Patricia McClain said, 'Do you know why Hawthorne was in that elevator, riding up to your floor? I'll tell you. To arrest you.'

'No,' Pete said. 'He told me on the vidphone last night that they'd gotten Luckman's murderer, a man back East.'

The McClains glanced at each other but said nothing.

'You killed an innocent man,' Pete said.

'Not Hawthorne,' Patricia said. 'Hardly innocent. I wish we could have gotten that E. B. Black at the same time but it wasn't along. Well, maybe later on.'

'That damn Mary Anne,' Allen McClain said as they got into the car parked at the curb; it was not Pete's car. Evidently the McClains had come in it. 'Somebody ought to wring her neck.' He started the car and it spun upward into the morning haze. 'That age is amazing. When you're eighteen you believe you know everything, you possess absolute certitude. And then when you're one hundred and fifty you know you don't.'

'You don't even know you don't,' Patricia said. 'You just have a queasy intimation that you don't.' She sat in the back seat, behind Pete, still holding the heat-needle pointed at him.

'I'll make a deal with you,' Pete said. 'I want to be sure Carol and the baby are all right. Whatever you want me to do – '

Patricia interrupted, 'You've already made that deal; Carol and the baby are all right. So don't worry about them. Anyhow, the last thing we would want to do is hurt them.'

'That's right,' Allen said, nodding. 'It would defeat everything we stand for, so to speak.' He smiled at Pete. 'How does it feel to have *luck*?'

'You ought to know,' Pete said. 'You've got more children than any other man in California.'

'Yes,' Allen McClain agreed, 'but it's been over eighteen years since that first time, many years indeed. You really went out and tied one on last night, didn't you? Mary Anne said you were in a trance. Absolutely blind.'

Pete said nothing. Gazing down at the ground below, he tried to make out the direction of the car's motion. It seemed to be heading inland, toward the hot central valley-region of California and the Sierras beyond. The utterly desolated Sierras, where no one lived.

'Tell us a little more about Doctor Philipson,' Patricia said to him. 'I catch some ill-formed thoughts. You called him last night after you got home?'

'Yes.'

To her husband, Patricia said, 'Pete called him up and asked him if he – Doctor Philipson – was a vug.'

Grinning, Allen McClain said, 'What did he say?'

'He said that he is not a vug,' Patricia said. 'And then Pete called Joe Schilling and told him the news; you know, that we're entirely surrounded by them, and Joe Schilling suggested he call Hawthorne. Which he did. And that's why Hawthorne came over this morning.'

'I'll tell you who you should have called, instead of

Wade Hawthorne,' McClain said to Pete. 'Your attorney, Laird Sharp.'

'Too late now,' Patricia said. 'But we'll probably run into Sharp somewhere along the line anyhow. You can talk to him then, Pete. Tell him the whole story, how we're an island of humans swamped in a sea of non-terrestrials.' She laughed, and so did her husband.

'I think we're scaring him,' McClain said.

'No,' Patricia said. 'I'm scanning him and he's not scared, at least not like he was last night.' To Pete she said, 'That was an ordeal for you, wasn't it, that trip home with Mary Anne? I'll bet you never get over it as long as you live.' To her husband she said, 'His two frames of reference kept switching back and forth; first he'd see Mary Anne as a girl, as an attractive eighteen-year-old Terran, and then he'd peek over, out of the corner of his eye – '

'Shut up!' Pete said savagely.

Patricia continued, 'And there it would be. The amorphous mass of cytoplasm, spinning its web of illusion, to mix a metaphor. Poor Pete Garden. It sort of takes the romance out of life, doesn't it, Pete? First you couldn't find a bar that would serve Mary Anne and then – '

'Stop it,' her husband said. 'That's really enough; he's gone through enough already. This rivalry of yours with Mary Anne, it's bad for both of you. You shouldn't be competing with your own daughter.'

'Okay,' Pat said, and was silent as she lit a cigarette.

Below them, the Sierras passed slowly. Pete watched them drop behind.

'Better call him,' Patricia said to Allen.

'Right.' Her husband clicked on the radio transmitter. 'This is Dark Horse Ferry,' he said into the microphone. 'Calling Sea Green Lamb. Come in, Sea Green Lamb. Come in, Dave.'

A voice from the radio said, 'This is Dave Mutreaux. I'm at the Dig Inn Motel in Sparks, waiting for you.'

'Okay, Dave; we'll be right there. Another five minutes.' Allen McClain switched his transmitter off. 'All set,' he said to Patricia. 'I can preview it; there won't be any gaffs.'

'Splendid,' Patricia said.

'By the way,' Allen McClain said to Pete, 'Mary Anne will be there; she came direct, in her own car. And several other people, one of whom you know. It'll be interesting for you, I think. They're all Psis. Mary Anne, by the way, is not a telepath, as her mother is. Despite what she told you. That was irresponsible of her. A good deal of what she told you was hogwash. For instance, when she said – '

'Enough,' Patricia said, firmly.

McClain shrugged. 'He'll know in another half hour; I can preview that.'

'It just makes me nervous, that's all. I'd rather wait until we're at the Dig Inn.' To Pete, she said, 'By the way, you would have been better off if you had listened to her and kissed her goodnight, as she asked you to.'

'Why?' Pete said.

'Then you would have known what she was.' She added, 'Anyhow, how many opportunities do you get in your lifetime to kiss stunningly-beautiful girls?' Her voice, as before, was bitter.

'You're eating your heart out for nothing,' Allen McClain told her. 'Christ, I'm sorry to see you do it, Pat.'

Pat said, 'And I'm going to do it again later on with Jessica, when she's older.'

'I know,' McClain said, nodding. 'I can preview that even without my talent.' He looked morose.

On the flat sand outside the Dig Inn Motel the car landed. With the heat-needle the McClains ushered Pete Garden

131

out and toward the single-story Spanish-style adobe building.

A long-limbed man, well-dressed, middle-aged, strode toward them from the motel, his hand extended. 'Hi, McClain. Hi, Pat.' He glanced at Pete. 'Mr Garden, the one-time owner of Berkeley, California. You know, Garden, I darn near came to Carmel to play in your group, but, sorry to say, you scared me off with your EEG machine.' He chuckled. 'I'm David Mutreaux, formerly on Jerome Luckman's staff.' He held out his hand to Pete, but Pete did not accept it. 'That's right,' Mutreaux drawled, 'you don't understand the situation. Yet I'm a little muddled about what's happened and what's shortly to come. Old age, I suppose.' He led the way up the flagstone path, to the open doorway of the motel office. 'Mary Anne got in a few minutes ago. She's taking a swim in the pool.'

Hands in her pockets, Pat walked over to the swimming pool and stood watching her daughter. 'If you could read my mind,' she said, to no one in particular, 'you'd see envy.' She turned away from the pool. 'You know, Pete, when I first met you I lost some of that. You're one of the most innocent people I've ever known. You helped me purge myself of my shadow-side, as Jung – and Joe Schilling – call it. How is Joe, by the way? I enjoyed seeing him again last night. How'd he feel being awakened at five-thirty in the morning?'

'He congratulated me,' Pete said shortly, 'on my *luck*.'

'Oh yes,' Mutreaux said in a jolly tone of voice; he slapped Pete good-naturedly on the back. 'Lots of best wishes on the pregnancy.'

Pat said, 'That was an awful remark your ex-wife made, that to Carol about "hoping it was a baby." And that daughter of mine she relished it; I suppose she derives that cruel streak from me. But don't blame Mary Anne too much for what she said last night, Pete, because most

132

of what you experienced was not Mary's fault; it was in your mind. Hallucinated. Joe Schilling was right in what he told you; the amphetamines were responsible. You had an authentic psychotic occlusion.'

'Did I?' Pete said.

She met his gaze. 'Yes, you did.'

'I doubt it,' Pete said.

'Let's go inside,' Allen McClain said. He cupped his hands and shouted, 'Mary Anne, get out of the pool!'

Splashing, the girl approached the rim of the pool. 'Go to hell.'

McClain knelt down. 'We have business; get inside! You're still my child.'

In the air above the surface of the pool a ball of shiny water formed, whipped toward him, broke over his head, splattering him; he jumped back, cursing.

'I thought you were such a great pre-cog,' Mary Anne called, laughing. 'I thought you couldn't be taken by surprise.' She caught hold of the ladder, hoisted herself lithely from the pool.

The mid-morning Nevada sun sparkled from her moist, smooth body as she ran and picked up a white terry cloth bath towel. 'Hello, Pete Garden,' she said, as she ran by him. 'Nice to see you again when you're not sick to your stomach; you were actually a dark green color, like old moldy moss.' Her white teeth glinted as again she laughed.

Allen McClain, brushing drops of water from his face and hair, walked over to Pete. 'It's now eleven o'clock,' he said. 'I'd like you to call Carol and say you're all right. However, I can look ahead and see you won't, or at least probably won't.'

'That's right,' Pete said. 'I won't.'

McClain shrugged. 'Well, I can't see what she'll do; possibly she'll call the police, possibly not. Time will tell.' They walked toward the motel building, McClain still shaking himself dry. 'An interesting element about Psionic abilities is that some tend to invalidate others. For instance, my daughter's psycho-kinesis; as she aptly demonstrated, I can't predict it. Pauli's synchronicity comes in, an acausal connective event that throws someone like me entirely off.'

To Dave Mutreaux, Patricia said, 'Did Sid Mosk actually confess to having killed Luckman?'

'Yes,' Mutreaux answered. 'Rothman put pressure on him, to take pressure off Pretty Blue Fox; the police out in California were probing a little too deeply, we felt.'

'But they'll know after a while that it's spurious,' Patricia said. 'That vug E. B. Black will get into his mind telepathically.'

'It won't matter then,' Mutreaux said, 'I hope.'

Inside the motel office an air-conditioner roared; the room was dark and cool and seated here and there Pete saw a number of individuals talking together in muted tones. It looked, for an instant, as if he had stumbled into a Game-playing group here in the middle of the morning, but of course it was not. He had no illusions about that. These were not Bindmen.

He seated himself, warily, wondering what they were saying. Some of them sat utterly silent, staring straight ahead as if preoccupied. Telepaths, perhaps, communicating with one another. They seemed to be in the majority. The others – he could only guess. Pre-cogs, like McClain, psycho-kinesists, like the girl Mary Anne. And Rothman, whoever he was. Was Rothman here? He had a feeling, deep and intuitive, that Rothman was very much here, and in control.

From a side room, Mary Anne appeared, now wearing a T-shirt and blue cotton shorts and sandals and no bra; her breasts were high-pointed, small. She seated herself beside Pete vigorously rubbing her hair with a towel to dry it. 'What a bunch of jerks,' she said quietly to Pete. 'I mean, don't you agree? They – my mother and dad – made me come here.' She frowned. 'Who's that?' Another man had entered the room and was looking around him. 'I don't know him. Probably from the East Coast, like that Mutreaux.'

'You're not a vug,' Pete said to her. 'After all.'

'No, I'm not. I never said I was; you asked me what I was and I told you, "you can see," and you could. It was true. See, Peter Garden, you were an involuntary tele-path; you were psychotic, because of those pills and the drinking, and you picked up my marginal thoughts, all my anxieties. What they used to call the subconscious. Didn't my mother ever warn you about that? She ought to know.'

'I see,' Pete said. Yes, she had.

'And before me you picked up that psychiatrist's sub-conscious fears, too. We're all afraid of the vugs. It's natural. They're our enemies; we fought a war with them and didn't win and now they're here. See?' She dug him in the ribs with her sharp elbow. 'Don't look so stupid; are you listening or not?'

Pete said, 'I am.'

'Well, you gape like a guppy. I knew last night you were hallucinating like mad along a paranoid line, having to do with hostile, menacing conspiracies of alien crea-tures. It interfered with your perceptions, but fundamen-tally *you were right*. I actually was feeling those fears, thinking those thoughts. Psychotics live in a world like that all the time. Anyhow, your interval of being a telepath was unfortunate because it happened around me and I know about this.' She gestured at the group of people in the motel room. 'See? So from then on you were dangerous. And you had to go right away and call the police; we got you just in time.'

Did he believe her? He studied her thin, heart-shaped face; he could not tell. If telepathic talent it had been, it certainly had deserted him now.

'See,' Mary Anne said quietly, swiftly, 'everyone has the potentiality for Psionic talent. In severe illness and in deep psychic regression – ' She broke off. 'Anyhow, Peter Garden, you were psychotic and drunk and on amphetamines and hallucinating, but basically you perceived the reality that confronts us, the situation this group knows about and is trying to deal with. You see?' She smiled at him, her eyes bright. 'Now you know.'

He did not see; he did not *want* to see.

Petrified, he drew away from her.

'You don't want to know,' Mary Anne said thoughtfully.

'That's right,' he said.

'But you do know,' she said. 'Already. It's too late not to.' She added, in her pitiless tone, 'And this time you're not sick and drunk and hallucinating; your perceptions are not distorted. So you have to face it head-on. Poor Peter Garden. Were you happier last night?'

'No,' he said.

'You're not going to kill yourself about this, are you? Because that wouldn't help. You see, we're an organization, Pete. And you have to join, even though you're non-P, not a Psi; we'll have to take you in anyway or kill you. Naturally, no one wants to kill you. What would happen to Carol? Would you leave her for Freya to torment?'

'No,' he said, 'not if I could help it.'

'You know, the Rushmore Effect of your car told you I wasn't a vug; I don't understand why you didn't listen to it; they're never wrong.' She sighed. 'Not if they're working properly, anyhow. Haven't been tampered with. That's how you can always sort out the vugs; ask a Rushmore. See?' Again she smiled at him, cheerfully. 'So things aren't really so bad. It's not the end of the world or anything like that; we just have a little problem of knowing who our friends are. They have the same problem, too; they get a little mixed up at times.'

'Who killed Luckman?' Pete asked. 'Did you?'

'No,' Mary Anne said. 'The last thing we'd do is kill a man who's had so much *luck*, so many offspring; that's the whole point.' She frowned at him.

'But last night,' he said slowly, 'I asked you if your people had done it. And you said – ' He paused, trying to think clearly, trying to sort out the confusion of those events. 'I know what you said. "I forget," you said. And – you said our baby is next; you called it a thing, you said it was *not* a baby.'

For a long time Mary Anne stared at him. 'No,' she whispered, stricken and pale. 'I didn't say that; I know I didn't.'

'I heard you,' he insisted. 'I remember that; it's a mess, but honest to god, I have that part clear.'

Mary Anne said, 'Then they've gotten to me.' Her words were scarcely audible; he had to bend toward her to hear. She continued to stare at him.

Opening the door of the sun-drenched kitchen, Carol Holt Garden said, 'Pete – are you in there?' She peered in.

He was not in the kitchen. Bright, yellow and warm, it was empty.

Going to the window she looked out at the street below. Pete's car and hers, at the curb; he had not gone in his car then.

Tying the cord of her robe she hurried out of the apartment and down the hall to the elevator. I'll ask it, she decided. The elevator will know whether he went out, whether anyone was with him and if so who. She pressed the button, and waited.

The elevator arrived; the doors slid back.

137

On the floor of the elevator lay a man, dead. It was Hawthorne.

She screamed.

'The lady said no help was necessary,' the Rushmore circuit of the elevator said, apologetically.

With difficulty Carol said, 'What lady?'

'The dark-haired lady.' It did not elaborate.

'Did Mr Garden go with them?' Carol asked.

'They came up without him but returned with him from his apartment, Mrs Garden. The man, not Mr Garden, killed this person here. Mr Garden then said, "They've kidnapped me and they've killed a detective. Get help."'

'What did you do?'

The elevator said, 'The dark-haired lady said, "Cancel that last request. We don't need any help. Thank you." So I did nothing.' The elevator was silent for a moment. 'Did I do wrong?' it inquired.

Carol whispered, 'Very wrong. You should have gotten help, as he said.'

'Can I do anything now?' the elevator asked.

'Call the San Francisco Police Department and tell them to send someone here. Tell them what happened.' She added, 'That man and woman kidnapped Mr Garden and you didn't do anything.'

'I'm sorry, Mrs Garden,' the elevator apologized.

Turning, she made her way step by step back to the apartment; in the kitchen she seated herself unsteadily at the table. Those stupid, maddening Rushmore circuits, she thought; they seem so intelligent and they actually aren't. All it takes is something unusual, something unexpected. But what did I do? Not much better. I slept while they came and got Pete, the man and woman. It sounds like Pat McClain, she thought. Dark-haired. But how do I know?

The vidphone rang.

She did not have the energy to answer it.

* * *

138

Trimming his red beard, Joe Schilling sat by his vidphone, waiting for an answer. Strange, he thought. Maybe they're still asleep. It's only ten-thirty. But –

He did not think so.

Hurriedly, he finished trimming his beard; he put on his coat and strode from his apartment and downstairs to Max, his car.

'Take me to the Gardens' apartment,' he instructed as he slid in.

'Up yours,' the car said.

'It's curtains for you if you don't take me there,' Schilling said.

The car, reluctantly, started up and drove down the street, making the trip the hard way, by surface. Schilling impatiently watched the buildings and maintenance equipment pass, one by one, until at last they reached San Rafael.

'Satisfied?' the car Max said, as it pulled to a bucking, clumsy halt before the Gardens' apartment building.

Pete's car and Carol's car were both parked at the curb, he noticed as he got out. And so were two police cars.

By elevator he ascended to their floor, rushed down the hall. The door to the Gardens' apartment was open. He stepped inside.

A vug met him.

'Mr Schilling.' Its thought-propagation was questioning in tone.

'Where are Pete and Carol?' he demanded. And then he saw, past the vug, Carol Garden seated at the kitchen table, her face waxen. 'Is Pete okay?' he said to her, pushing past the vug.

The vug said, 'I am E. B. Black; probably you remember me, Mr Schilling. Be calm. I catch from your thoughts a complete innocence of this, so I will not bother to interrogate you.'

Raising her head, Carol said starkly to Schilling, 'Wade Hawthorne, the detective, has been murdered and Pete's gone. A man and woman came and got him, according to the elevator. They killed Hawthorne. I think it was Pat McClain; the police checked at her apartment and nobody's there. And their car is gone.'

'But – do you know why they would take Pete?' Schilling asked her.

'No, I don't know why they would take Pete; I don't even know who "they" are, really.'

With a pseudopodium, the vug E. B. Black held something small; it extended it toward Joe Schilling. 'Mr Garden wrote this interesting inscription,' the vug said. '"We are entirely surrounded by vugs." That, however, is not so, as Mr Garden's disappearance testifies to. Last night Mr Garden called my ex-colleague Mr Hawthorne and told him that he knew who had killed Mr Luckman. At that time we imagined we had the killer and so we were not interested. Now we have learned we were in error. Mr Garden did not say who had killed Mr Luckman, unfortunately, because my ex-colleague refused to listen.' The vug was silent a moment. 'Mr Hawthorne has paid for his foolishness rather fully.'

Carol said, 'E. B. Black thinks that whoever killed Luckman came and got Pete and ran into Hawthorne in the elevator on their way out.'

'But it doesn't know who that is,' Schilling said.

'Correct,' E. B. Black said. 'From Mrs Garden, I have managed to learn a great deal, however. For instance, I have learned whom Mr Garden saw last night. A psychiatrist in Pocatello, Idaho, first of all. Also Mary Anne McClain; we have not been able to locate her, however. Mr Garden was drunk and confused. He told Mrs Garden that the murder of Mr Luckman had been committed by six members of Pretty Blue Fox, the six with defective memories. This would include himself. Do you have any comment on that, Mr Schilling?'

'No,' Joe Schilling murmured.

'We hope to get back Mr Garden alive,' E. B. Black said. It did not sound very confident.

Chapter 12

Patricia McClain picked up her daughter's frightened thoughts. At once she said, 'Rothman, we've been infiltrated. Mary Anne says so.'

'Is she right?' Rothman, old, hard-eyed and tough, demanded from where he, as their leader, sat.

Looking into Pete Garden's mind, Patricia saw his memory of the visit to Doctor E. R. Philipson, the strange sense of lightness, of fractional gravity as he walked down the corridor. 'Yes,' Patricia said. 'Mary's right. *He's been on Titan.*' She turned to the two pre-cogs, Dave Mutreaux and her husband Allen. 'What's going to happen?'

'A variable,' Allen murmured, ashen-faced. 'Clouds it up.'

Mutreaux said hoarsely, 'Your daughter, she's going to do something; impossible for us to tell what.'

'I have to get out of here,' Mary Anne said to them all. She rose to her feet, her thoughts scattered by her terror. 'I'm under vug influence. That Doctor Philipson, Pete must have been right. He asked me what I saw in the bar and I thought he was hallucinating. But it wasn't my fear he was picking up. He saw reality.' She started toward the door of the motel room, panting. 'I have to get away. I'm dangerous to the organization.'

As Mary Anne went out the door, Patricia said urgently to her husband, 'The heat-needle; set it on low. So it doesn't injure her.'

'I'll cut her down,' Allen said, and pointed the heat-needle at his daughter's back. Mary Anne turned for an instant, and saw the heat-needle.

The heat-needle jumped from Allen McClain's hand,

142

climbed and reversed its flight. It smashed against the wall.

'Poltergeist effect,' Allen said. 'We can't stop her.' Now the heat-needle in Patricia's hands quivered, struggled and tore loose from her fingers. 'Rothman,' he said, appealing to the highest authority in the organization present. 'Ask her to stop.'

'Leave my mind alone,' Mary Anne said to Rothman.

Pete Garden, on his feet, sprinted after Mary Anne. The girl saw that, too.

'No,' Patricia called after her. 'Don't!'

Rothman, his forehead bulging, concentrated on Mary Anne, his eyes virtually shut. But all at once Pete Garden flopped forward, like a rag doll, boneless, danced in the air, his limbs jiggling. He drifted, then, toward the wall of the motel room, and Patricia McClain screamed at Mary Anne. The dangling figure hesitated, briefly, and then swooped into the wall; it passed through the wall until only its outstretched arm and hand remained, projecting absurdly.

'Mary Anne!' Patricia shouted. *'For god's sake bring him back!'*

At the door, Mary Anne halted, turned in panic, saw what she had done with Pete Garden, saw the expression on her mother's face and on Allen's face, the horror of everyone in the room. Rothman, focussing everything which he possessed on her, was trying to persuade her. She saw that, too. And –

'Thank god,' Allen McClain said, and sagged. From the wall, Pete Garden tumbled back out, fell in a heap on the floor, intact; he got up almost at once and stood shaking, facing Mary Anne.

'I'm sorry,' Mary Anne said, and sighed.

Rothman said, 'We hold the dominant possibility here, Mary Anne; believe that. Even if they have gotten in. We'll examine everyone in the organization, person by

143

person. Shall we start with you?' To Patricia he said, 'Try and find out for me just how deeply they've penetrated her.'

'I'm trying,' Patricia said. 'But it's in Pete Garden's mind that we'll find the most.'

'He's going to leave,' Allen and Dave Mutreaux said, almost at once. 'With her, with Mary Anne.' Mutreaux said, 'She can't be predicted but I think he's going to make it.'

Rothman rose to his feet and walked toward Pete Garden. 'You see our situation; we're in a desperate match with the Titanians and losing ground to them steadily. Prevail on Mary Anne McClain to stay here so we can regain what we've lost; we have to or we're doomed.'

'I can't make her do anything,' Pete said, white and trembling, almost unable to speak.

'Nobody can,' Patricia said, and Allen nodded.

'You p-ks,' Rothman said to Mary Anne. 'So willful and stubborn; nobody can tell you anything.'

'Come on, Pete,' Mary Anne said to him. 'We have to get a long way from here, because of me and because of you, too; they're into you just as they are in me.' Her face was drawn with despair and fatigue.

Pete said to her, 'Maybe they're right, Mary Anne; maybe it would be wrong to go. Wouldn't that split up your organization?'

'They don't really want me,' Mary Anne said. 'I'm weak; this proves it. I can't stand up against the vugs. The damn vugs, I hate them.' Tears filled her eyes, tears of impotence.

The pre-cog Dave Mutreaux said, 'Garden, I can preview one thing; if you do leave here, alone or with Mary Anne McClain, your car will be intercepted by the police. I foresee a vug detective moving toward you; its name is – ' Mutreaux hesitated.

144

'E. B. Black,' Allen McClain, also pre-cog, agreed, finishing for him. 'Wade Hawthorne's partner, attached to the West Coast division of the national law-enforcement agency. One of the best they have,' he said to Mutreaux, and Rothman nodded.

'Let's do this carefully,' Rothman said. 'At what point in time did the vug authority penetrate our organization? Last night? Previous to last night? If we could establish that fact, maybe we'd have something to go on. I don't think they've gotten very deep; they haven't reached me, haven't reached any of our telepaths and we have four of them in this room and a fifth on the way here. And our pre-cogs are free, at least so it would seem.'

Mary Anne said, 'You're trying to probe into me and influence me, Rothman.' But she returned slowly to where she had been sitting. 'I can feel your mind at work.' She smiled a little. 'It's reassuring.'

To Pete Garden, Rothman said, 'I'm the main bulwark against the vugs, Mr Garden, and it'll be a long time before they penetrate me.' His leatherlike face was impassive. 'This is a dreadful discovery we've made here today, but our organization can surmount it. What about you, Garden? You're going to need our help. For an individual it's different.'

Somberly, Pete nodded.

'We must kill E. B. Black,' Patricia said.

'Yes,' Dave Mutreaux said. 'I agree.'

Rothman said, 'Go easily, here. We've never killed a vug. Killing Hawthorne was bad enough, sufficiently dangerous but necessary. As soon as we destroy a vug – any vug – it'll become clear to them not only that we exist but what our final intentions are. Isn't that so?' He looked around at the organization for confirmation.

'But,' Allen McClain said, 'they obviously know about us already. They could hardly penetrate us without knowing of our existence.' His voice was sharp, edged with exasperation.

The telepath Merle Smith spoke up from her seat in the corner; she had taken no part in the colloquy so far. 'Rothman, I have been scanning each person here in the motel and I find no indication that anyone has been penetrated in addition to Mary Anne McClain and the non-P Garden whom she wanted brought here, although there is a peculiar inert area in David Mutreaux' mind which should be looked into. I wish you other telepaths would do that, right now.'

At once, Patricia turned her attention on Dave Mutreaux.

Merle, she discovered, was correct; there was an anomaly in Mutreaux' mind and she felt at once that it implied a situation unfavorable to the interests of the organization. 'Mutreaux,' she said, 'can you turn your thoughts to – ' It was difficult to know what to call it. She had, in her hundred years of scanning, never run into anything quite like it. Puzzled, she passed over Mutreaux' surface thoughts and probed into the deeper levels of his psyche, into the involuntary and repressed syndromes which had been excluded as part of his ego-character, of the conscious self-system.

Now she was in a region of ambivalent drives, and of nebulous and stillborn wishes, anxieties, doubts interwoven with regressive beliefs and libido wishes of a fantastic nature. It was not a pleasant region but each person had it; she was accustomed to it, by now. This was what made her existence so rife with difficulty, running into this hostile area of the human mind. Each perception and observation which Dave Mutreaux had rejected in himself existed here, imperishable, living on in a kind of half-life, feeding deeply on his psychic energy.

He could not be held responsible for these, and yet there they were anyhow, semi-autonomous and – feral. Opposed to everything Mutreaux consciously, deliberately believed in. In opposition to all his life aims.

146

Much could be learned about Mutreaux' psyche by this examination of what he chose to – or had to – reject from consciousness.

'The area in question,' Patricia said, 'simply will not open up to scanning. Can you control it, Dave?'

Mutreaux said haltingly, a bewildered expression on his face, 'I don't understand what's being discussed. Everything in me is open to you, as far as I know; I'm certainly not deliberately holding back.'

Now she had picked up the pre-cognitive region of Mutreaux' mind, and by entering it she made herself, temporarily, a pre-cog; it was an eerie sensation to possess this talent as well as her customary one.

She saw, as if arranged in neat boxes, a supple, viable sequence of time-possibilities, each one obviating all the others, strung so as to be knowable simultaneously. It was pictorial, and oddly static rather than dramatic. Patricia saw herself, frozen in a variety of actions; some she blanched at – they were hideous, sequences in which she yielded to her most deranged suspicions and –

My own daughter, she thought bleakly. So it's possible that I might do that to her, possible but not probable. The majority of sequences showed a *rapprochement* with Mary Anne, and a healing of the split within the organization rather than a widening. And yet – it could happen.

And, in addition, she saw in one swift instant a scene in which the telepaths within the organization pounced on Mutreaux. And Mutreaux himself certainly was aware of this; the scene after all existed in his consciousness. But why? Patricia wondered. What could he do that would warrant this? Or what could we discover?

Mutreaux' thoughts became diffused, all at once.

'You're evading,' Patricia said, and glanced at Merle and then at the other telepaths in the room. 'It's the arrival of Don,' she said to them. Don was the missing telepath, on his way now from Detroit; he would arrive

147

any time. 'In Mutreaux' pre-cog area there's a sequence in which Don will, on his arrival here, ferret out the inert area involved, will open and explore it. And – ' She hesitated, but the three other telepaths had picked up her thought anyhow.

And will destroy Mutreaux because of it, she had thought.

But why? There was nothing to suggest the vuggish power about it or about him; this was something else, and it completely baffled her.

Was it certain that Don would do this? No, only probable. And how did Mutreaux feel, knowing this, knowing that his death was imminent? *What did a pre-cog do under such circumstances?*

The same as anyone else, she discovered as she scanned Mutreaux' mind. The pre-cog ran.

Mutreaux, rising to his feet, said huskily, 'I've got to get back to the New York Area I'm afraid.' His manner was easy, but inside the opposite. 'Sorry I can't stay,' he said to Rothman.

'Don is our best telepath,' Rothman said meditatively. 'I'm going to have to ask you to remain until he gets here. Our only defense against the penetration of our organization is the existence of four telepaths who can dig in and tell us what's going on. So you must sit down, Mutreaux.'

Mutreaux reseated himself.

Closing his eyes, Pete Garden listened to the discussion between Patricia McClain, Mutreaux and Rothman. This secret organization, composed of Psi-people, stands between us and the Titanian civilization, its domination over us or some such thing; his thoughts ran together muddily. He still had not recovered from last night and the manner in which he had been awakened this morning – that, and Hawthorne's pointless, shocking death.

I wonder if Carol's all right, Pete thought.

148

God, he thought, I wish I could get out of here. He thought of the moment when Mary Anne, through her psycho-kinetic talent, had made him a floating particle, had tossed him into and through the material wall of the room, and then somehow, for reasons unclear to him, had let him come back; she had changed her mind at the last instant.

I'm afraid of these people, he said to himself. Of them and their talents.

He opened his eyes.

In the motel room, discoursing in shrill, chattery voices, sat nine vugs. And one human being besides himself. Dave Mutreaux.

He and Dave Mutreaux, standing in opposition to the rest of them. Hopeless and impossible. He did not stir; he simply stared at the nine vugs.

One vug – it spoke in the voice of Patricia McClain – said agitatedly, 'Rothman! I've picked up an incredible thought from Garden.'

'I have, too,' another vug said in agreement. 'Garden perceives us all as – ' It hesitated. 'He sees us, with the exception of Mutreaux, as *vugs*.'

There was silence.

The vug which spoke as Rothman said, 'Garden, this implies then that the penetration of our group is complete? Is that right? Complete with the exception of David Mutreaux, at least.'

Pete said nothing.

'How can we consider this,' the vug calling itself Rothman said, 'and keep on being sane? We've already lost, if Garden's perceptions are to be believed. We must try to consider rationally; possibly there's some hope. What do you say, Mutreaux? If Garden is right, you're the only authentic Terran among us.'

Mutreaux said, 'I have no understanding of this.' He glanced at Pete. 'Ask him, not me.'

'Well, Mr Garden?' the vug Rothman said, calmly. 'What do you say?'

'Please answer,' the Patricia McClain one pleaded. 'Pete, in the name of all we hold holy – '

Pete said, 'I think you know now what there is in Mutreaux that your telepaths couldn't scan. He's a human being and you're not. That's the difference. And when your last telepath gets here – '

'We'll destroy Mutreaux,' the Rothman vug said slowly, thoughtfully.

Chapter 13

Joseph Schilling said to the homeostatic informational circuit of the vidphone, 'I want the attorney-at-law Laird Sharp. He's somewhere on the West Coast; I don't know any more than that.'

It was past noon, now. Pete Garden had not returned home and Joe Schilling knew that he was not going to. There was no point in contacting the other members of Pretty Blue Fox; Pete wasn't with any of them. Whoever had taken him lay outside the group.

If this identity problem has actually been solved, he thought, if Pat and Al McClain did it, then *why*? And killing the detective Hawthorne, a mistake, whatever their reasons. No one could convince him of the rightness of such an action as that.

Going into the bedroom of the apartment he asked Carol, 'How are you feeling?'

She sat by the window, wearing a gaily-colored cotton print dress, listlessly watching the street below. 'I'm okay, Joe.'

The detective E. B. Black had temporarily gone out of the apartment, so Joe Schilling shut the bedroom door and said to Carol, 'I know something about the McClains that the police aren't to know.'

Raising her eyes, Carol regarded him. 'Tell me.'

Joe Schilling said, 'She's mixed up in some kind of extra-legal activity, has been apparently for some time. That would fit in with the murder of Hawthorne. I'll make a guess; I think it's connected with her being a Psi. And her husband, too. But other than that, and it isn't much, I can't account for them murdering, especially a police

151

detective. Now look what they've got on their hands: a nation-wide search by all police agencies. They must be desperate.' Or fanatic, he thought to himself. 'There's no one the police hate more than a cop-killer,' he murmured. 'It was a stupid thing to do.' Fanatic and stupid, he thought. A bad mixture.

The vidphone rang and said, 'Your party, Mr Schilling. The attorney Laird Sharp.'

Schilling at once snapped the screen on. 'Laird,' he said. 'Good.'

'What's happened?' Sharp said.

'Your client's gone, Pete Garden.' He explained, tersely, what had happened. 'And I have an intuitive distrust of the police,' Schilling said. 'For some reason it seems to me they're not trying. Maybe it's because of the vug, E. B. Black.' The instinctive aversion of the Terran was there, operating within himself, he realized.

Sharp said, 'Um, let's make a run up to Pocatello. What did you say the psychiatrist's name is?'

'Philipson,' Joe Schilling said. 'He's world-famous. What do you expect to find up there?'

'I don't know,' Sharp said. 'After all, I'm getting everything third-hand, but I have a hunch. I'll fly to San Rafael and meet you there; stay put for another ten minutes. I'm in San Francisco.'

'Right,' Schilling said, and broke the connection.

'Where are you going?' Carol asked him as he started for the door of the apartment. 'You told Pete's attorney you'd meet him here.'

'I'm going to get a gun,' Schilling said. He shut the door after him and hurried down the hall. I only need one, he realized. Because if I know Laird Sharp he's carrying his own at all times.

As he and Sharp flew northeast in Sharp's car, Schilling said, 'On the vid last night Pete said some strange things.

152

First, that this situation was going to kill Pete, as it had killed Luckman. That he should be especially careful of Carol's safety. And – ' He glanced at Sharp. 'Pete said that Doctor Philipson is a vug.'

'So?' Sharp said. 'There are vugs all over the planet.'

'But I know something about Philipson,' Joe Schilling said. 'I've read his articles and read about his therapeutic techniques. There's never been any mention of him being a Titanian. Something's wrong. I don't think Pete saw Doctor Philipson; I think he saw someone or something else. A man of Philipson's stature wouldn't be available in the middle of the night, like a common GP. And where did Pete get the one hundred and fifty dollars he remembers paying Philipson? I know Pete; he never carries money on him. No Bindman does; they think in terms of real estate deeds, not cash. Money is for us non-Bs.'

'Did he actually say he had *paid* this doctor? Possibly he simply ran up a bill for that amount.'

'Pete said that he had paid him, and paid him last night. And he said he'd gotten his money's worth.' Joe Schilling brooded about it for a moment. 'In Pete's condition, drunk and drug-stimulated and in a manic phase because of Carol's pregnancy, he wouldn't have known what he really saw, if it actually was Philipson or not that sat facing him. And it's always possible that he hallucinated the entire episode. That he never went to Pocatello at all.' He got out his pipe and his pouch of tobacco. 'The whole episode doesn't ring right. Pete may be one sick cookie; that may be the root of the whole problem.'

'What do you use in your pipe these days?' Sharp asked. 'Still nothing but white burley, rough-cut?'

'Not any more. This is a mixture called Barking Dog. It never bites.'

Sharp grinned briefly.

At the outskirts of Pocatello Doctor Philipson's psychiatric clinic lay below, a square of dazzling white surrounded by lawns and trees, and in the rear, a rose

153

garden. Sharp landed his car on the gravel driveway and continued by surface up into the parking lot at the side of the large central building. The place, quiet and well-tended, seemed deserted. The only car in the parking lot appeared to be Doctor Philipson's own.

Peaceful, Schilling thought. But obviously it's enormously expensive to come here. The rose garden attracted him and he meandered toward it, sniffing the air and smelling the deep, heavy scent of roses and organic fertilizers. A sprinkler, homeostatic and efficient, rotated as it watered a lawn, causing him to step from the path and onto the thick, springy grass itself. Just being here would cure me, he thought. Getting the smells, feeling the textures of the pastoral community. Ahead he saw tied to a post a nodding gray donkey.

'Look,' he said to Laird Sharp, who had followed behind him. 'Two of the finest roses ever developed. *Peace* and *Star of Holland*. In the twentieth century they were rated something like nine points in rose-growing circles.' He explained, 'Nine was extremely good. And then of course they developed the more modern patented rose, *Space Voyager*.' He pointed to it, the huge orange and white buds. 'And *Our Land*.' That was a red, so dark as to be virtually black, with spatters of lighter dots across the petals.

While they were inspecting *Our Land*, the door of the clinic building flew open and a bald, friendly-looking elderly man stepped out, smiling at them in greeting. 'Can I help you?' he asked, eyes twinkling.

Sharp said, 'We're looking for Doctor Philipson.'

'That's I,' the elderly man said. 'I'm afraid the rose garden needs spraying; I see grefi on several bushes.' He brushed at a leaf with the side of his hand. 'Grefi, a mite that slipped in here from Mars.'

Joe Schilling said, 'Where can we go that we could talk to you?'

'Right here,' Doctor Philipson said.

'Did a Mr Peter Garden visit you late last night?' Schilling asked.

'He certainly did.' Doctor Philipson smiled wryly. 'And vidphoned me even later.'

'Pete Garden has been kidnapped,' Schilling said. 'His abductors killed a policeman on the way, so they must be serious.'

The smile on Doctor Philipson's face vanished. 'That so.' He glanced at Schilling and then at Laird Sharp. 'I was worried about something on this order. First Jerome Luckman's death, now followed by this. Come in.' He held the door to the clinic building open, then abruptly changed his mind. 'Perhaps it would be better if we sat in the car. So no one overhears.' He led the way back to the parking lot. 'There are several matters I'd like to discuss with you.'

Presently the three of them were seated tensely in Doctor Philipson's car.

'What's your relationship to Peter Garden?' the doctor asked.

Schilling, briefly, told him.

'Probably,' Philipson said, 'you'll never see Garden alive again. I'm deeply sorry to say that, but it's almost certainly the truth. I tried to warn him.'

'I know that,' Schilling said. 'He told me.'

'I knew too little about Pete Garden,' the doctor said. 'I'd never seen him before in my life; I couldn't get an accurate background history from him because last night he was drunk and sick and scared. He phoned me at my home; I had gone to bed. I met him in downtown Pocatello at a bar. I forget the name of it, now. It was a bar at which he had stopped. He had an attractive young girl with him but she didn't come in. Garden was actively hallucinating and needed major psychiatric help. I could

155

scarcely supply that to him in the middle of the night at a bar, needless to say.'

'His fear,' Joe Schilling said, 'was of the vugs. Pete believed they were – closing in on us.'

'Yes, I realize that. He expressed those fears last night to me. A number of times in a variety of ways. It was touching. At one point he very laboriously scratched himself a message on a match folder and hid it – with great ceremony – in his shoe. "The vugs are after us," it said, or words to that effect.' The doctor eyed Schilling and Laird Sharp. 'What do you know, at this moment, about the internal problems on Titan?'

Taken by surprise, Joe Schilling said, 'Not a damn thing.'

Doctor Philipson said, 'Titan civilization is sharply divided into two factions. The reason I know this is simple; I have, in the clinic here, several Titanians who hold high posts here on Earth. They're undergoing psychiatric treatment with me. It's somewhat unorthodox, but I discover I can work with them well enough.'

Alertly, Sharp said, 'Is that why you wanted to talk here in the car?'

'Yes,' Philipson said. 'Here, we're out of range of their telepathic ability. All four of them are moderates, politically speaking. That's the dominant force in Titan politics and has been for decades. But there is also a war party, a faction of extremists. Their power has been growing, but no one, including the Titanians themselves, seems to know precisely how strong they've become. In any case, their policy toward Terra is hostile. I have a theory. I can't prove this, but I've hinted at it in several papers I've done.' He paused. 'I think – just think, mind you – that the Titanians, on the instigation of their war party elements, are tinkering with our birth rate. On some technological level – don't ask me quite how – they're responsible for holding our birth rate down.'

156

There was silence. A long, strained one.

'As far as Luckman goes,' Doctor Philipson said, 'I'd guess that he was killed either directly or indirectly by Titanians, but not for the reason you think. True, he had just come out to California after sewing up the East Coast thoroughly. True, he probably would have assumed economic domination of California as he did with New York. But that was not why the Titanians killed him. It was because they had been trying to get to him probably for months, possibly even years; when Luckman left the sanctuary of his organization and came out to Carmel where he had no pre-cogs, no human Psi-people to protect him – '

'Why'd they kill him?' Sharp asked quietly.

'Because of his *luck*,' the Doctor replied. 'His fertility. His ability to have children. That's what menaces the Titanians. Not his success at The Game; they don't give a god damn about that.'

'I see,' Sharp said.

'And any other human who has *luck* stands to be wiped out, if the war party has its way. Now listen. *Some humans know this or suspect this.* There's an organization, based on the prolific McClains of California; perhaps you've heard of them, Patricia and Allen McClain. They have three children. Therefore their lives are acutely in danger. Pete Garden has demonstrated the ability to be fertile and that puts him and his pregnant wife also in automatic jeopardy, and I so warned him. And I warned him that he was facing a situation about which he could do little. I firmly believe that. And – ' Doctor Philipson's voice was steady. 'I think the organization formed around the McClains is futile if not dangerous. It has probably already been penetrated by the Titanian authority, here, which is quite effective at that sort of business. Their telepathic faculty works to their advantage; it's almost impossible to keep anything – such as the existence of a secret, militant, patriotic organization – secret from them for long.'

Schilling said, 'Are you in touch with the moderates? Through your vug patients, here?'

Hesitating, Doctor Philipson said, 'To some extent. In the most general way I've discussed the situation with them; it's come up during therapy.'

Schilling said to Laird Sharp, 'I think we've found out what we came for. We know where Pete is, who kidnapped him and killed Hawthorne. The McClain organization, whatever it's called. Wherever it is.'

With an expression of keen wariness, Laird Sharp said, 'Doctor, your explanation is extremely interesting. There's another interesting matter, however, that has not as yet been raised.'

'Oh?' Doctor Philipson said.

Sharp said, 'Pete Garden thought you were a vug.'

'I realize that,' Doctor Philipson said. 'To some extent I can explain that. On an unconscious intuitive level, Garden perceived the dangerous situation. His perceptions, however, were disordered, a mixture of involuntary telepathy and projection, his own anxiety plus – '

'*Are* you a vug?' Laird Sharp asked.

'Of course not,' Doctor Philipson said brusquely.

To the Rushmore Effect of the car in which they were seated, Laird Sharp said, 'Is Doctor Philipson a vug?'

'Doctor Philipson is a vug,' the auto-auto mech replied. 'That is correct.'

And it was Doctor Philipson's own car.

'Doctor,' Joe Schilling said, 'do you have any reaction to that?' He held his gun, an ancient but efficient .32 revolver, pointed at Doctor Philipson. 'I'd like your comment, please.'

'Obviously it's a false statement by the circuit,' Doctor Philipson said. 'But I admit there is more I haven't told you. The organization of Psi-persons around the McClains, I'm a part of that.'

'You're a Psi?' Schilling said.

'Correct,' Doctor Philipson said, nodding. 'And the girl with Pete Garden last night is also a member, Mary Anne McClain. She and I conferred briefly as to policy regarding Garden. It was she who arranged for me to see Garden; at such a late hour at night I normally – '

'What is your Psionic talent?' Sharp said, breaking in. Now he also held a gun pointed at the doctor; it was a small .22 pistol.

Doctor Philipson glanced at him and then at Joseph Schilling. He said, 'An unusual one. It will surprise you when I tell you. Basically it's related to Mary Anne's, a form of psycho-kinesis. But it is rather specialized, compared with hers. I form one end of a two-way underground system between Terra and Titan. Titanians come here, and on occasion, certain Terrans are transmitted to Titan. This procedure is an improvement on the standard spacecraft method because there is no time lapse.' He smiled at Joe Schilling and Laird Sharp. 'May I show you?' He leaned forward.

'My god,' Sharp said. 'Kill him.'

'Do you see?' Doctor Philipson's voice came to them but they could not make him out; an extinguishing curtain had blotted the fixed images of the objects around them, had blotted them into waste. Junk, like a billion golf balls, cascaded brightly, replacing the familiar reality of substantial forms. It was, Joe Schilling thought, like a fundamental breakdown of the act of perception itself. In spite of himself, his determination, he felt fear.

'I'll shoot him,' Laird Sharp's voice came, and then the racket of a gun fired several times in quick succession. 'Did I get him? Joe, did I – ' Sharp's voice faded. Now there was only silence.

Joe Schilling said, 'I'm scared, Sharp. What is this?' He

did not understand and he reached out, groping in the stream of atom-like sub-particles that surged everywhere. Is this the understructure of the universe itself? he wondered. The world outside of space and time, beyond the modes of cognition?

He saw now a great plain, on which vugs, unmoving, rested at fixed spaces. Or was it that they moved incredibly slowly? There was an anguish to their situation; the vugs strained, but the category of time did not move and the vugs remained where they were. Is it forever? Joe Schilling wondered. There were many of the vugs; he could not see the termination of the horizontal surface, could not even imagine it.

This is Titan, a voice said inside his head.

Weightless, Joe Schilling drifted down, wanting desperately to stabilize himself but not knowing how. Dammit, he thought, this is all wrong; I shouldn't be here, doing this. 'Help,' he said aloud. 'Get me out of this. Are you there some place, Laird Sharp? What's happening to us?'

No one answered.

More rapidly now he fell. Nothing stopped him in the usual sense and yet all at once he was there; he experienced it.

Around him formed the hollowness of a chamber, a vast enclosure of some nebulous sort, and across from him, facing him across a table, were vugs. He counted twenty of them and then gave up; the vugs were everywhere in front of him, silent and motionless but somehow doing something. They were ceaselessly busy and at first he could not imagine what they were doing. And then, all at once, he understood.

Play, the vugs thought-propagated.

The board was so enormous that it petrified him. Its sides, its two ends, faded, disappeared into the understructure of the reality in which he sat. And yet, directly

160

before him, he made out cards, clear-cut and separable. The vugs waited; he was supposed to draw a card.

It was his turn.

Thank god, Joe Schilling said to himself, that I'm able to play, that I know how. It would not matter to them if I didn't; this Game has been going on too long for that to matter. How long? No knowing. Perhaps the vugs themselves did not know. Or remember.

The card he drew read twelve.

And now, he thought, the sequence which is the heart of The Game. The moment in which I bluff or do not bluff, in which I advance my piece either twelve or null-twelve. But they can read my thoughts, he realized. How can I play The Game with them, then? It's not fair!

And yet he had to play anyhow.

That's the situation we're in, he said to himself. And we can't extricate ourselves, any of us. And even great Game-players, such as Jerome Luckman, can die at it. Die trying to succeed.

We have been waiting a long time for you, a vug thought-propagated to him. *Please don't keep us waiting any longer.*

He did not know what to do. And what was the stake? What deed had he put up? He looked around but he saw nothing, no pot or hopper.

A bluffing game in which telepaths participate for stakes which do not exist, Joe Schilling realized. What a travesty. How can I get out of this? *Is* there a way out? He did not even know that much.

This, the Platonic ultimate template of The Game, a reproduction of which had been impressed on Terra for Terrans to play; he understood. And yet it did not help him to understand because he still could not get out of it. He picked up his piece and began to advance it, square by square. Twelve squares ahead. He read the inscription.

Gold rush on your land! You win $50,000,000 in royalties from two producing mines!

No need to bluff, Joe Schilling said to himself. What a square; the best he had ever heard of. No such square existed on the boards of Earth.

He placed his piece on that square and sat back.

Would anyone challenge him? Accuse him of bluffing?

He waited. There was no motion, no indication of life from the near infinite row of vugs. Well? he thought. I'm ready. Go ahead.

It is a bluff, a voice declared.

He could not make out which vug had challenged him; they seemed to have expressed themselves in unison. Had their telepathic ability become faulty at this critical moment? he wondered. Or had the talent been deliberately suspended for purposes of playing The Game? 'You're wrong,' he said, and turned over his card. 'Here it is.' He glanced down.

It was no longer a twelve.

It was an eleven.

You are a bad bluffer, Mr Schilling, the corporate group of vugs thought. *Is this how you generally play?*

'I'm under tension,' Joe Schilling said. 'I misread the card.' He was furious and badly frightened. 'There's some kind of cheating going on,' he said. 'Anyhow, what's the stakes in this?'

The vugs answered, *In this Game, Detroit.*

'I don't see the deed,' Joe Schilling said, looking up and down the table.

Look again, the vugs said.

In the center of the table he saw what appeared to be a glass ball, the size of a paperweight. Something complex and shiny and *alive* flickered within the globe and he bent to scrutinize it. A city, in miniature. Buildings and streets, houses, factories . . .

It was Detroit.

162

We want that next, the vugs told him.

Reaching out, Joe Schilling moved his piece back one square. 'I really landed on that,' he said.

The Game exploded.

'I cheated,' Joe Schilling said. 'Now it's impossible to play. Do you grant that? I've wrecked The Game.'

Something hit him over the head and he fell, dropped instantly, into the engulfing grayness of unconsciousness.

Chapter 14

The next he knew Joseph Schilling stood on a desert, feeling the reassuring tug of Terra's gravity once more. The sun, blinding him, spilled down in gold-hot familiar torrents and he squinted, trying to see, holding up his hand to ward off its rays.

'Don't stop,' a voice said.

He opened his eyes and saw, walking beside him across the uneven sand, Doctor Philipson; the elderly, sprightly little doctor was smiling.

'Keep moving,' Doctor Philipson said in a pleasant, conventional tone of voice, 'or we'll die out here. And you wouldn't like that.'

'Explain it to me,' Joe Schilling said. But he kept on walking. Doctor Philipson remained beside him, walking with easy, long strides.

'You certainly broke up The Game,' Doctor Philipson chuckled. 'It never occurred to them that you'd cheat.'

'They cheated first. They changed the value of the card!'

'To them, that's legitimate, a basic move in The Game. It's a favorite play by the Titanian Game-players to exert their extra-sensory faculties on the card; it's supposed to be a contest between the sides; the one who's drawn the card struggles to keep its value constant, you see? By yielding to the altered value you lost, but by moving your piece in conformity to it you thwarted them.'

'What happened to the stake?'

'Detroit?' Doctor Philipson laughed. 'It remains a stake, unclaimed. You see, the Titanian Game-players believe in following the rules. You may not believe that but it's true. Their rules, yes; but rules nonetheless. Now I don't know what they'll do; they've been waiting to play against you in particular for a long time, but I'm sure they won't try again after what just happened. It must have been psychically unnerving for them; it'll be a great while before they recover.'

'What faction do they represent? The extremists?'

'Oh no; the Titanian Game-players are exceptionally moderate in their political thinking.'

'What about you?' Schilling said.

Doctor Philipson said, 'I admit to being an extremist. That's why I'm here on Terra.' In the blinding mid-day sunlight his heat-needle sparkled as it rose and fell with his long strides. 'We're almost there, Mr Schilling. One more hill and you'll see it. It's built low to the ground, attracts little attention.'

'Are all the vugs here on Earth extremists?'

'No,' Doctor Philipson said.

'What about E. B. Black, the detective?'

Doctor Philipson said nothing.

'Not of your party,' Schilling decided.

There was no answer; Philipson was not going to say.

'I should have trusted it when I had the chance,' Schilling said.

'Perhaps so,' Doctor Philipson said, nodding.

Ahead, Schilling saw a Spanish-style building with tile roof and pale adobe walls, contained by an ornamental railing of black iron. The Dig Inn Motel, the neon sign – turned off and inert – read.

'Is Laird Sharp here?' Schilling asked.

'Sharp is on Titan,' Doctor Philipson said. 'Perhaps I will bring him back, but certainly not at this time.' Doctor Philipson, briefly, scowled. 'An agile-brained creature, that Sharp. I must admit I don't care for him.' With a white linen handkerchief he mopped his red and perspiring forehead, slowing down a little now, as they came up

165

onto the flagstone path of the motel. 'And as for your cheating, I didn't much care for that either.' He seemed tense and irritable, now. Schilling wondered why.

The door of the motel office was open, and Doctor Philipson went toward it, peering into the darkness within. 'Rothman?' he said, in a hesitant, questioning voice.

A figure appeared, a woman. It was Patricia McClain.

'Sorry I'm late,' Doctor Philipson began. 'But this man here and a companion showed up at the – '

Patricia McClain said, 'She's out of control. Allen couldn't help. Get away.' She ran past Doctor Philipson and Joe Schilling, across the parking lot toward a car parked there. Then all at once she was gone. Doctor Philipson grunted, cursed, stepped back from the motel door as swiftly as if he had been seared.

High in the mid-day sky Joe Schilling saw a dot, rising and then disappearing toward invisibility. On and on it rushed, away from Earth, away from the ground until finally he could no longer see it. His head ached from the glare and the effort of seeing, and he turned to Doctor Philipson. 'My god, was that – ' he started to say.

'Look,' Doctor Philipson said. He pointed, with his heat-needle, at the motel office, and Joe Schilling looked inside; he could not see at first and then by degrees his eyes accustomed themselves to the gloom.

On the floor lay twisted bodies of men and women, tangled together like multi-armed monsters, as if they had been shaken and then dropped there, discarded, the remains jammed together, forced into an impossible fusion. Mary Anne McClain sat on the floor in the corner, curled up, her face buried in her hands. Pete Garden and a well-dressed middle-aged man whom Schilling did not know stood together, silently, their faces blank.

'Rothman,' Doctor Philipson choked, staring at one of

the shattered bodies. He turned toward Pete Garden. 'When?' he said.

'She just now did it,' Pete Garden murmured.

'You're lucky,' the well-dressed middle-aged man said to Doctor Philipson. 'If you had been here she would have killed you, too. You're fortunate; you missed your appointment.'

Doctor Philipson, shaking, lifted his heat-needle and pointed it unsteadily at Mary Anne McClain.

'Don't,' Pete Garden said. 'They tried that. At the end.'

'Mutreaux,' Doctor Philipson said, 'why didn't she – '

'He's a Terran,' Pete Garden said. 'The only one of you who was. So she didn't touch him.'

'The best thing,' the well-dressed man, Mutreaux, said, 'is for none of us to do anything. Move as little as possible; that's the safest.' He kept his eyes fixed on the huddled shape of Mary Anne McClain. 'She didn't even miss her father,' Mutreaux said. 'But Patricia got away; I don't know what happened to her.'

'The girl got her, too,' Doctor Philipson said. 'We watched; we didn't understand, then.' He tossed the heat-needle away; it rolled across the floor and came to rest against the far wall. His face was gray. 'Does she understand what she's done?'

Pete Garden said, 'She knows. She understands the dangerousness of her talent and she doesn't want to use it again.' To Joe Schilling he said, 'They couldn't seem to manage her; they had partial control but it kept slipping away. I watched the struggle. It's been going on here in this room for the last few hours. Even when their last member came.' He pointed to a squashed, crumpled body, a man with glasses and light hair. 'Don, they called him. They thought he'd turn the tide, but Mutreaux threw his talent in with hers. It all happened in a second; one minute they were sitting on their chairs, the next she just simply began flinging them around like rag dolls.' He added, 'It wasn't pleasant. But,' he shrugged, 'anyhow, that's what happened.'

Doctor Philipson said, 'A dreadful loss.' He glanced at Mary Anne with hatred. 'Poltergeist,' he said. 'Unmanageable. We knew but because of Patricia and Allen we accepted her as she was. Well, we'll have to begin all over again, from the start. Of course I have nothing personally to fear from her; I can return to my primary nexus, Titan, whenever I wish. Presumably, her talent doesn't extend that far, and if it does there's not much we can do. I'll take the chance, I have to.'

'I think she can freeze you here, if she wants to,' Mutreaux said. 'Mary Anne,' he said sharply. In the corner the girl raised her head; her cheeks, Joe Schilling saw, were tear-stained. 'Do you have any objection if this last one returns to Titan?'

'I don't know,' she said listlessly.

Joe Schilling said, 'They've got Sharp there.'

'I see,' Mutreaux said. 'Well, that makes a difference.' To Mary Anne he said, 'Don't let Philipson go.'

'All right,' she murmured, nodding.

Doctor Philipson shrugged. 'A good point. Well, it's agreeable to me. Sharp can return here, I'll go to Titan.' His tone was calm, but, Schilling saw, the man's eyes were opaque with shock and tension.

'Arrange for it now,' Mutreaux said.

'Of course,' Doctor Philipson said. 'I don't want to be around this girl; that must be obvious even to you. And I can hardly say I envy you and your people, depending on a crude, erratic power of this sort; it's apt to rebound or be turned deliberately against you at any moment.' He added, 'Sharp is now back from Titan. At my clinic in Idaho.'

'Can that be verified?' Mutreaux said to Joe Schilling.

'Place a call to your car, there,' Doctor Philipson said. 'He should be in it or close by it, by now.'

Going outdoors, Joe Schilling found a parked car. 'Whose are you?' he asked it, opening its door.

'Mr and Mrs McClain's,' the Rushmore Effect stated.

'I want to use your vidphone.' Seated within the sun-scorched interior of the car, Joe Schilling placed a call to his own car at Doctor Philipson's clinic in the outskirts of Pocatella, Idaho.

'What the hell do you want now?' the voice of Max, his car, answered after a wait.

'Is Laird Sharp there?' Joe Schilling asked.

'Who cares.'

'Listen,' Schilling began, but all at once Laird Sharp's features formed on the small vidscreen. 'You're okay?' Schilling asked him.

Sharp curtly nodded. 'Did you see the Titanian Game-players, Joe? How many were there? I couldn't seem to count them.'

'I not only saw them, I conned them,' Joe Schilling said. 'So they right away bumped me back here. Take Max – you know, my car – and fly back to San Francisco; I'll meet you there.' To the old, sullen car he said, 'Max, you cooperate with Laird Sharp, goddam it.'

'All right!' Max said irritably. 'I'm cooperating!'

Joe Schilling returned to the motel room.

'I previewed your narration about the attorney,' Mutreaux said. 'We let Philipson go.'

Schilling looked around. It was so. There was no sign of Doctor E. R. Philipson.

'It's not over,' Pete Garden said. 'Philipson is back on Titan. Hawthorne is dead.'

'But their organization,' Mutreaux said. 'It's abolished. Mary Anne and I are the only ones remaining. I couldn't believe it when I saw her destroy Rothman; he was the pivot of the organization's power.' He now bent down beside Rothman's body, touching it.

'What's the wisest thing to do now?' Joe Schilling said to Pete. 'We can't pursue them to Titan, can we?' He did not want to face the Game-players of Titan again. And yet –

Pete said, 'We'd better bring in E. B. Black. It's the only thing I can think of at this point that might help. Otherwise, we're finished.'

'We can trust Black, can we?' Mutreaux said.

Schilling said, 'Doctor Philipson implied that we could.' He hesitated. 'Yes, I vote we take the chance.'

'So do I,' Pete said, and Mutreaux, after a pause, brusquely nodded. 'What about you, Mary?' Pete turned to the girl, who still sat curled up in a rigid, stricken ball.

'I don't know,' she said, finally. 'I don't know who to believe in or trust anymore; I don't even know about myself.'

'It's got to be done,' Joe Schilling said to Pete. 'In my opinion, anyhow. He or it is looking for you; he's with Carol. If he's not reliable – ' Schilling broke off and scowled.

'Then he's got Carol,' Pete agreed, stonily.

'Yes,' Schilling nodded.

Pete said, 'Call him. From here.'

Together, they went outside to the McClains' parked car. Joe Schilling placed the call to the apartment in San Rafael. If we're making a mistake, Joe Schilling thought, it probably means Carol's death and the death of their baby. I wonder which it is? he asked himself. A boy or a girl? They have those tests now; they can tell after the third week. Pete, of course, would accept either. He smiled a little.

Pete said tensely, 'I've got him.' On the screen the image of a vug formed, and Joe Schilling reflected that it looked – to him at least – like any other vug. This is what

170

Doctor Philipson really looks like, he knew. What Pete saw. And he thought he was hallucinating.

'Where are you, Mr Garden?' the vug's query came to them from the speaker. 'I see you have Mr Schilling there with you. What do you require from the Coast police authority? We are ready to dispatch a ship when and where you tell us.'

'We're coming back,' Pete said. 'We don't need any ship. How is Carol?'

'Mrs Garden is anxiously concerned, but physically in satisfactory condition.'

'There are nine dead vugs here,' Joe Schilling said.

E. B. Black said instantly, 'Of the Wa Pei Nan? The extremist party?'

'Yes,' Schilling said. 'One returned to Titan; he had been here a Doctor E. R. Philipson of Pocatello, Idaho. You know, the well-known psychiatrist. We urge you to take his clinic at once; there could be others entrenched there.'

'We will shortly do that,' E. B. Black promised. 'Are the killers of my colleague, Wade Hawthorne, among the dead?'

'Yes,' Joe Schilling said.

'A relief,' E. B. Black said. 'Give us your location and we will send someone out to undertake whatever dispositionary chores are necessary.'

Pete gave him the information.

'That's that,' Schilling said, as the screen faded. He did not know how to feel. Had they done the right thing? We will know before very long, he said to himself. Together, they walked back to the motel room, neither of them saying anything.

'If they get us,' Pete said, pausing at the door of the room, 'I still say we did the best we could. You can't know everything. This is all – ' He gestured. 'Blurred and

171

twisting, people and things merging back and forth into each other. Maybe I haven't recovered from last night.'

Joe Schilling said, 'Pete, *I saw the Game-players of Titan*. It was enough.'

'What should we do?' Pete said.

'Get Pretty Blue Fox back into being.'

'And then what?'

Joe Schilling said, 'Play.'

'Against?'

'The Titanian Game-players,' Joe Schilling said. 'We have to; they're not going to give us any choice.'

Together, they re-entered the motel room.

As they flew back to San Francisco, Mary Anne said faintly, 'I don't feel their control over me as strongly as I did. It's waned.'

Mutreaux glanced at her. 'Let's hope so.' He looked utterly tired. 'I preview,' he said to Pete Garden, 'your effects to get your group restored. Want to know the outcome?'

'Yes,' Pete said.

'The police will grant it. By tonight you'll be a legal Game-playing body again, as before. You will meet at your condominium apartment in Carmel and plan your strategy. At this point there is a division into parallel futures. They hinge in a disputed fact. Whether your group permits you to bring Mary Anne McClain in as a new Game-playing Bindman.'

'What are the two futures branching from that?' Pete asked.

'I can see the one without her very clearly. Let's simply say it's not good. The other – it's blurred because Mary is a variable and can't be previewed within casual frameworks; she introduces the acausal principle of synchronicity.' Mutreaux was silent a moment. 'I think, on the basis

172

of what I preview, I would advise you to make the attempt to bring her into the group. *Even though it's illegal.*'

'That's right,' Joe Schilling said, nodding. 'It's strictly against the bylaws of Bluff-playing entities. No Psi of any description can be admitted. But our antagonists aren't non-Psi humans; they're Titans and telepaths. I see her value. With her in our group the telepath factor is balanced. Otherwise, they hold an absolute advantage.' He recalled the altercation in the card which he had drawn, its change from twelve to eleven. We couldn't win against that, he realized. And even with Mary –

'I should be admitted, too, if possible,' Mutreaux said. 'Although, again, legally I'm also inadmissible. Pretty Blue Fox must be made to comprehend the issues involved, what the stakes are this time. It's not just an exchange of property deeds, not a competition among Bindmen to see who's top man. It's our old struggle with an enemy, renewed after all these years. If it ever ceased in the first place.'

'It never did cease,' Mary Anne spoke up. 'We knew that, the people in our organization. Whether we were vugs or Terrans; we agreed on that.'

'What can you see us obtaining from E. B. Black and the police power?' Pete asked Mutreaux.

'I preview a meeting between the Area Commissioner, U. S. Cummings, and E. B. Black. But I can't seem to foresee the outcome. There is something which U. S. Cummings is involved in that introduces another variable. I wonder, U. S. Cummings may be an extremist. What is it called?'

'The Wa Pei Nan,' Joe Schilling said. 'That's what E. B. Black called it.' He had never heard the words before the vug detective had said them; he rolled them around in his mind, trying to get the flavor of them. But they were impenetrable, shut tight to him. He gave up.

He could not imagine what such a party was like or how it felt to belong to it.

I can't empathize with them, he realized. And that's bad because if we can't put ourselves in their places we can't predict what they're going to do. Even with the use of our pre-cog.

He did not feel very confident. However, he did not tell that to the people in the car with him.

Soon, he thought, we – the augmented Game-playing group Pretty Blue Fox – will make our first move against the Titanians. We'll have, perhaps, the help of Mutreaux and Mary Anne McClain; will that be enough? Mutreaux can't see, and no one can count on Mary Anne, as Doctor Philipson pointed out. And yet he was glad they had her. Without Mary Anne, he thought caustically, Pete and I would be back there at the motel, in the middle of the Nevada Desert. Sitting in on Titanian strategy.

'I'll be glad to contribute title deeds to both of you,' Pete said to Mary Anne and Dave Mutreaux. 'Mary, you can have San Rafael. Mutreaux, you can have San Anselmo. Those will bring you to the table. I hope.'

No one spoke; no one felt optimistic enough to.

'*How do you bluff*,' Pete said, '*against telepaths?*'

It was a good question. It was, in fact, the question on which everything depended.

And none of them could answer it. They can't alter the values of the cards we draw, Schilling said to himself, because we've got Mary Anne to exert a contra-pressure stabilizing them as we hold them. But –

'If we can develop a strategy,' Pete said, 'we'll need the collective minds of everyone in Pretty Blue Fox. Among all of us there must be an idea we can use.'

'You think so?' Schilling said.

'It's got to be,' Pete said, harshly.

Chapter 15

At ten o'clock that night they met in the group condominium apartment in Carmel. First came Silvanus Angst, this time – for perhaps the first time in his life – sober and silent, but as always carrying a paper bag containing a fifth of whiskey. He set it on the sideboard and turned to Pete and Carol Garden who followed him.

'I just can't see letting Psis in,' Angst murmured. 'I mean, you're talking about something that'll make Game-playing impossible forever.'

Bill Calumine said drily, 'Wait until everyone's here.' His tone, to Angst, was unfriendly. 'I want to meet the two of them,' he said to Pete, 'before I decide. The girl and the pre-cog, who, I understand, is on Jerome Luckman's staff back in New York.' Although now voted out as spinner, Calumine automatically assumed the position of authority. And perhaps it was well he did, Pete reflected.

'That's right,' Pete murmured absently. At the sideboard he looked to see what Silvanus Angst had brought. Canadian whiskey, this time, and very good. Pete got himself a glass, held it under the ice machine.

'Thank you sir,' the ice machine piped.

Pete mixed himself a drink, his back to the room as it slowly, steadily, filled with people. Their murmuring voices came to him.

'And not just one Psi but two!'

'Yes, but the issue involved; it's patriotic.'

'So what. Game-playing ends when Psis come in.'

'It can be with the proviso that they terminate as Bindmen as soon as this fracas with the – what're they called? The Woo Poo Non? Something like that, according to the *Chronicle* this evening. Anyhow, the vug firebrands. You know. The ones we thought we beat.'

'You saw that article? The homeopape system at the *Chronicle* inferred that it's been these Woo Poo Noners who've kept our goddam birth rate down.'

'Implied.'

'Pardon?'

'You said "inferred." That's grammatically unsound.'

'Anyhow, my point is, without quibbling, that it's our *duty* to let these two Psi-people into Pretty Blue Fox. That vug detective, that E. B. Black, told us that it was to our national advantage to – '

'You believe him? A vug?'

'He's a good vug. Didn't you grasp that point?' Stuart Marks tapped Pete urgently on the shoulder. 'That was the whole point you were trying to make to us, wasn't it?'

'I don't know,' Pete said. He really didn't, now. He was worn-out. Let me drink my drink in peace, he thought, and turned his back once more on the roomful of arguing men and women. He wished Joe Schilling would arrive.

'Let them in this once, I say. It's for our own protection; we're not playing against *each other*, we're all on the same side in this, playing against the vug-bugs. And they can read our minds so they automatically win unless we can come up with something new. And anything new would have to be derived from the two Psi-people, right? Because where else is it going to come from? Straight ozone?'

'We can't play against vugs. They'll just laugh at us. Look, they got six of us right here in this room to gang together and kill Jerome Luckman; if they can do that – '

'Not me. I wasn't one of the six.'

'But it could have been. They just didn't happen to choose you.'

'Anyhow, if you read the article in the homeopape you know the vugs mean business. They slaughtered Luckman and that detective Hawthorne and kidnapped Pete Garden and then – '

'But newspapers exaggerate.'

'Aw, there's no use talking to you.' Jack Blau stalked away; he appeared beside Pete and said, 'When are they getting here? These two Psi-people.'

Pete said, 'Any time now.'

Coming up, slipping her smooth, bare arm through his, Carol said, 'What are you drinking, darling?'

'Canadian whiskey.'

'Everyone's been congratulating me,' Carol said. 'About the baby. Except of course Freya. And I think even she would, except – '

'Except she can't stand the idea,' Pete said.

'Do you actually think it's been the vugs – or at least a segment of them – who've been keeping our birth rate down?'

'Yes,' Pete said.

'So if we win, our birth rate might go up.'

He nodded.

'And our cities would have something in them besides a billion Rushmore circuits all saying, "Yes sir, no sir."' Carol squeezed his arm.

Pete said, 'And if we don't win, there pretty soon won't be any births on our planet at all. And the race will die out.'

'Oh.' She nodded wanly.

'It's a big responsibility,' Freya Garden Gaines said, from behind him. 'To hear you tell it, anyhow.'

Pete shrugged.

'And Joe was on Titan, too? You both were?'

'Joe and I and Laird Sharp,' Pete said.

'Instantly.'

'Yes.'

177

'Quaint,' Freya said.

Pete said, 'Get away.'

'I'm not going to vote to admit the two Psi-people,' Freya said. 'I can tell you that now, Pete.'

'You're an idiot, Mrs Gaines,' Laird Sharp said; he had been standing nearby, listening. 'I can tell you that, at least. Anyhow, I think you'll be outvoted.'

'You're fighting against a tradition,' Freya said. 'People don't lightly and easily set aside one hundred years.'

'Not even to save their species?' Laird Sharp asked her.

'No one's seen these Game-playing Titans except Joe Schilling and you,' Freya said. 'Even Pete doesn't claim to have seen them.'

'They exist,' Sharp said quietly. 'And you'd better believe it. Because soon you're going to see them, too.'

Carrying his glass, Pete walked through the apartment and outside, into the cool California evening air; he stood by himself in the semi-darkness, his drink in his hand, waiting. He did not know for what. For Joe Schilling and Mary Anne to arrive? Perhaps that was it.

Or perhaps it was for something else, something even more meaningful to him than that. I'm waiting for The Game to begin, he said to himself. The last Game we Terrans may ever play.

He was waiting for the Titanian Game-players to arrive.

He thought, Patricia McClain is dead, but in a sense she never really existed; what I saw was a simulacrum, a fake. What I was in love with, if that's the proper word . . . it wasn't there anyhow, so how can I really say I've lost it? You have to possess it first to lose it.

Anyhow we can't think about that, he decided. We've got other matters to worry about. Doctor Philipson said that the Game-players are moderates; it's an irony that what we ultimately have to defeat is not the fringe of extremists but the great center group itself. Maybe it's just as well; we're taking on the core of their civilization,

178

vugs not like E. R. Philipson but more like E. B. Black. The reputable ones. The ones who play by the rules.

That's all we can count on, Pete realized, the fact that these players are law-abiding. If they weren't, if they were like Philipson and the McClains –

We would not be facing them across a Game-board. They would simply kill us, as they killed Luckman and Hawthorne, and that would be that.

A car descended, now, its headlights flashing; it came to rest at the curb, behind the other cars, and its lights switched off. The door opened and shut and a single figure, a man, came striding toward Pete.

Who was this? He strained to see, not recognizing him.

'Hi,' the man said. 'I dropped by. After I read the article in the homeopape. It looks interesting, here. No fnool, I say, buddy-friend. Correct?'

'Who are you?' Pete said.

The man said coolly, 'You don't recognize me? I thought everyone knew who I am. Awop awop woom. May I sit in on your group, tonight? Buddy, buddy, buddy; I know I'd enjoy it.' He approached the porch, stood now beside Pete, his movements confident and alert, hand extended. 'I'm Nats Katz.'

Bill Calumine said, 'Of course you can sit in on our Game, Mr Katz. It's an honor to have you here.' He waved the members of Pretty Blue Fox into momentary silence. 'This is the world-renowned disc jockey and recording star Nats Katz, whom we all watch on TV; he's asked to sit in on our meeting tonight. Does anybody mind?'

The group was watching, uncertain how to react.

What was it Mary Anne had said about Katz? Pete thought. *Is Nats Katz the center of all this?* he had asked her. And she had said yes. And, at the time, it had seemed true.

Pete said, 'Wait.'

Turning, Bill Calumine said, 'Surely there's no valid reason to object to this man's presence here. I can't believe you'd seriously – '

'Wait until Mary Anne gets here,' Pete said. 'Let her decide about Katz.'

'She's not even a part of the group,' Freya Gaines said. There was silence.

'If he comes in,' Pete said, 'I go out.'

'Out where?' Calumine said.

Pete said nothing.

'A girl who isn't even part of our group – ' Calumine began.

'What's your basis for opposing him?' Stuart Marks asked Pete. 'Is it rational? Something you are able to express?' They were all watching him, now, wondering what his reason was.

Pete said, 'We're in a much worse position than any of you realize. There's very little chance that we can win against our opponents.'

'So?' Stuart Marks said. 'What's that have to do – '

'I think,' Pete said, 'that Katz is on their side.'

After a moment Nats Katz laughed. He was handsome, dark, with sensuous lips and strong, intelligent eyes. 'That's a new one,' he said. 'I've been accused of just about everything, but hardly that. Awop woom! I was born in Chicago, Mr Garden. I assure you; I'm a Terran. Woom, woom, *woom*!' His round, animated face radiated a potent cheerfulness. Katz did not seem offended, only surprised. 'What will you see, my birth certificate? You know, buddy-friend Garden woom, I really am well-known here and there, no fnool. If I were a vug it probably would have come to light before now. Wouldn't you think? Correct?'

Pete sipped his drink; his hands, he found, were shaking. *Have I lost contact with reality?* he asked himself. Maybe so. Maybe I never fully recovered from my binge, my temporary psychotic interlude. Am I the person to judge about Katz?

Should I be here at all? he wondered.

Maybe this is the end for me, he said to himself. Not for them; for me. Personally. At last.

Aloud, he said, 'I'm going out. I'll be back later.' Turning, he set his drink glass down and left the room; he descended the porch steps and arrived at his car. Getting in, he slammed the door and sat in silence for a long, long time.

Maybe I'm more of a detriment to the group than an asset at this point, he said to himself. He lit a cigarette, then abruptly dropped it into the disposal chute of the car. For all I know, Nats might even come up with the idea we need; he's an imaginative guy.

Someone was standing on the porch, calling him; the voice drifted to him faintly. 'Hey, Pete, what're you doing? Come on back inside!'

Pete started up the car. 'Let's go,' he ordered it.

'Yes, Mr Garden.' The car moved forward, then lifted from the pavement, skimmed above the other parked cars, deep-beeping, then above the rooftops of Carmel; at last, it headed toward the Pacific, a quarter mile west.

All I have to do, Pete thought idly, is give it the command to land. Because in another minute we'll be over water.

Would the Rushmore circuit do that? Probably.

'Where are we?' he asked it, to see if it knew.

'Over the Pacific Ocean, Mr Garden.'

'What would you do,' he said, 'if I asked you to set down?'

There was a moment of silence. 'Call Doctor Macy at – ' It hesitated; he heard the unit clicking, trying different combinations. 'I would set down,' it decided. 'As instructed.'

It had chosen. Had he?

I shouldn't be this depressed, he told himself. I shouldn't be doing things like this; it isn't reasonable.

But he was.

For a time he managed to look down at the dark water below. And then, with a turn of the tiller, he steered the car into a wide arc until it was skimming back toward land. This way isn't for me, Pete said to himself. Not the ocean. I'll pick up something at the apartment, something I can take; a bottle or so of phenobarbital, maybe. Or Emphytal.

He flew above Carmel, going north, and presently his car was passing above South San Francisco. And a few minutes later he was over Marin County. San Rafael lay directly ahead. He gave the Rushmore circuit the instructions to land at his apartment building; settling back, he waited.

'Here we are, sir.' The car bumped the curb slightly. The motor clicked itself off; the car dutifully opened its door.

Pete stepped out, walked to the building door, put his key in the lock and then entered.

Upstairs, he reached the door of his and Carol's apartment; the door was unlocked and he opened it and passed on inside.

The lights were on. In the living room a lanky, middle-aged man sat in the center of the couch, legs crossed, reading the *Chronicle*.

'You forget,' the man said, tossing the newspaper down, 'that a pre-cog previews every possibility that he's later going to know about. And a suicide on your part would be big news.' Dave Mutreaux rose to his feet, hands in his pockets; he seemed completely at ease. 'This would be an especially unfortunate time for you to kill yourself, Garden.'

'Why?' Pete demanded.

Mutreaux said quietly, 'Because if you don't, you're on

the verge of finding an answer to the Game-problem. The answer to how one bluffs a race of telepaths. I can't give it to you; only you can think it up. But it's going to be there. Not, however, if you're dead ten minutes from now.' He nodded in the direction of the bathroom and its medicine cabinet. 'I've done a little rigging along the lines of the alternate future I'd like to see become actual; while I've been here I've disposed of your pills. The medicine cabinet is empty.'

Pete went at once into the bathroom and looked.

Not even the aspirin remained. He saw only bare shelves.

To the medicine cabinet he said, angrily, 'You let him do this?'

Its Rushmore Effect answered cringingly, 'He said it was for your own good, Mr Garden. And you know how you are when you're depressed.'

Slamming the cabinet door, Pete walked back into the living room.

'You've got me, Mutreaux,' he conceded. 'At least in one respect. The way I had in mind – '

'You can find some other way, of course,' Mutreaux said calmly. 'But emotionally you lean toward suicide by oral means. Poisons, narcotics, sedatives, hypnotics and so forth.' He smiled. 'There's a resistance to doing it by any other means. For instance, by dropping into the Pacific.'

Pete said, 'Can you tell me anything about my solution to the Game-playing problem?'

'No,' Mutreaux said. 'I can't. That's entirely up to you.'

'Thanks,' Pete said sardonically.

'I'll tell you one thing, however. A hint. One which may cheer you or it may not. I can't preview it because you aren't going to show your reaction visibly. Patricia McClain is not dead.'

Pete stared at him.

'Mary Anne didn't destroy her. She set her down somewhere. Don't ask me where because I don't know. But I preview Patricia's presence in San Rafael within the next few hours. At her apartment.'

Pete could think of nothing to say; he continued to stare at the pre-cog.

'See?' Mutreaux said. 'No palpable reaction of any sort. Perhaps you're ambivalent.' He added, 'She'll only be there a short time; then she's going to Titan. And not by Doctor Philipson's Psionic means but in the more conventional manner, by interplan ship.'

'She's really on their side, isn't she? There's no doubt of that.'

'Oh yes,' Mutreaux said, nodding. 'She's really on their side. But that's not going to stop you from going, is it?'

'No,' Pete said, and started from the apartment.

'May I come along?' Mutreaux asked.

'Why?'

'To keep her from killing you.'

Pete was silent a moment. 'It's really like that, is it?'

Mutreaux nodded. 'It certainly is, and you know it. You watched them shoot Hawthorne.'

'Okay,' Pete said. 'Come with me.' He added, 'Thanks.' It was hard to say it.

They left the apartment building together, Pete slightly ahead of David Mutreaux.

As they reached the street, Pete said, 'Did you know that Nats Katz, the disc jockey, showed up at the con-apt in Carmel?'

Nodding, Dave Mutreaux said, 'Yes. I met him an hour or so ago and talked to him; he looked me up. It was the first time I had ever run into him, although of course I had heard of him.' He added, 'It's because of him that I crossed over.'

'Crossed over?' Halting, Pete turned toward Mutreaux, who followed after him.

184

And found himself, incredibly, facing a heat-needle.

'With Katz,' Mutreaux said calmly. 'The pressure simply was too much on me, Pete. I couldn't effectively resist it. Nats is extraordinarily powerful. He was chosen to be leader of the Wa Pei Nan here on Terra for a good reason. Come on, let's continue on our way to Patricia McClain's apartment.' He gestured with the heat-needle.

After a moment Pete said, 'Why didn't you just let me kill myself? Why intervene at all?'

'Because,' Dave Mutreaux said, 'you're coming over to our side, Pete. We can make good use of you. The Wa Pei Nan doesn't approve of this Game-playing solution; once we manage to penetrate Pretty Blue Fox, by means of you, we can call The Game off from this end.' He added, 'We've already discussed it with the moderate faction on Titan and they're determined to play; they like to play and they feel this controversy between the two cultures ought to be resolved within a legal framework. Needless to say, the Wa Pei Nan does not agree.'

They continued along the dark sidewalk, toward the McClain apartment, Dave Mutreaux slightly behind Pete.

'I should have guessed,' Pete said. 'When Katz showed up, I had an intuition but I didn't act on it.' They had penetrated the group and directly, it seemed, through him. He wished now that he had managed to find the courage to drop his car into the sea; he had been right; it would have been better for everyone concerned. Everyone and everything he believed in.

'When The Game begins,' Mutreaux said, 'I will be there and you, too, Pete, and we will decline to play. And perhaps by that time Nats will have managed to persuade others. I can't see that far ahead; the alternative courses are obscure to me, for reasons I can't make out.' They had almost reached the McClain apartment, now.

When they opened the door to the apartment they

found Pat McClain busy packing two suitcases; she hardly paused to acknowledge their presence.

'I picked up your thoughts as you came down the hall,' she said, carrying an armload of clothes to the suitcases from the dresser in the bedroom. Her face, Pete saw, had a craven, caved-in look on it; in every way she had collapsed from the disastrous clash with Mary Anne. She worked feverishly to complete her packing, as if struggling against an inexorable and yet unclearly seen deadline.

'Where are you going?' Pete asked. 'Titan?'

'Yes,' Patricia answered. 'As far away from that girl as I possibly can get. She can't hurt me there; I'll be safe.' Her hands, Pete saw, shook as she tried, and failed, to close the suitcases. 'Help me,' she said, appealing to Mutreaux.

Obligingly, Dave Mutreaux closed the suitcases for her.

'Before you leave,' Pete said to her, 'let me ask you something. How do the Titanians play The Game being telepaths?'

'Do you think you're going to care?' Patricia said, pausing, lifting her head and regarding him bleakly. 'After Katz and Philipson are through with you?'

'I care now,' he said. 'They've been playing The Game for a long time, so evidently they've found a way to incorporate their faculty or – '

Patricia said, 'They hobble it, Pete.'

'I see,' he said. But he did not see. Hobble it how? And to what extent?

Patricia said, 'Through drug-ingestion. The effect is similar to what the phenothiazine class does to a Terran.'

'Phenothiazines,' Mutreaux said. 'In big doses that's given to schizophrenics; in quantity it becomes an anti-psychotic medication.'

'It lessens the schizophrenic delusions,' Patricia said, 'because it obliterates the involuntary telepathic sense; it eradicates the paranoiac response to the picking up of subconscious hostilities in others. The Titanians possess medication which acts along the same lines on them and the rules of The Game, as they practise it, require them to lose their talent or at least to abort it by some extent.'

Mutreaux, glancing at his watch, said, 'He should be here any time now, Patricia. Surely you're going to wait for him.'

'Why?' she said, still gathering up articles here and there in the apartment. 'I don't want to stay; I just want to get out. Before something else happens. Something more that has to do with *her*.'

'We'll need all three of us to exert sufficient influence on Garden, here,' Mutreaux pointed out.

'You get Nats Katz, then,' Patricia said. 'I'm telling you I'm not going to stay one minute longer than I have to!'

'But right now Katz is in Carmel,' Mutreaux said, patiently. 'And we want to have Garden thoroughly with us when we go there.'

'I can't help,' Patricia said, paying no attention to him; she could not seem to stop her headlong flight, her rushing blindly. 'Listen, Dave, honest to god, there's only one thing that matters to me; I don't want to undergo again what we went through in Nevada. You were there, you know what I'm talking about. And next time she won't spare you, because you're with us. I really advise you to get out, too; let E. R. Philipson handle this, since he's immune to her. But it's your life; you have to decide.' She went on, then, and Mutreaux somberly seated himself, with the heat-needle, waiting for Doctor Philipson to show up.

To himself Pete thought, *Hobble* it. Hobble the Psionic talents on both sides, as Patricia said. It could be an agreement with them; we make use of the phenothiazines, they use whatever it is they're accustomed to. So they were cheating when they read my mind. And then he thought, And they'll cheat again. We can't trust them to hobble themselves. They seem to feel that their moral obligations end when they encounter us.

'That's right,' Patricia said, picking up his thoughts. 'They're not going to hobble themselves when they play you, Pete. And you can't compel them to because in your own playing you don't recognize such a stipulation; you can't show them a legal basis on your side for demanding that.'

'We can show them that we've never allowed Psionic talents at the board,' he said.

'But you are now. Your group is voting that daughter of mine in and Dave Mutreaux in, right?' She smiled at him crookedly, heartlessly, her eyes lusterless and black. 'So that's that, Pete Garden. Too bad. At least you made the try.'

Bluffing, he thought. Telepaths. Hobbling through medication that acts as a thalamic suppressor, dulls the extrasensory area of the brain. It could be dulled to various degrees, damped to some extent but not entirely; gradations can be obtained, depending on the amount of medication. Ten milligrams of a phenothiazine would dampen it; sixty would obliterate it.

And then he thought, his mind careening, Suppose we didn't look at the cards we drew? There would be nothing in our minds for the Titanians to read because we wouldn't know what number we'd obtained . . .

To Mutreaux, Patricia said, 'He's almost managed it, Dave. He forgets that he's not going to be playing on the Terran side, that he's going to belong to us by the time he seats himself at the Game-board.' She brought out a little overnight bag, now, hurrying to fill it.

Pete thought, If we had Mutreaux, if we could regain him, we could win. Because I know how, finally.

'You know,' Patricia said, 'but how is it going to help you?'

Aloud, Pete said, 'We could dampen his pre-cog faculty

to an undetermined degree. So that it becomes unpredictable.' Through the use of phenothiazine spansules, he realized, which act over a period of hours at a variable rate. Mutreaux himself would not know if he were bluffing or not, how accurate his guess was. He would draw a card, and, without looking at it, move our piece. If his pre-cog faculty were operating at maximum force at that instant his guess would be accurate; it would not be a bluff. But if at that instant the medication had a greater rather than a lesser effect on him –

It would be a bluff. And Mutreaux himself would not know. That could easily be arranged; someone else would prepare the phenothiazine spansule, fix the rate at which it would release its medication.

'But,' Patricia said softly, 'Dave isn't on your side of the Game table, Pete.'

Pete said, 'But I'm right. That's how we could play against the Titanian telepaths and win.'

'Yes,' Patricia said, and nodded.

'He's worked it out now, has he?' Mutreaux asked her.

'He has,' she said. 'I feel sorry for you, Pete, because you've got it and it's too late in coming. Your people would have a lot of fun, wouldn't they? Preparing the grains of medication within the spansule, using all kinds of complex tablets and formulae to work out the rate of release. It could be random, too, if you want it that way, or at a fixed but so elaborate rate that – '

To Mutreaux, Pete said, 'How can you sit there and know you're betraying us? You're not a Titanian national; you're a Terran.'

Calmly, Mutreaux said, 'Psychic dynamisms are real, Pete, as real as any other kind of force. I foresaw my meeting with Nats Katz; I foresaw what was going to happen, but I couldn't prevent it. Remember, I didn't seek him out, he found *me*.'

189

'Why didn't you warn us?' Pete said. 'When you were still on our side of the board.'

'You would have killed me,' Mutreaux said. 'I previewed that particular alternative future. In several, I did tell you. And – ' He shrugged. 'I don't blame you; what other course would you have? My going over to Titan determines the outcome of The Game. Our acquiring you proves that.'

'He wishes,' Patricia said, 'that you had left the Emphytal in his medicine cabinet; he wishes he had taken them. Poor Pete, always a potential suicide, aren't you? Always, as far as you're concerned, that's the ultimate way out. The one solution to everything.'

Mutreaux said restlessly, 'Doctor Philipson should have been here by now. Are you certain the arrangements were understood? Could the moderates have sequestered his services? Legally, they hold the – '

'Doctor Philipson would never yield to the cowards in our midst,' Patricia said. 'You're familiar with his attitude.' Her voice was sharp, laden with dread and concern.

'But he's not here,' Mutreaux said. '*Something's wrong.*'

They looked at each other, silently.

'What do you preview?' Patricia demanded.

'Nothing,' Mutreaux said. His face, now, was pale.

'*Why not?*'

'If I could preview, I could preview, period,' Mutreaux said bitingly. 'Isn't that obvious? I don't know and I wish I did.' He got to his feet and went over to the window to look out. For a moment he had forgotten Pete; he held the heat-needle slackly, squinting to see in the evening darkness that lay outside. His back was to Pete, and Pete jumped toward him.

'Dave!' Patricia barked, dropping her armload of books.

Mutreaux turned, and a bolt from the heat-needle

zoomed past Pete; he felt the peripheral effects from it, the dehydrating envelope that surrounded the laser beam itself, the narrow, effective beam that was so useful both in close quarters and at a distance.

Raising his arms, Pete struck the man with both elbows, in the unprotected throat.

The heat-needle rolled away from both of them across the floor. Patricia McClain, sobbing, scrambled after it. 'Why? Why couldn't you predict this?' She clutched at the small cylinder, frantically.

His face sickly and dark, Mutreaux shut his eyes and dwindled into physical collapse, pawing at himself, inhaling raucously, no longer concerned with anything else beyond the massive, difficult effort to live.

'I'm killing you, Pete,' Patricia McClain gasped, backing away from him, holding the heat-needle waveringly pointed at him. Sweat, he saw, stood out on her upper lip; her mouth quivered violently and tears filled her eyes. 'I can read your mind,' she said huskily, 'and I know, Pete, I know what you'll do if I don't. You've got to have Dave Mutreaux back on your side of the board to win and you can't have him back; he's ours.'

Throwing himself away from her he tumbled out of the path of the laser, snatching at anything. His fingers closed over a book and he hurled it; the book fluttered open and dropped at Patricia McClain's feet, harmlessly.

Panting, Patricia backed away, still. 'Dave will recover,' she whispered. 'If you had killed him perhaps it wouldn't matter so much, because then you couldn't get him for your side and we wouldn't – '

She broke off. Swiftly turning her head she listened, not breathing.

'The door,' she said.

The knob turned.

Patricia raised the heat-needle. Slowly, her arm bent

and twisted, inch by inch, until the muzzle of the heat-needle was pointing at her face. She stared down at it, unable to take her eyes from it. She said, 'Please don't, okay? I gave birth to you. Please – '

Her fingers, against her will, moved the stud. The laser beam flicked on.

Pete looked away.

When he looked back at last the door of the apartment stood open. Mary Anne, framed in the outline of darkness, walked in, slowly, hands deep in the pockets of her long coat. Her face was expressionless. She said to Pete, 'Dave Mutreaux is alive, isn't he?'

'Yes.' He did not look at the heap which had been Patricia McClain; he averted his eyes from it and said, 'We need him so leave him alone, Mary.' His heart labored slowly, horribly.

'I realize that,' Mary Anne said.

'How did you know about – this?'

Mary Anne said, after an interval, 'When I got to the condominium apartment in Carmel, with Joe Schilling I saw Nats and of course I understood. I knew that Nats was the organization's overall superior. He outranked even Rothman.'

'What did you do there?' Pete said.

Joe Schilling, his face puffy with tension, entered the apartment and went up to Mary Anne; he put his hand on her shoulder but she jerked away, going alone over to the corner to stand and watch. 'When she came in,' Schilling said, 'Katz was fixing himself a drink. She – ' He hesitated.

Mary Anne said tonelessly, 'I moved the glass which he held. I made it go five inches, that's all. He was – holding it at chest level.'

'The glass is inside him,' Schilling said. 'It very simply cut his heart, or part of his heart, out of his circulatory system. There was a good deal of blood, because the glass didn't go in all the way.' He was silent then; neither he nor Mary Anne spoke.

On the floor, Dave Mutreaux, gargling, struggled, his face blue, trying to get air into his lungs. He had stopped stroking his throat now, and his eyes were open. But he did not seem able to see.

'What about him?' Schilling said.

Pete said, 'With Patricia dead and Nats Katz dead, and Philipson – ' He understood, now, why Doctor Philipson had failed to appear. 'He knew you would be here,' he said to Mary Anne. 'So he was afraid to leave Titan. Philipson saved himself, at their expense.'

'I guess so,' Mary Anne murmured.

Joe Schilling said, 'I can hardly blame him.'

Bending down, Pete said to Mutreaux, 'Will you be all right?'

Mutely, Dave Mutreaux nodded.

Pete said to him, 'You must show up at the Gameboard. On our side. You know why; you know what I intend to do.'

Staring at him, Mutreaux nodded.

'I can manage him,' Mary Anne said, walking over to watch. 'He's too much afraid of me to do anything more for them. Aren't you?' she said to Mutreaux in the same inert, neutral tone. And prodded him with her toe.

Mutreaux, dully, managed to nod.

'Be glad you're alive,' Schilling said to him.

'He is,' Mary Anne said. To Pete she said, 'Will you do something about my mother, please?'

'Sure,' Pete said. He glanced at Joe Schilling. 'Why don't you go downstairs and wait in the car?' he said to Mary Anne. 'We'll call E. B. Black; we don't need you for a while.'

'Thank you,' Mary Anne said. Turning, she walked slowly out of the apartment; Pete and Joe Schilling watched her until she was gone.

'Because of her,' Joe Schilling said, 'we're going to win, there at the board.'

Pete nodded. Because of her and because Mutreaux was still alive. Alive – and no longer in a position to act for the Titanian authority.

'We're lucky,' Joe Schilling said. 'Someone had left the door of the con-apt open; she saw Katz before he could see her. She was standing outside and he couldn't make her out until too late. I think he had counted on Mutreaux' pre-cog faculty, forgetting or not understanding that she's a variable as far as that faculty is concerned. He was as unprotected by Mutreaux' talent as if Mutreaux had never existed.'

And so are we, Pete thought to himself. That unprotected.

But he could not bother to worry about that now. The Game against the Titanians lay directly ahead; he did not need to be a pre-cog to see that. Everything else would have to wait.

Joe Schilling said, 'I have confidence in her. I'm not concerned about what she might do, Pete.'

'Let's hope you're right,' Pete said. He bent down beside the body of Patricia McClain. This was Mary's mother, he realized. And Mary Anne did this to her. And yet we have to depend on Mary Anne; Joe is right. We have no choice.

Chapter 16

To Mutreaux, Pete Garden said, 'This is what you have to face and accept. As we play, Mary Anne McClain will be at the board beside you at all times. If we lose, Mary will kill you.'

Mutreaux said woodenly, 'I know. It was obvious as soon as Pat died that my life now depends on our winning.' He sat massaging his throat and drinking hot tea. 'And more indirectly, so do your lives, too.'

'That's so,' Joe Schilling said.

'It should begin any time,' Mary Anne said, 'if I understand them, anyhow. They should begin to arrive on Terra within the next half hour.' She had seated herself at the far end of the kitchen of the McClain apartment; in the living room the amorphous shape of E. B. Black could be made out through the open door consulting with human members of the West Coast police agency. At least six people were active in the living room now. And more were arriving.

'We've got to start for Carmel,' Pete said. By vidphone he had arranged with his psychiatrist, Doctor Macy at Salt Lake City, for the phenothiazine spansules to be prepared; the spansules would be flown to Carmel from one of the pharmaceutical houses in San Francisco direct to the condominium apartment, to be received by Bill Calumine acting for the group, as he always did.

'How long does it take for the phenothiazine to begin acting?' Joe Schilling asked Pete.

'Once he's taken it into his system it should take effect immediately,' Pete said. 'Assuming Mutreaux hasn't been

195

taking any up to now.' And, since it acted to blunt his Psitalent, that was highly unlikely.

The four of them, checked out by E. B. Black, left San Rafael for Carmel in Joe Schilling's ill-tempered old car, Pete's following directly behind them, empty. On the trip almost nothing was said. Mary Anne stared blankly out the window. Dave Mutreaux sat slumped inertly, occasionally touching his injured throat. Joe Schilling and Pete sat together in the front seat.

This may be the final time we make this trip, Pete realized.

They reached Carmel reasonably quickly. Pete parked the car, shut off the motor and the creaky Rushmore circuit, and the four of them got out.

Standing in the dark, waiting for them, he saw a group of people.

Something about them chilled him. There were four of them, three men and a woman. Getting a flashlight from the glove compartment of his own car, which had come to a halt at the curb behind Max, he shone the light on the soundless, waiting group.

After a long pause Joe Schilling muttered, 'I see.'

'That's right,' Dave Mutreaux said. 'That's exactly how it will be played. I hope for all our sakes you can go on.'

'Hell,' Pete said shortly, 'we can.'

The four noiseless figures waiting for them were Titanian simulacra.

Of themselves. A vug Peter Garden, a vug Joe Schilling, a vug Dave Mutreaux, and, slightly behind the others, a vug Mary Anne McClain. The last was not as effective, not as substantial, as the others. Mary Anne was a problem for the Titanians. Even in this regard.

To the four simulacra, Pete said, 'And if we lose?'

His counterpart, the vug Peter Garden, said in precisely the same tone, 'If and when you lose, Mr Garden, your

196

presence is no longer required in The Game and I replace you. It's as simple as that.'

'Cannibalism,' Joe Schilling said gratingly.

'No,' the vug Joe Schilling contradicted. 'Cannibalism occurs when a member of a species feeds on other members of that species. We are not of the same species as you.' The vug Joe Schilling smiled, and it was the smile familiar from years back to Pete Garden; it was a superb imitation.

The group upstairs in the apartment, Pete thought, the others of Pretty Blue Fox, have simulacra appeared for them, too?

'Correct,' the vug Peter Garden answered. 'So shall we proceed on up? The Game should begin at once; there is no reason for further delay.' It started toward the stairs, knowing the way.

That was the terrible part, the part which sickened Pete Garden: the alacrity of the vug as it ascended the stairs. Its certitude, as if it had made this climb a thousand times before.

It was already at home, here on Terra, in the midst of their customary lives. Shuddering, he watched the other three simulacra follow equally rapidly. And then he and his companions started into reluctant motion.

Above them the door opened; the vug Peter Garden entered the con-apt of the Game-playing group Pretty Blue Fox.

'Hello!' it greeted those within the room.

Stuart Marks – or was it the simulacrum of Stuart Marks? – regarded it with horror and then stammered, 'I guess everybody's here, now.' He – or it – stepped out onto the porch and peered down. 'Hi.'

'Greetings,' Pete Garden said, laconically.

They faced one another across the table, the Titanian simulacra on one side, Pretty Blue Fox plus Dave Mutreaux and Mary Anne McClain on the other.

197

'Cigar?' Joe Schilling said to Pete.

'No thanks,' Pete murmured.

Across from them the vug simulacrum of Joe Schilling turned to Pete Garden beside it and said, 'Cigar?'

'No thanks,' the vug Pete Garden answered.

Pete Garden said to Bill Calumine, 'Did the shipment arrive from the San Francisco pharmaceutical house? We've got to have it before we can begin. I hope no one intends to dispute that.'

The vug Pete Garden said, 'A noteworthy idea you have fastened onto, in this erratic crippling of your pre-cog's sensory apparatus. You are absolutely correct; it will go a great distance toward evening our relative strengths.' It grinned at the group Pretty Blue Fox, up and down the Game table. 'We have no objection to waiting until your medication arrives; anything else would be unfair.'

Answering it, Pete Garden said, 'I believe you've got to wait; we obviously won't begin to play until then. So don't make it appear that you're doing us a big favor.' His voice shook, slightly.

Leaning over, Bill Calumine said, 'Sorry. It's already there, in the kitchen.'

Rising from his chair, Pete Garden went with Dave Mutreaux into the kitchen of the condominium apartment. In the center of the kitchen table, with trays of half-melted ice, lemons, bottles of mixer, glasses and bitters, he saw a package wrapped in brown paper, sealed with tape.

'Just think,' Mutreaux said meditatively, as Pete unwrapped the package, 'if this doesn't work, what happened to Patricia and the others in the organization, there in Nevada, will happen to me.' He seemed relatively calm, however. 'I don't sense the ominous disregard of all order and legality in these moderates,' he said, 'that I do in the Wa Pei Nan, with Doctor Philipson and those like him. Or rather, like *it*.' He scrutinized Pete as Pete took a phenothiazine spansule from the bottle. 'If you know the time-phasing of the granules within,' he said, 'the vugs will be able to – '

'I don't,' Pete said shortly, as he filled a glass with water at the tap. 'The ethical house making up these spansules was told that the range could vary between instantaneous full action to any sequence of partial action to no action whatsoever. In addition, it was told to make up several spansules, one varying from another.' He added, 'And I've picked a spansule at random. Physically it's identical in appearance to the others.' He held out the spansule and the glass of water to Mutreaux.

Somberly, Mutreaux swallowed the spansule.

'I will tell you one thing,' Mutreaux said, 'for your own information. Several years ago, as an experiment, I tried a phenothiazine derivative. It had a colossal effect on my pre-cognitive ability.' He smiled fleetingly at Pete. 'As I told you before we went over to Pat McClain's this idea of yours is an adequate solution to our problems, as nearly as I can foresee. Congratulations.'

'Do you say that,' Pete asked, 'as someone genuinely with us, or merely as someone forced to play on this side of the table?'

'I don't know,' Mutreaux said. 'I'm in transition, Pete. Time will tell.' Turning, he walked back into the living room without another word. Back to the great Gameboard and the two opposing parties.

The vug Bill Calumine rose to its feet and announced, 'I suggest our side roll first and then your side.' It took the spinner and spun with expert vigor.

The pointer stopped at nine.

'All right,' Bill Calumine said, also rising and facing his simulacrum; he, too, rolled. For him the pointer slowed as it came close to twelve, then started to pass on toward one.

To Mary Anne, Pete said, 'Are you resisting any efforts on their part at psycho-kinesis?'

'Yes,' she said, concentrating on the barely-moving pointer.

The pointer stopped on one.

'It's fair,' Mary Anne said, in a scarcely audible voice.

'You Titanians initiate play, then,' Pete conceded. He managed to suppress his discouragement; he kept it out of his voice.

'Good,' his simulacrum said. It regarded him, grinning mockingly. 'Then we will transport the field of interaction from Terra to Titan.' It added, 'We trust that you Terrans will not object.'

'What?' Joe Schilling said. 'Wait!' But the transforming activity had begun; it was already too late.

The room trembled and became hazed over. And the simulacra seated opposite them had, Pete thought, begun to attain a disrupted, oblique quality. As if, he thought, their physical shapes no longer functioned adequately, as if, like archaic, malformed exoskeletons, they were now in the process of being discarded.

His simulacrum, seated directly across from him, all at once lurched hideously. Its head lolled and its eyes became glazed, empty of light, filmed over with a destructive membrane. The simulacrum shivered, and then, up its side, a long rent appeared.

The same process was occurring in the other simulacra.

The Pete Garden simulacrum quivered, vibrated, and then, from the head-to-foot rent, something tentative popped quaveringly.

Out of the rent squeezed the protoplasmic organism within. The vug, in authentic shape, no longer requiring the artificial hull, was emerging. Forcing its way out into the gray-yellow light of the weakened sun.

Out of each discarded human husk a vug emerged, and the husks teetered and one by one, as if blown by an impalpable wind, writhed and then danced away, weightless, already without color. Bits and flakes of the discarded husks blew in the air; particles drifted across the Game-board, and Pete Garden, horrified, hurriedly brushed them away.

The Titanian Game-players had appeared in their actual shapes, at last. The business of The Game had begun in earnest. The fraud of the simulated Terran appearance had been abolished; it was no longer needed because The Game was no longer being played on Earth.

They were now on Titan.

In as calm a voice as possible, Pete Garden said, 'All our plays will be made by David Mutreaux. Although we will, in turn, draw the cards and perform the other chores of The Game.'

The vugs, opposite them, seemed to thought-propagate a derisive, meaningless laughter. Why? Pete wondered. It was as if, once the simulacra shapes had been discarded, communication between the two races had at once suffered an impairment.

'Joe,' he said to Joe Schilling, 'if it's all right with Bill Calumine, I'd like you to move our pieces.'

'Okay,' Joe Schilling said, nodding.

Tendrils of gray smoke, cold and damp, sifted onto the Game table and the vug shapes opposite them dimmed into an irregular obscurity. Even physically, the Titanians had retreated, as if desiring as little contact with the Terrans as possible. And it was not out of animosity; it seemed to be a spontaneous withdrawal.

Maybe, Pete thought, we were doomed to this encounter from the very start. It was the absolutely-determined outcome of the initial meeting of our two cultures. He felt hollow and grim. More determined than ever to win The Game before them.

'Draw a card,' the vugs declared, and their propagations seemed to merge, as if there was in actuality only

201

one vug against whom the group played. One massive, inert organism opposing them, ancient and slow in its actions, but infinitely determined.

And wise.

Pete Garden hated it. And feared it.

Mary Anne said aloud, 'They are beginning to exert influence on the deck of cards!'

'All right,' Pete said. 'Keep your attention as fully formed as you can.' He himself felt overwhelmingly tired. Have we lost already? he wondered. It felt like it. It felt as if they had been playing for an endless time now. And yet they had barely begun.

Reaching out, Bill Calumine drew a card.

'Don't look at it,' Pete warned.

'I understand,' Bill Calumine said irritably. He slid the card, unexamined, to Dave Mutreaux.

Mutreaux, in the flickering half-light, sat with the card face down before him, his face wrinkled with concentration.

'Seven squares,' he said, then.

Joe Schilling, on a signal from Calumine, moved their piece ahead, seven squares. The square on which it came to rest read: *Rise in fuel costs. Pay bill to utility company of* $50.

Raising his head, Joe Schilling faced the Titanian authority squatting opposite them on the far side of the board.

There was no call. The Titanians had decided to allow the move to pass; they did not believe it to consist of a bluff.

All at once Dave Mutreaux turned to Pete Garden and said, 'We've lost. That is, we're going to lose; I preview it absolutely, it's there in every alternative future.'

Pete Garden stared at him.

'But your ability,' Joe Schilling pointed out. 'Have you

202

forgotten? It's now highly impaired. A new experience for you; you're disoriented. Isn't that it?'

Mutreaux said haltingly, 'But it does not feel impaired.'

The vug authority facing them said, 'Do you wish to withdraw from The Game?'

'Not at this point,' Pete answered, and Bill Calumine, white and stricken, reflexively nodded in agreement.

What is this? Pete asked himself. What's going on? *Has Dave Mutreaux, despite the threat from Mary Anne, betrayed us?*

Mutreaux said, 'I spoke aloud because they – ' He indicated the vug opponent. 'They can read my mind anyhow.'

That was true; Pete nodded, his mind laboring furiously. What can we salvage here? he asked himself. He tried to control his plunging panic, his intuition of defeat.

Joe Schilling, lighting a cigar, leaned back and said, 'I think we'd better go on.' He did not appear worried. And yet of course he was. But Joe Schilling, Pete realized, was a great Game-player; he would not show his emotions or capitulate in any way. Joe would go on to the end, and the rest of them would, too. Because they had to. It was as simple as that.

'If we win,' Pete said to the vug opponent, 'we obtain control of Titan. You have as much to lose. You have as much at stake as we do.'

The vug drew itself up, shivered, replied, 'Play.'

'It's your turn to draw a card,' Joe Schilling reminded it.

'True.' Admonished, the vug now drew a card. It paused, and then on the board its piece advanced one, two, three . . . nine squares in all.

The square read: *Planetoid rich in archeological treasures, discovered by your scouts. Win $70,000.*

203

Was it a bluff? Pete Garden turned toward Joe Schilling, and now Bill Calumine leaned over to confer. The others of the group, too, bent closer, murmuring.

Joe Schilling said, 'I'd call it.'

Up and down the table the members of Pretty Blue Fox hesitantly voted. The vote ran in favor of calling the move as a bluff. But it was close.

'Bluff,' Joe Schilling stated, aloud.

The vug's card at once flipped over. It was a nine.

'It's fair,' Mary Anne said in a leaden voice. 'I'm sorry, but it is; no Psi-force that I could detect was exerted on it.'

The vug said, 'Prepare your payment, please.' And again it laughed, or seemed to laugh; Pete could not be certain which.

In any case it was a violent and quick defeat for Pretty Blue Fox. The vuggish side had won $70,000 from the bank for having landed on the square and an additional $70,000 from the group's funds due to the inaccurate call of bluff. $140,000 in all. Dazed, Pete sat back, trying to keep himself composed, at least externally. For the sake of the others in the group he had to.

'Again,' the vug said, 'I ask your party to concede.'

'No, no,' Joe Schilling said, as Jack Blau shakily counted out the group's funds and passed them over.

'This is a calamity,' Bill Calumine stated quietly.

'Haven't you survived such losses in The Game before?' Joe Schilling asked him, scowling.

'Have you?' Calumine retorted.

'Yes,' Schilling said.

'But not in the end,' Calumine said. 'In the end, Schilling, you didn't survive; in the end you were defeated. Exactly as you're losing for us, now, here at this table.'

Schilling said nothing. But his face was pale.

'Let's continue,' Pete said.

Calumine said bitterly, 'It was your idea to bring this jinx here; we never would have had this bad luck without him. As spinner – '

'But you're not our spinner any longer,' Mrs Angst spoke up in a low voice.

'Play,' Stuart Marks snapped.

Another card was drawn, passed unread to Dave Mutreaux; he sat with it face down before him and then, slowly, he moved their piece ahead eleven places. The square read: *Pet cat uncovers valuable old stamp album in attic. You win $3,000.*

The vug said, 'Bluff.'

Dave Mutreaux, after a pause, turned over the card. It was an eleven; the vug had lost and therefore had to pay. It was not a huge sum but it proved something to Pete that made him tremble. The vug could be wrong, too.

The phenothiazine-crippling was working effectively.

The group had a chance.

Now the vug drew a card, examined it, and its piece moved ahead nine spaces. *Error in old tax return. Assessed by Federal Government for $80,000.*

The vug shuddered convulsively. And a faint, barely audible moan seemed to escape from it.

This, Pete knew at once, could be a bluff. If it was, and they did not call it, the vug – instead of losing that sum – collected it. All it had to do was turn over its card, show that it had not drawn a nine.

The vote of Pretty Blue Fox, member by member, was taken.

It was in favor of not calling the move as a bluff.

'We decline to call,' Joe Schilling stated.

Reluctantly, with agonized slowness, the vug paid from its pile of money $80,000 to the bank. It had not been a bluff, and Pete gasped with relief. The vug had now lost back over half of what it had won on its great previous move. It was in no sense whatsoever an infallible player.

And, like Pretty Blue Fox, the vug could not conceal its dismay at a major setback. It was not human, but it was alive and it had goals and desires and anxieties. It was mortal.

Pete felt sorry for it.

'You're wasting your affect,' the vug said tartly to him, 'if you pity me. I still hold the edge over you, Terran.'

'For now,' Pete agreed. 'But you're involved in a declining process. The process of losing.'

Pretty Blue Fox drew another card, which, as before, was passed to Dave Mutreaux. He sat, this time, for an interval that seemed forever.

'Call it!' Bill Calumine blurted, at last.

Mutreaux murmured, 'Three.'

The Terran piece was moved by Joe Schilling. And Pete read: *Mud slide endangers house foundations. Fee to construction firm:* $14,000.

The vug did not stir. And then, suddenly, it stated, 'I – do not call.'

Dave Mutreaux glanced at Pete. He reached out and turned over the card.

It was not a three. It was a four.

The group had won – not lost – $14,000. The vug had failed to call the bluff.

'Astonishing,' the vug said, presently, 'that such a handicapping of your ability would actually enable you to win. That you could profit by it.' It savagely drew a card, then shoved its piece ahead seven squares. *Postman injured on your front walk. Protracted lawsuit settled out of court for the sum of* $300,000.

Good god in heaven, Pete thought. It was a sum so staggering that The Game certainly hinged on it. He scrutinized the vug, as everyone else in Pretty Blue Fox was doing, trying to discover some indication. Was it bluffing or was it not?

If we had one single telepath, he thought bitterly. If only –

But they could never have had Patricia, and Hawthorne was dead. And, had they possessed a telepath, the vug authority would undoubtedly have summoned up some system of neutralizing it, just as they had neutralized its telepathic factor; that was obvious. Both sides had played The Game too long to be snared as simply as that; both were prepared.

If we lose, Pete said to himself, I will kill myself before I let myself fall into the hands of the Titanians. He reached into his pocket, wondering what he had there. Only a couple of methamphetamines, perhaps left over from his *luck*-binge. How long ago had it been? One day? Two? It seemed like months ago, now. Another world away.

Methamphetamine hydrochloride.

On his binge it had made him temporarily into an involuntary telepath; a meager one, but to a decisive degree. Methamphetamine was a thalamic stimulator; its effect was precisely the opposite from that of the phenothiazines.

He thought, *Yes!*

Without water he managed – gagging – to gulp down the two small pink methamphetamine tablets.

'Wait,' he said hoarsely to the group. 'Listen; I want to make the decision on this play. Wait!' They would wait at least ten minutes he knew for the methamphetamine to take effect.

The vug said, 'There is cheating on your side. One member of your group has ingested drug-stimulants.'

At once, Joe Schilling said, 'You previously accepted the phenothiazine class; in principle you accepted the use of medication in this Game.'

'But I am not prepared to deal with a telepathic faculty emanating from your side,' the vug protested. 'I scanned

207

your group initially and saw none in evidence. And no plan to obtain such a faculty.'

Joe Schilling said, 'That appears to have been an acute error on your part.' He turned to watch Pete; all the members of Pretty Blue Fox were watching Pete now. 'Well?' Joe asked him, tensely.

Pete Garden sat waiting, fists clenched, for the drug to take effect.

Five minutes passed. No one spoke. The only sound was Joe Schilling drawing on his cigar.

'Pete,' Bill Calumine said abruptly, 'we can't wait any longer. We can't stand the strain.'

'That's true,' Joe Schilling said. His face was wet and florid, shiny with perspiration; now, his cigar had gone out, too. 'Make your decision. Even if it's the wrong one.'

Mary Anne said, 'Pete! The vug is attempting to shift the value of its card!'

'Then it was a bluff,' Pete said, instantly. It had to be, or the vug would have left the value strictly alone. To the vug he said, '*We call your bluff.*'

The vug did not stir. And then, at last, it turned over the card.

The card was a six.

It had been a bluff.

Pete said, 'It gave itself away. And,' he was shaking wildly, 'the amphetamines didn't help me and the vug can tell that; it can read my mind, so I'm happy to say it aloud. It turned out to be a bluff on our part, on my part. I didn't have enough of the amphetamines and there wasn't any alcohol to speak of in my system. It was not successfully developing a telepathic faculty in my system; I wouldn't have been able to call it. But I had no way of knowing that.'

The vug, palpitating and a dark slate color, now, bill by bill paid over the sum of $300,000 to Pretty Blue Fox.

The group was extremely close to winning The Game.

They knew it and the vug opposing them knew it. It did not have to be said.

Joe Schilling murmured, 'If it hadn't lost its nerve – ' With trembling fingers he managed to relight his cigar. 'It would at least have had a fifty-fifty chance. First it got greedy and then it got scared.' He smiled at the members of the group on both sides of him. 'A bad combination, in Bluff.' His voice was low, intense. 'It was the combination in me, many years ago, that helped wipe me out. In my final play against Bindman Lucky Luckman.'

The vug said, 'It seems to me that I have, for all intents and purposes, lost this Game against you Terrans.'

'You don't intend to continue?' Joe Schilling demanded, removing his cigar from his lips and scrutinizing the vug; he had himself completely under control. His face was hard.

To him, the vug said, 'Yes, I intend to continue.'

Everything burst in Pete Garden's face; the board dissolved and he felt dreadful pain and at the same time he knew what had happened. The vug had given up, and in its agony it intended to destroy them along with it. It was continuing – but in another dimension. Another context entirely.

And they were here with it, on Titan. On its world, not their own.

Their luck had been bad in that respect.

Decisively so.

Chapter 17

Mary Anne's voice reached him, coolly and placidly. 'It's attempting to manipulate reality, Pete. Using the faculty by which it brought us to Titan. Shall I do what I can?'

'Yes,' he agreed. He could not see her; he lay in darkness, in a darkened pool which was not the presence of matter around him but its absence. Where are the others? he wondered. Scattered, everywhere. Perhaps over millions of miles of vacant, meaningless space. And – over millennia.

There was silence.

'Mary,' he said aloud.

No answer.

'Mary!' he shouted in desperation, scratching at the darkness. 'Are you gone, too?' He listened. There was no response.

And then he heard something, or rather felt it. In the darkness, some living entity was probing in his direction. Some sensory extension of it, a device feeling its way; it was aware of him. Curious about him in a dim, limited, but shrewd, way.

Something even older than the vug against which they had played.

He thought, It's something that lives here between the worlds. Between the layers of reality which make up our experience, ours and the vugs'. Get away from me, he thought. He tried to scramble, to move rapidly or at least repel it.

The creature, interested even more now, came closer.

'Joe Schilling,' he called. 'Help me!'

'I *am* Joe Schilling,' the creature said. And it made its

210

way toward him urgently, now, unwinding and extending itself greedily. 'Greed and fear,' it said. 'A bad combination.'

'The hell you're Joe Schilling,' he said in terror; he slapped at it, twisting, trying to roll away.

'But greed alone,' the thing continued, 'is not so bad; it's the prime motivating pressure of the self-system. Psychologically speaking.'

Pete Garden shut his eyes. 'God in heaven,' he said. It was Joe Schilling. What had the vugs done to him?

What had he and Joe become, out here in the darkness?

Or had the vugs done this? Was it, instead, just showing them this?

He bent forward, found his foot, began feverishly to unlace his shoe; he took off the shoe and, reaching back, clouted the thing, Joe Schilling, as hard as he could with it.

'Hmmm,' the thing said. 'I'll have to mull this over.' And it withdrew.

Panting, he waited for it to return.

He knew that it would.

Joe Schilling, floundering in the immense vacuity, rolled, seemed to fall, caught himself, choked on the smoke of his cigar and struggled to breathe. 'Pete!' he said loudly. He listened. There was no direction, no up or down. No here. No sense of what was him and not him. No division into the I and the not-I.

Silence.

'Pete Garden,' he said again, and this time he sensed something, sensed it but did not actually hear it. 'Is that you?' he demanded.

'Yes, it's me,' the answer came. And it was Pete.

Yet, it was not.

'What's going on?' Joe said. 'What's the damn thing doing to us? It's cheating away a mile a minute, isn't it?

211

But we'll get back to Earth; I have faith we'll find our way back. After all, we won The Game, didn't we? And we were positive we weren't going to be able to do that.'
Again he listened.

Pete said, 'Come closer.'

'No,' Schilling said. 'For some darn reason I – don't trust you. Anyhow, how can I come closer? I'm just rolling around here, right? You, too?'

'Come closer,' the voice repeated, monotonously.

No, Joe Schilling said to himself.

He did not trust the voice; he felt frightened. 'Get away,' he said and, paralyzed, listened.

It had not gone away.

In the darkness, Freya Gaines thought, It's betrayed us; we won and got nothing. That bastard organism – we never should have trusted it or put any faith in Pete's idea of playing it.

I hate him, she said to herself. It's his and Joe's fault.

I'd kill them, both of them, she thought, furiously. I'd crunch them to death. She reached out, groping with both hands in the darkness. I'd kill anyone, right now.

I want to kill!

Mary Anne McClain said to Pete, 'Listen, Pete; it's deprived us of all our modes of apprehending reality. It's *us* that it's changed. I'm sure of it. Can you hear me?' She cocked her head, strained to hear.

There was nothing. No answer.

It's atomized us, she thought. As if we're each of us in an extreme psychosis, isolated from everyone else and every familiar attribute in our method of perceiving time and space. This is frightened, hating isolation, she realized. It must be that. What else can it be?

It can't be real. And yet –

Perhaps this is fundamental reality, beneath the conscious layer of the psyche; maybe this is the way we really

212

are. They're showing us this, killing us with the truth about ourselves. Their telepathic faculty and their ability to mold and reform minds, to infuse them; she retreated from the thought.

And then, below her, she saw something that lived.

Stunted, alien creatures, warped by enormous forces into miserably malformed, distorted shapes. Crushed down until they were blinded and tiny. She peered at them; the waning light of a huge, dying sun lit and relit the scene and then, even as she watched, it faded into dark red and at last utter blackness snuffed it out once more.

Faintly luminous, like organisms inhabiting a vast depth, the stunted creatures continued to live, after a fashion. But it was not pleasant.

She recognized them.

That's us. Terrans, as the vugs see us. Close to the sun, subject to immense gravitational forces. She shut her eyes.

I understand, she thought. No wonder they want to fight us; to them we're an old, waning race that's had its period, that must be compelled to abandon the scene.

And then, the vugs. A glowing creature, weightless, drifted far above, beyond the range of the crushing pressures, the blunted, dying creatures. On a little moon, far from the great, ancient sun.

You want to show us this, she realized. This is how reality appears to you, and it's just as real as our own view.

But – no more so.

Do you grasp that? she asked the glowing, weightless presence that was the spiraling Titanian. That our view of the situation is equally true? Yours can't replace ours. Or can it? Is that what you want?

She waited for the answer, her eyes squeezed shut with fear.

'Ideally,' a thought came to her drily, 'both views can be made to coincide. However, in practicality, that does not work.'

Opening her eyes she saw a blob, a mound of sagging, gelatinous protoplasm – ludicrously, with its name *stitched* to its front, in red thread. E. B. Black.

'What?' she demanded, and looked around.

E. B. Black thought-radiated to her, 'There are difficulties. We have not resolved them ourselves; hence, the contradictions within our culture.' It added, 'I've prevailed over the Game-players whom your group was pitted against. You're here on Terra, in your family's apartment in San Rafael where I am currently conducting my criminal investigation.'

Light, and the force of gravity; both were acting on her. She sat up, warily. 'I saw – '

'You saw the view which obsesses us. We can't repudiate it.' The vug flowed closer to her, anxious to make its thoughts truly clear. 'We're aware that it's partial, that it's unfair to you Terrans because you have, as you say, an equal and opposite and as completely binding a view of us in return. However, we continue to perceive as you just now experienced.' It added, 'It would have been unfair to leave you in that frame of reference any longer.'

Mary Anne said, 'We won The Game. Against you.'

'Our citizens are aware of that. We repudiate punitive efforts by our distraught Game-players. Logically, having won, you must be returned to Terra. Anything else is unthinkable. Except of course to our extremists.'

'Your Game-players?'

'They will not be punished. They are too highly-placed in our culture. Be glad you're here; be content, Miss McClain.' Its tone was harsh.

Mary Anne said, 'And the other members of our group? Where are they now?' They were not here in San Rafael, obviously. 'At Carmel?'

214

'Scattered,' E. B. Black said, irritably. She could not tell if it were angry at her, at the members of the group, or at its fellow vugs. The whole situation appeared to annoy it. 'You'll see them again, Miss McClain. Now, if I may return to my investigation . . .'

It moved toward her and she retreated, not wanting to come into bodily contact with it. E. B. Black reminded her too much of the *other*, the one against which they had played – played and won and then been cheated out of their victory.

'Not cheated,' E. B. Black contradicted. 'Your victory has merely been – held back from you. It is still yours and you will obtain it.' It added, 'In time.' There was a faint tinge of relish in its tone. E. B. Black was not particularly saddened by the plight of Pretty Blue Fox, the fact that its members were scattered, frightened and confused. In chaos.

'May I go to Carmel?' she asked.

'Of course. You may damn well go anywhere you wish, Miss McClain. But Joe Schilling is not in Carmel; you'll have to search elsewhere.'

'I will,' she said. 'I'll look until I find him. Pete Garden too.' Until the group is back together again, she thought. As it was before, when we sat across the board from the Titanian Game-players; as we were in Carmel, just a little while ago this evening.

A little while – and a long way ago.

Turning, she left the apartment. And did not look back.

A voice, eager and querulous, prodded at Joe Schilling; he moved away from it – tried to, anyhow – but it crept after him.

'Um,' it gibbered. 'Uh, say, Mr Schilling, you got a minute?' In the darkness he floated closer, always closer until it was right on him, throttling him; he was unable to breathe. 'I'll just take a little of your time. Okay?' It

215

paused. He said nothing. 'Well,' the voice resumed, 'I'll tell you what I'd like. As long as you're here, visiting us and I mean, it's *really* a distinct honor, you know.'

Schilling said, 'Get away from me.' He pawed at it and it was as if his hands broke through webs, sticky, mislinked sections of webs. And accomplishing nothing.

The voice bleated, 'Oh, here's what we both wanted to ask, Es and I. I mean, you hardly ever get out to Portland, right? So by any chance do you have that Erna Berger recording of – what's it called? From *Die Zauberflöte* you know.'

Breathing heavily, Joe Schilling said, 'The Queen of the Night aria.'

'Yes! That's it!' Greedily, the voice crept over him, pressing him inexorably; it would never turn back, now.

'Da dum-dum DUM, da dee-dee da-da dum dum,' another voice, a woman's, joined in; both voices clamored at him.

'Yes, I have it,' Joe Schilling said. 'On Swiss HMV. Both of the Queen of the Night arias. Back to back.'

'Can we have them?' the voices chimed together.

'Yes,' he said.

Light, gray and fragmented, fluttered before him; he managed to get to his feet. My record shop in New Mexico? he asked himself. No. The voices had said he was in Portland, Oregon. What am I doing here? he asked himself. Why did the vug set me down here? He looked around.

He stood in the unfamiliar living room of an old house, on bare, soft wooden floors, facing a moth-scavenged old red and white couch on which sat two familiar figures, short, squat, with ill-cut hair, a man and woman leering at him with avidity.

'You don't actually have the record with you, by any chance?' Es Sibley squawked. Beside her, Les Sibley's eyes glowed with eagerness; he could not sit still and he got to his feet to pace about the barren, echoing living room.

In the corner, a phonograph played, loudly, *The Cherry Duet*; Joe Schilling, for once in his life, wished he could stuff his fingers in his ears, could cut out all such sound. It was too screechy, too blaring; it made his head ache and he turned away, taking a deep, unsteady breath.

'No,' he said. 'It's back at my shop.' He wished like hell for a cup of hot black coffee or tea; for good oolong tea.

Es Sibley said, 'You all right, Mr Schilling?'

He nodded. 'I'm okay.' He wondered about the rest of the group; had all of them been dispersed, dropped like dry leaves to flutter over the plains of Earth? Evidently so. The Titanian could not quite give up.

But at least the group was back. The Game was over.

Schilling said, 'Listen.' He phrased his question carefully, word by word. 'Is – my – car – outside?' He hoped so. Prayed so.

'No,' Les Sibley said. 'We picked you up and brought you out here to Oregon; don't you remember?' Beside him Es giggled, showing her large, sturdy teeth. 'He doesn't remember how he got here,' Les said to her and they both laughed, now, together.

'I want to call Max,' Joe Schilling said. 'I have to go. I'm sorry.' He got totteringly to his feet. 'Goodbye.'

'But the Erna Berger record!' Es Sibley protested, dismayed.

'I'll mail it.' He made his way step by step toward the front door; he had a vague memory – or sense – of its location. 'I have to find a vidphone. Call Max.'

'You can call from here,' Les Sibley said, guiding him toward the hall to the dining room. 'And then maybe you can stay a little – '

'No.' Schilling found the vidphone and, snapping it on, dialed the number of his car.

Presently Max's voice sounded. 'Yeah?'

'This is Joe Schilling. Come and get me.'

'Come and get your fat-assed self,' the car said.

Joe Schilling gave it the address. And then he made his way back down the hall to the living room once more. He reseated himself on the chair where he had been sitting and groped reflexively, hopefully, for a cigar or at least his pipe. The music, even more than before, filled his ears and made him cringe.

He sat, hands clasped together, waiting. But, each minute, feeling a little better. A little more certain what had happened to them. How they had come out.

Standing in the grove of eucalyptus trees, Pete Garden knew where he was; the vugs had released him and he was in Berkeley. In his old, original bind, which he had lost to Walt Remington who had turned it over to Pendleton Associates who had in turn sold it to Luckman who now was dead.

On a rough-hewn bench, among the trees, directly ahead of him sat a silent, motionless girl. It was his wife.

He said, 'Carol. Are you all right?'

She nodded thoughtfully. 'Yes, Pete. I've been here a long time, going over things in my mind. You know, we're very fortunate to have had her on our side, that Mary Anne McClain, I mean.'

'Yes,' he agreed. He walked up to her, hesitated, and then seated himself beside her. He was glad, more so than he could say, to see her.

Carol said, 'Have you any idea what she could have done to us, if she were malevolent? I'll tell you, Pete; she could have whisked the baby out from inside me. Do you realize that?'

He had not; he was sorry, now, to even hear about it. 'True,' he admitted, his heart becoming cold with fear again.

218

'Don't be afraid,' Carol said. 'She's not going to do it. Any more than you go about running people down and killing them with your car. After all, you could do it. And as a Bindman you might even get away with it.' She smiled at him. 'Mary Anne isn't a danger to either of us. In many ways, Pete, she's more sensible than we are. More reasonable and mature. I've had a lot of time to think this out, sitting here. It seems like years.'

He patted her on the shoulder, then bent and kissed her.

Carol said, 'I hope you can win Berkeley back. I guess Dotty Luckman owns it, now. You should be able to. She's not such a good player.'

'I guess Dotty could spare it,' Pete said. 'She's got all the East Coast titles that Lucky left her.'

'Do you think we'll be able to keep Mary Anne in the group?'

'No,' he said.

'That's a shame.' Carol looked around her, at the huge old eucalyptus grove. 'It's nice, here in Berkeley. I can see why you were so unhappy at losing it. And Luckman didn't really enjoy it for itself; he just wanted it as a base for playing and winning.' She paused. 'Pete, I wonder if the birth rate will return to normal, now. Since we beat them.'

'God help us,' he said, 'if it doesn't.'

'It will,' Carol said. 'I know it will. I'm the first of many women. Call it a Psionic talent, pre-cognition on my part, but I'm positive of it. What'll we call our child?'

'In my opinion, it depends on whether it's a boy or a girl.'

Carol smiled. 'Maybe it'll be both.'

'Then,' he said, 'Freya would be right, in her schizoid jibe when she said she hoped it was a baby, implying she wasn't convinced of it.'

'I mean of course one of each. Twins. When was the last pair of twins born?'

He knew the answer by heart. 'Forty-two years ago. In Cleveland. To a Mr and Mrs Toby Perata.'

'And we could be the next,' Carol said.

'It's not likely.'

'But we won,' Carol said softly. 'Remember?'

'I remember,' Pete Garden said. And put his arms around his wife.

Stumbling in the darkness, over what appeared to be a curb, David Mutreaux reached the main street of the small Kansas country town in which he found himself. Ahead, he saw lights; he sighed with relief and hurried.

What he needed was a car; he did not even bother to call his own. God knew where it was and how long he would have to wait for its arrival, assuming he could contact it. Instead, he strode up the single main street of the town – Fernley, it was called – until he came to a homeostatic car-rental agency.

There, he rented a car, drove it away at once and then parked at the curb and sat, by himself, getting his courage together.

To the Rushmore Effect of the car, Mutreaux said, 'Listen, am I a vug or a Terran?'

'Let's see,' the car said, 'you're a Mr David Mutreaux of Kansas City.' Briskly, the Rushmore continued, 'You are a Terran, Mr Mutreaux. Does that answer your question?'

'Thank god,' Mutreaux said. 'Yes, that answers my question.'

He started up the car then, and headed by air toward the West Coast and Carmel, California.

It's safe for me to go back to them, he said to himself. Safe in regards to them, safe period. Because I've thrown off the Titanian authority. Doctor Philipson is on Titan,

220

Nats Katz was destroyed by the psycho-kinetic girl Mary Anne McClain, and the organization – which was subverted from the start – has been obliterated. I have nothing to fear. In fact I helped win; I played my part well in The Game.

He previewed his reception. There they would be, the members of Pretty Blue Fox, trickling in one by one from the various points on Earth at which the Titanians had summarily deposited them. The group re-formed, everyone back together; they would open a bottle of Jack Daniel's Tennessee whiskey and a bottle of Canadian whiskey –

As he piloted his car toward California he could taste it, hear the voices, see the members of the group, now.

The celebration. Of their victory. Everyone was there.

Or was it everyone? *Almost* everyone, anyhow. That was good enough for him.

Tramping across the sand, the wasteland which was the Nevada Desert, Freya Garden Gaines knew that it would be a long time before she got back to the condominium apartment in Carmel.

And anyway, she thought to herself, what did it matter? What did she have to look forward to? The thoughts she had had as she floundered in the intermediate regions into which the Titanian Game-players had hurled them . . . *I don't repudiate those thoughts*, she said to herself with envenomed bitterness. Pete has his pregnant mare, his wife Carol; he'll never notice me again as long as I live.

In her pocket she found a strip of rabbit-paper; getting it out, she removed the wrapper and bit it. With the light cast by her cigarette lighter she examined it and then crumpled it up and violently flung it away from her. Nothing, she realized. And it'll always be like this for me. It's Pete's fault; if he made it with that Carol Holt creature he could have made it with me. God knows we tried it

221

enough times; it must have been several thousand. Evidently he just didn't want to succeed.

Twin lights flashed ahead of her. She halted, cautiously, gasping for breath. Wondering what she had arrived at.

A car lowered itself warily to the surface of the desert, its signal lights flashing on and off. It landed, stopped.

The door opened.

'Mrs Gaines!' a cheerful voice called.

Peering, Freya walked toward the car.

Behind the wheel sat a balding, friendly-looking elderly man. 'I'm glad I found you,' the elderly man said. 'Get in and we'll drive out of this dreadful desert-area. Where exactly do you want to go?' He chuckled. 'Carmel?'

'No,' Freya said. 'Not Carmel.' Never again, she thought.

'Where, then? What about Pocatello, Idaho?'

'Why Pocatello?' Freya demanded. But she got into the car; it was better than continuing to wander aimlessly across the desert, alone in the darkness, with no one – certainly none of the group – to help her. To give a damn about what happened to her.

The elderly man, as he started up the car, said pleasantly, 'I'm Doctor E. R. Philipson.'

She stared at him. She knew – she was positive she knew – who he was. Or rather, who *it* was.

'Do you want to get out?' Doctor Philipson asked her. 'I could, if you wish, set you back down there again where I found you.'

'N-no,' Freya murmured. She sat back in her seat, scrutinized him thoroughly, thinking to herself many thoughts.

Doctor E. R. Philipson said to her, 'Mrs Gaines, *how would you like to work for us, for a change*?' He glanced her way, smiling, a smile without warmth or humor. A smile utterly cold.

Freya said, 'It's an interesting proposal, but I'd have to

222

think it over. I couldn't decide just like that, right now.'
Very interesting indeed, she thought.

'You'll have time,' Doctor Philipson said. 'We're patient. You'll have all the time in the world.' His eyes twinkled.

Freya smiled back.

Humming confidently to himself, Doctor Philipson drove the car toward Idaho, skimming across the dark night sky of Earth.